PRAISE FOR KATHERINE SLEE'S
THE LOVE WE LEFT BEHIND

T0051094

The
Other
Half
Of
Me

ALSO BY KATHERINE SLEE

The Love We Left Behind

The Other Half Of Me

Katherine Slee

LAKE UNION
PUBLISHING

Text copyright © 2022 by Katherine Slee
All rights reserved.

Published by Lake Union Publishing, Seattle

www.apub.com

Amazon, the Amazon logo, and Lake Union Publishing are trademarks of Amazon.com, Inc., or its affiliates.

ISBN-13: 9781542034616
ISBN-10: 1542034612

Cover design by Emma Rogers

Printed in the United States of America

For Dylan & Scarlett

'If music be the food of love, play on.'

William Shakespeare

1.

Last night, just like every night, I dreamt of Lucy. No matter how late I go to bed, how many vodkas I've drunk or whose arms I curl up in, she always finds a way to sneak into my dreams.

The dreams themselves are always frantic, a muddle of memories and make-believe with a few flashbacks thrown in. But they all end the same way: with the two of us running through the woods back home, heading for the river. Lucy, being older and taller, runs ahead, then disappears into the trees, and I call out, asking her to wait. Coming out of all that green, I stand by the riverbank, looking every which way, then down to the perpetual current to see my own blurred reflection staring back.

I step into the wet, feeling the cold pull of water tempting me towards the sea. My feet suck and slick against the boggy riverbed and I try to turn, to look for Lucy. For a second, I think I see her, then I stumble, fall back and go under as the sky overhead becomes too far away to reach. I feel the dank water hit the back of my throat, flooding my lungs and making me scrabble for the air I cannot breathe. That is when I wake, clutching at my neck and wishing I had actually drowned.

Waking is the worst part of my day. For a split second before the world slips back into place, I don't remember. Then I look around, figuring out where I spent the night, and the feeling returns, like a cloak that's pulled too tight around my neck.

I don't recognise the room I have woken up in, nor do I know who the man still asleep beside me is. This in itself isn't unusual, far from it, but I swore to myself I was going to stop, to get better. Empty words I've been saying to myself for years – *No more, Beth. No more men who can't give you what you need.*

Easing myself from under the covers, I pad across the floor, picking up clothes that I have no memory of removing as I go. In the bathroom, I splash my face with cold water and scrape my hair into a knot on top of my head. The mirror shows me the error of my ways and I hunt in a cabinet for something that might help. I discover lotions and potions, oils and waxes, an old-fashioned shaving kit just like my dad's, and an expensive bottle of cologne. After helping myself to a generous dollop of moisturiser I open the bottle, breathing in the woody scent. Immediately I am rewarded with a memory from last night, the two of us in a cab, him with his hand up my top, and my head leaning back, watching through the rear window as the streets flashed past.

I need to leave. I need to be out of here before he wakes up. Tom? No. Tristan? No, it wouldn't be Tristan. But then again that would have been my perfect justification for choosing him.

'Babe,' he says, knocking on the door, and I wonder if he has forgotten my name too.

'Just a second,' I call back, putting the bottle of cologne in the cabinet, then I pinch my cheeks and push back my eyelashes with my fingertips, just like my sister once taught me to do.

'Hey,' he says as I open the door.

'Hey,' I reply, looking from his face down to a St Christopher's charm he is wearing around his neck then back up to his face. Definitely not as cute as I remember, but I seem to have fallen into the habit of going home with less than desirable men.

'You all right?'

There's a lilt to his voice and I half remember asking him about it at the same time as I reached inside his shirt and pulled out that charm.

'I have to go,' I say, but he makes no effort to step aside to let me do as I ask.

'Will you come back?' He's looking at me as if I'm something tasty to eat, making me feel both nauseous and also more than a little ashamed of myself.

'I'm not sure that's such a good idea,' I say, edging past him and out to the open-plan living area. It's all high ceiling, exposed brick walls and oversized windows, a glance through one showing me a view of the Thames. Just like that, I'm back inside my dream that is a nightmare, swimming in the river and catching fireflies with the one person who swore to me she would never leave.

'We had fun, didn't we?' He tries to take my hand, but I swat him away, picking up my ancient pair of pixie boots and doing my best to ignore the empty bottle of whiskey on the coffee table.

'That's the problem,' I say, shouldering my bag and heading for the door. 'I'm only ever pretending to have fun.' It sounds like the beginning of a song, one that once I would have written down, played around with, tended to like a farmer does their crops. But that Beth, the person I used to be, is gone.

Outside it's all too bright, too real, so I rummage in my bag for my sunglasses. A man jogs past, turns around to give me a disparaging look, before turning again and heading for the bridge. They never used to look at me but would always stare at her, even more so when they discovered Lucy and I were sisters.

But you're so different, was the most common response. To the untrained eye it would be true – Lucy was tall, ethereal even, with platinum hair and delicate features, whilst I was all messy curls and skinny legs. But if you looked closer, you'd see the same pronounced cupid's bow and dimples when we smiled. I used to hate being compared to my sister and all her brilliance. Now, I'd give anything just to hear her voice.

I look along the river, where a boat skims across the surface, two rowers lifting their oars in unison, no more than a soft slap of wood on water as they go. A quick check of Google Maps confirms I'm all the way on the other side of London and mentally I map out my route to work. Except my job was never supposed to be playing piano in the bar of a decidedly old-fashioned London hotel, although I don't think I ever had a clue what the plan, the way to get to where I wanted to be, should have actually been. Lucy was always the diligent one, the doer, the one who knew exactly where she wanted to be in ten years' time.

Where will I be in ten years' time? I keep looking for a sign, for something to tell me which future I should be heading towards, but most of the time I feel like a hamster on a wheel, constantly moving but never getting anywhere.

My mother's voice pops into my head – *So much potential*, was a phrase she tended to overuse on me, along with a tut and a look. *Just a shame you choose to waste it.*

But it's not as easy as that. Some people are born lucky, have everything they ever wanted simply fall into their laps. The rest of us have to hope for the best, make do with whatever life throws at us.

Pushing all thoughts of my mother and our unresolved issues aside, I open up the astrology app on my phone. It's a habit that started years ago, and even though part of me knows it's silly to have a random stranger dictate your future, the other half of me likes the idea that there's someone out there giving me a bit of a heads-up as to what's coming my way.

> Many little things make a whole. Any one of them
> could be important enough to break a loop that has
> been keeping you unhappy or static for a long time.

Which seems kind of serendipitous, or more likely ridiculous, because I'm not convinced waking up in the arms of a stranger (again), is in any way going to help pave the path to enlightenment.

Another check through my phone tells me not only that I have less than half an hour before my shift starts but I tried sending Lucy a string of rambling, nonsensical texts just before one a.m. It's become a bit of a habit, and even though I know she won't text me back, I can't stop myself telling her a little bit about my day.

Today is April first, the day of fools, and six weeks since Lucy, my utterly perfect sister, died. I used to say my white rabbits for luck on the first day of the month, curse myself if I forgot, but what's the point in wishing if the only thing you want will never come true?

When you lose someone, you lose the version of yourself that you were to them. Not only that, but all the memories and jokes, all the years that we were a part of together. My grief feels like it has nowhere to go, because everything I did, Lucy was a part of too.

That's why I keep sending her texts, even though I know she'll never reply. It's the hardest part about her being gone, because how do you talk to someone who can't answer you? When the person who knew you best, who shared so many jokes and ideas and your whole entire life is gone, then a part of you vanishes too.

I am with the living, but part of me wants to be with the dead.

I wish I could go back, start again, be more than the sum of all my mistakes. With one last look along the river, I pop in my headphones, then cross the street and head towards the Tube.

'You look like shit,' Sam says as I come through the staff entrance to the hotel and hang my coat on its usual peg.

'Lovely to see you too,' I say, going through to the bar and reaching under the counter for my spare make-up bag. I then turn on the coffee machine and fill the water container to the brim.

'Late night or early morning?'

'Bit of both.'

'Was it worth it?'

'I'm not in the mood for a lecture.' Sam is my boss, but he's also elected himself as my resident agony uncle, which is somewhat hypocritical given I know all about his own questionable past.

'Then call it a gentle warning. From someone who knows.' He looks from me to the triple espresso I am in the process of making, then over to my open make-up bag, from which a near-empty packet of Nurofen is protruding.

He's right. Of course, he's right. But it's temporary, a way of blocking out what happened to Lucy.

'Hey, Beth.' One of the waitresses, Natalie, comes through from the kitchen and the smell of her perfume makes me suppress the urge to vomit. 'We still on for later?'

'Sure,' I reply, pretending to rummage through my bag in search of some eye drops whilst I try to remember what I've apparently agreed to do with Natalie.

'Fab,' she says with a glossy smile. 'But remember, Jack is off limits, so if he tries flirting with you, tell him you're seeing someone.'

'Jack. Got it.' I have some vague recollection of Natalie telling me all about a guy she'd met at the gym, which was (I think) the whole reason for the party I now remember she is throwing tonight.

'I thought you were teaching tomorrow?' Sam says, licking the end of a cigarette paper and twisting it into a tight cylinder. I'm tempted to make a comment about all those joints he used to roll still coming in handy, but it feels like too much effort right now.

'I am,' I say, turning back to the coffee machine and immediately closing my eyes as the room starts to spin. 'But it's not until eleven, so I'll have plenty of time.'

'If you say so,' Sam replies, though he doesn't sound convinced. Granted, my recent track record is hardly pristine, but it's an hour's lesson with someone who no longer needs my help. Not like I'm trying to land a real job, one that I'd actually need to have studied for.

You deserve more than helping other people achieve their dreams, is what Lucy used to say to me whenever I told her about a new student I'd enrolled. Which was sweet and kind, and completely untrue.

The feeling originates from somewhere behind my heart, a hot ball of pain that pulses erratically, and I press my hands against my eyes to try and block out the picture of Lucy's face.

'You ok?' Sam asks, and I force myself to nod and smile. 'You sure?' He looks at me with a tilted head and I hate to see so much pity on his face. It's the same whenever anyone finds out about my sister, a constant reminder that she is never coming back.

'I'm fine,' I lie, because it's not getting any better. Every day it's the same and no matter what I do I can't find a way to forget or move on.

'If you need to take a day, we can manage.'

'I'm fine,' I say, a little too loud and shrill, but it's enough to make Sam raise his hands and back away.

'Oh my god, it's Tristan King,' Natalie exclaims, and a jolt of panic shoots right through me as I spin round and scan the room.

'I used to have such a crush on him,' Natalie says, and I realise she's staring at the TV screen behind the bar. On it is the image of a ruined mansion, in front of which the five band members of SuperKing are standing. I hold my breath as Natalie bends down to turn up the volume on the main stereo system and suddenly the bar is filled with the intricate melody that once spilt from every radio station, every pub, every home.

'I remember this,' Sam says, hovering in the doorway with a cigarette dangling from his lips. 'It played on repeat that last year I was in Ibiza. Even the ravers loved it.'

'*Galaxy of Angels* is, like, the album of my youth,' Natalie says, leaning on the counter and watching as the camera cuts to a scene of Tristan wading into a river, where a half-naked model is waiting.

'He was mesmerising on stage,' Sam says, tucking his cigarette behind one ear and checking his watch. 'All the girls wanted to screw him and all the lads wanted to be him.'

'Actually,' I say, peeling my eyes away from the screen, 'he was a bit of a twat.'

'You know him?' Sam asks, watching as I add two spoonfuls of sugar to my coffee.

'I used to.' He was the first boy I ever fell for, and the person who set so many things in motion that I wish pretty much every single day I could go back and undo.

'No way,' Natalie says, leaning on the bar and staring up at me with heavily kohled eyes.

'Yes, way.' I take a long, slow sip of my coffee as I think back to the time I spent with someone who went from nobody to rock god overnight.

'So what happened to the band?' Sam asks, taking a tray of glasses out of the dishwasher and stacking them on a shelf up high. 'They just fell off the map after several years riding the crescendo of rock glory.'

'Are the rumours true?' Natalie says, grabbing my hand. 'Did Tristan have a nervous breakdown after their second album got scrapped?'

'I wouldn't know,' I say, watching as the video comes to an end. The last shot is of Tristan standing on a rooftop and reaching one hand up to the heavens. It's ridiculously cheesy and nothing at all to do with what the song is actually about, but what would I know? 'We didn't stay in touch.'

'But still. Must have been amazing to know him.'

'I guess.' Actually, it was exhausting and incredible in equal measure because Tristan was always so very good at convincing people they were important to him.

'When did you know him?' Natalie asks.

'During my last year of school.' I take out my eyeliner and begin to draw a thin black line above my lashes, trying to ignore how much my hand is still shaking.

I can tell she's mentally calculating how long ago this was and I wish I'd kept my mouth shut because I already know what she's going to ask next. It's the same question I always get asked if I ever let slip that I was once acquainted with the infamous Tristan King.

'So, you were there when they were writing *Galaxy of Angels*?'

I was. I was there from the very beginning. Sat through countless rehearsals, went to every single one of their gigs in the back rooms of dodgy pubs, and put Tristan and his career ahead of everything else.

'He wanted to call the album *Sexy Dreamer*, but we talked him out of it.' He wanted it all to be about him. Claimed he was the glue that held the band together, that without him we were nothing more than a group of wannabe musicians who could barely play a note. Apart from me, but he was also rather good at ignoring other people's talent.

'That's so cool. Wait. Does that mean . . . Is "Hyacinth Girl" about you?'

'No.' It's not actually about me, or any other girl, despite what Tristan would later claim in every single magazine or television interview.

'Must have been weird.' Sam is watching me as I take another sip of coffee. 'I mean, to have your friend become that famous.'

I shrug again, because I have spent years trying to forget all the words to all the songs on an album that made SuperKing into a household name More than that, I miss the way it felt to be a part of something so creative, so full of possibility. I think we all knew the album was going to be big, that Tristan would stop at nothing until he was headlining gigs all over the country. Plus, he's always been one of the lucky ones; it was only a matter of time before he got everything he ever wanted. What I never anticipated was that the band's success wouldn't include me.

'It was years ago, Sam. We weren't that close and it's hardly relevant now.' Except it is. It's like living with a demon on your shoulder, one that bends to whisper in your ear every time a SuperKing song comes on the radio.

It could have been you, the creature likes to sneer. *But you weren't good enough, were you?*

'I'm going for a smoke.' Sam disappears out the back, swiftly followed by the sound of the fire door slamming shut.

'I wonder where Tristan is now,' Natalie says as she pops the cork on a bottle of champagne.

'No idea,' I say, which is another lie because of course I know. I have followed him ever since, both the highs and the lows of his short-lived career, telling myself that karma can indeed be such a bitch.

I walk through the bar and out to the internal courtyard beyond. The space is impressive, no matter how many times you see it – a fifty-foot atrium filled with palm trees and surrounded on all sides by overpriced hotel rooms that look down on the guests as

10

they eat. At its centre is a grand piano, waiting for me to take my seat at its helm.

Running my fingers over the keys, I feel the soft vibration of sound that always wakes me up better than any amount of caffeine. I would like nothing more than to play something other than the pre-agreed music that echoes around this space, but I'm not about to risk losing my job in the name of music preference. Instead, I begin with my usual Simon & Garfunkel, safe and inoffensive, although I've always been tempted to change the chorus to a different key.

There's a token round of applause when I finish, but I guarantee when these people go home and are asked about their trip to London not a single one of them will even remember me.

I can't help but think of all the times I would sit at the piano with Dad, of how he'd play me song after song, telling me to connect with, to feel the music that escaped from my fingertips. He's never been here, never heard me play all these songs that were written by someone else, because I know this isn't the kind of music he was trying to teach me.

I must have been no more than eight years old when he first showed me how to make sense of all the music I carried around in my head. It was the rain that woke me. A gentle tap, tap, tap against the windowpane that filtered through to my dreams. Slowly the tempo built, accompanied by a quick burst of wind that came through the open window and created goosebumps on my skin. I sat up in bed, breathing in the distinctive scent of summer rain and listening to the sound of all those droplets falling from the sky and hitting the ground below. My head began to nod in unison and a song appeared in my mind.

Slipping from the bed, I padded barefoot out of my room and downstairs.

Sitting at the piano, I brushed my fingertips over the keys, humming the melody to myself before playing the opening notes. The first few were slow, deliberate, as I figured out what came next, then I added in a few chords, going back to the beginning over and over again.

'What are you doing up so early?' Dad said as he came into the room, shutting the door behind him. He was wearing a t-shirt and boxers, his hair sticking out at odd angles and the remnants of sleep folded into his face. He smelt a little musty, his breath sour as he sat down beside me and yawned.

'I heard a song in the rain,' I said, looking out to the garden.

Dad cocked his head to listen, his own fingers tapping against the edge of the piano. 'Well I never,' he said with a smile, and kissed the top of my head.

'You told me there's music all around us,' I said, leaning into the warmth of him. 'And I remembered to listen.'

'I think you're going to need this,' he said, going over to the sideboard and opening a drawer. He came back, set down a notebook and a slim black box with buttons on the top and a clear panel on one side through which I could see the two wheels of a tiny cassette tape.

'Play it again,' he said, pressing down on two of the buttons and making those wheels turn. I did as he asked, and when I was done, he rewound the tape and played it back to me. The sound was imperfect but true, and in that moment my entire world changed.

'Carry it with you always,' he said, holding the machine out to me, and I took it, felt the weight of it in my palms. 'Inspiration can strike at any time. But now,' he continued, stretching his arms over his head and letting go a long yawn. 'Now it's time for breakfast. And coffee.'

'Daddy?' I said as he rose from the stool and opened the door to the hallway.

'Yes, pickle?'

'Do you think I could write a song? One good enough to be played on the radio?'

'I think you were born with music in your soul,' he said, looking at me in a way that made my insides smile. 'What you choose to do with it is up to you.'

My father gave me something that morning, a dream I never even knew I wanted. For a while it made me happy, it made me feel like I had a purpose. But the thing about dreams is that they can so easily be broken.

Natalie walks past, a stark reminder that I am so far away from the little girl who used to record her dreams on tiny cassettes. She's balancing a silver tray on one hand and I'm half tempted to swipe a drink, to find the bottom of the glass and its promise of oblivion.

'Let's make it a night to remember,' she says, and I raise my cup of coffee in response before playing the opening bars of the next song.

Problem is, all I really want to do is forget.

2.

If I stay still, if I don't move or breathe, then I think I can stop myself from being sick. Slowly, I turn my head to the side, feel sunlight on my skin, before tentatively opening one eye.

I'm home. Or at least in the flat that I have fashioned into some semblance of a home. Rolling on to my side, I use both hands to ease myself into a sitting position, then double over and retch on to the threadbare carpet. I'm not actually sick, but bile burns the back of my throat and I grab the omnipresent glass of water from my bedside table and gulp its contents down.

Swinging my legs out from under the duvet, I notice that I'm still wearing one sock. The other is over by the door next to a pile of clothes and a plastic bag from my local curry house. There is a graze on one knee and the beginnings of a bruise snaking up my thigh.

I vaguely remember climbing over a gate and kissing a stranger in a back alley. Shit, not a stranger, although technically he was to me, right up until I discovered he was called Jack. The same Jack who Natalie specifically asked me to stay away from, which means I owe Natalie an apology. Although I think she pushed me into the rosebushes at one point, which would explain all these scratches up my arm.

You have to stop doing this, Beth. You have to figure out a way to stop losing control and hurting the handful of friends you have left.

Picking up my phone, I see another missed call from Dad. I should call him, but what if Mum answers instead of him? It's been weeks since I saw her, thirty-six days to be precise, and our argument still rolls around my mind, stabbing me with the words neither of us have been able to apologise for.

I also have a string of messages from Natalie (best not deal with that right now), and a reminder that I should be on my way to Dulwich Village, not sitting here with a hangover pounding against my skull.

I shuffle through to the bathroom and turn on the shower. The mirror above the sink begins to cloud with steam as the water heats up, but that does nothing to disguise the mess that is my face. I'm rewarded with a memory of Lucy and I watching *It* one night whilst our parents went for drinks with friends. Lucy cowered behind the sofa, every so often sticking her head over the top then screaming at the sight of Pennywise the clown. Meanwhile, I sat eating an entire tub of Ben & Jerry's whilst describing in detail all the bits she was too scared to watch.

I miss her. I miss her all the time, but I know it's too late for me to do anything about it.

Stepping into the shower, I tilt back my head and rub honey-suckle shampoo into my scalp. The scent of it, just like everything else, makes me cry. Fat tears of guilt and remorse that mingle with soap and disappear down the plughole.

'I'm sorry,' I whisper to nobody at all, then proceed to comb conditioner through my curls, just like Lucy once showed me.

Wrapped in a towel, I go back to the bedroom and open the wardrobe door. Inside is a tangle of clothes, only some of which are wrinkle-free. Taking down a simple jersey dress, I toss it on the bed; its hem has come loose and I'm pretty sure I own neither needle nor thread. I settle on a pair of faux leather trousers, a plain white t-shirt and a velvet jacket bought from a charity shop years ago. The cuff is beginning to fray, but it's the best I can do. There's no time to style my hair, so I twist it into a chignon before pencilling in my brows and painting my lips the deepest shade of red.

Not bad, I tell myself as another message from Natalie appears on my phone, along with four bright numbers informing me that I am so very late.

Glancing around for my satchel, I spot it out in the hall, next to a small console table on which sits a pile of unopened post. Mostly bills, which is why I keep ignoring them. Underneath is a box wrapped up in brown paper, my name and address written in green ink and stamped with an Oxford postmark.

It's from Lucy. I know this because she wrote all her letters to me in green ink and she's the only person I know who lives in Oxford. Lived. She's not there any more, and there's nothing in this world that can change that. Which is precisely why that damned parcel has sat there, unopened, for the past month.

Ignoring the box, I look up to the wall above, where I have hung a collection of photos held in mismatched frames. Right in the centre is my favourite one of all: Lucy and me as children, sitting at the piano, my tongue caught between my teeth in concentration.

I can't remember the last time we sat down together and played. It all seems so long ago, the memories slipping over one another and making them feel like stills from a film rather than a life that once belonged to me.

Kissing my fingertips, I press them against Lucy's pixelated face, just as I do every time before leaving the flat, pick up my satchel and go.

I'm late. Which isn't unusual, and not always my fault given the unpredictability of London traffic. But being late isn't always an option, especially when it comes to my next client. It is also the reason I decided to get off the number 42 bus and run through Dulwich Village and, as a result, I am sweaty and out of breath when I reach my destination. The house is like every other one on the street – three storeys of Victorian red-brick with a Range Rover parked outside – all of them costing way more than I could ever afford. It's one more reminder that I seem to spend so much of my time playing music for other people, in places I will never quite fit.

'Elizabeth.' Mrs Miller looks me up and down as she stands aside to let me in. 'Is everything all right?'

'I'm fine,' I say, shrugging off my jacket and feeling a line of sweat trailing down my spine. 'The bus was late, so . . .' I don't offer up any more of an explanation and she seems not to need one, so I point along the hall towards the sound of a piano being played.

'Shall I go through?'

'Please,' she replies, shutting the front door and then heading for the stairs.

I go into the kitchen, bending down to placate the cat, and then turn right into the orangery (not conservatory, as I wrongly called it the first time I was here). Over by the back doors, which are open to the garden beyond, is a beautiful upright piano, sleek and glossy as a panther. A young woman is playing, her torso moving with the music as her fingers fly up and down the keys.

'Hi, Beth,' she says when she sees me, pushing back the stool and coming over to give me a hug. It's such a familiar gesture, one given the world over, but I've become unaccustomed to being touched, apart from sex, so it takes me by surprise.

Felicity (or Flick, as she'd rather be known) is as polished as her piano, but she hasn't fully grown into her looks. Despite being in her final year of school she still retains a certain innocence and vulnerability that I've long since forgotten. I want to capture it, preserve it for her somehow, even though when I was her age I longed for so much more than adolescence.

'Is there anything in particular you want to go through today?' I ask, opening my satchel and taking out a couple of song sheets.

'Not really.' Flick peers over my shoulder at the options I've brought along. 'But that might be fun,' she says, pointing at a collection of songs by Elton John.

I sit next to her on the stool and watch her play, every so often adding in a few notes of my own. She has no need to practise, not since the offer letter arrived a couple of months ago. Her mother called to thank me, said she'd had her reservations about my teaching methods but clearly they'd paid off. Then Flick called, leaving a voicemail heavy with tears, telling me how the Royal Academy had said her audition piece was as brilliant as it was unexpected.

Time has flown. Sometimes it feels like no time at all and yet it's been eight years since I stumbled across my first student. I remember how small he looked, perched on the very edge of the piano stool, his feet not quite reaching the floor.

One student turned into two, then more, enough for me to move out of my childhood home and into an ex-council flat in a part of London that Dad described as 'dodgy at best'. But it was mine, and gave me all the independence I thought I wanted.

Most of my students played because their parents wanted them to, one more thing to add to the list of after-school activities. Of them, only a handful would play through their teenage years, sheet music so easily replaced by CDs and downloads. But every so often I'd come across someone with an inherent understanding of music, a child who simply knew how to play without being taught.

Flick is one such child. Aged fifteen, she came to me with braces, spots and gangly limbs she didn't know what to do with. She was also painfully shy, unable to look directly at me and stood half hidden by her mother.

'I hear you're something of a piano whisperer,' Mrs Miller had said to me the first time we met, extending a slender hand decorated with diamonds. 'We need Felicity to go to the Royal Academy and her current teacher isn't really up to the job.'

It was a familiar complaint, one I'd heard from many parents who were convinced their little darling was a musical prodigy. But I knew better than to question the people who were paying my wages, and so I simply smiled and said I would do my best to help.

The moment Flick started to play, I felt it. There was something behind the notes, a feeling, a suggestion of more that I recognised all too well.

'Why did you change the last part?' I asked when she stopped, and she darted a look at me.

'It's wrong, I know. My previous teacher kept telling me not to.'

'But why?' I persisted, my own fingers reaching out to recreate the melody she'd just played.

'I guess . . .' she said with a shrug, looking down at her hands. 'It sounded better that way?' The last part came out as a question, like she wanted permission to do something other than what was written down in a rule book.

'How about . . .' I said, taking away the sheet music she'd been playing from and replacing it with something completely different. 'How about we try this instead?'

Flick looked at the music, then at me, then back to the music. She hesitated, perhaps nervous about what her mother might think of me asking her to play ABBA instead of Debussy.

'Anyone can play a pretty tune,' I said, running my fingers up and down the keys. 'But music, real music, is layered with feeling. You need to try it all, so that you can figure out a way to put yourself into whatever you play.'

Which is exactly what she did for her audition – the piece we composed was influenced by everything from jazz to classical and

19

even a bit of eighties glam rock. It was brave and daring to play something unconventional and we both knew it was a risk, but Flick was determined to try. It reminded me of Lucy, of how she would always push herself to be the very best version of herself she could possibly be.

'I can't believe next week's our last lesson,' Flick says, pulling me back to the here and now.

'Next week?' I reply. 'But you don't start college until September.'

'Mum didn't tell you?' she asks, and I shake my head, no. 'She wants me to focus on my A Levels. Thinks this might be too much of a distraction.'

'Right. I see.' Although I don't see, especially as Flick's offer from the Royal Academy is not dependent upon her getting three A* at A Level. But then I should know better than most about the need for a back-up, or a contingency plan, as my own mother used to call it.

I'm also trying not to think about the missed income from Flick's bi-weekly lessons. It's not much, but it does mean I need to start looking for new students to make up the shortfall. If it were anyone other than Flick it wouldn't sting so bad, because she gets music in a way most of my students don't. With her, it doesn't feel like teaching. With her, I allow myself, at least for the length of a lesson, to remember how music once made my life complete.

These past few months I've allowed myself to simply exist day to day, with no thought for the future. Now it seems I have to start planning for what comes next, even though I hate having to do so again and again.

'Any tips?' Flick asks, looking at me with a bucketload of expectation. 'For college?'

'I wouldn't know,' I say, registering the gentle pull of regret that always appears whenever anyone asks me about university. 'I never went.'

'Why not?'

'It's not what I wanted,' I reply, and she frowns.

'Then what did you want?'

It's the question I've been avoiding for eight long years, one that has persisted but which I've never been able to answer. Flick isn't the first student I've watched grow and develop into someone I once thought I could be. I also doubt she'll be the last, and despite the knowledge that I played a part in these metamorphoses, it stings, because I never found the courage to transform myself.

'I wanted . . .' I say with a sigh, looking around the room and thinking of all the music imprinted into the walls, music that I will no longer get to hear Flick play. 'I wanted something unattainable. Something that wasn't meant to be.'

On my way home, I stop off at the village bakery and treat myself to two large slices of lemon cake and a double-shot macchiato. I stroll through the park, side-stepping streams of kids and dogs and families, all living in middle-class suburbia and completely unaware of how fragile the world can make you. One wrong turn or bad decision, seemingly small and insignificant at the time, can set off a such cataclysmic chain of events in your life, making it impossible to go back and change it.

You might call it karma or fate or simply bad luck, but the fact I've lost my favourite student the night after I kissed someone I shouldn't leaves me feeling as if somehow I deserve it.

How did I get here? Sitting on a park bench, eating cake that's not a patch on Mum's and thinking about what might have been. I mean, there's always another student, there's always another piano to be played, or a bar to work in if all else fails. But I assumed that by now I'd be doing something more than sitting in the background of other people's lives. I thought that by now I would have figured out a way to be happy.

I'm twenty-six years old and it feels like I'm existing instead of living. If Lucy were here, she'd tell me to buck up, or take a breath, do something about the situation I now find myself in. She was always the lucky one, the golden child whose life seemed blessed by the gods, whilst my life has been a constant battle against everything that gets thrown at me.

My eye falls upon a dirty penny and I pick it up without thinking. I could do with some luck, something to help me try and figure out what on earth I'm supposed to do with the rest of my life.

I used to have a dream, I used to believe that one day I'd be sitting in the kitchen and hear my song come on the radio. More than that, I wanted to be at a festival, a stranger in a sea of people, all listening to a band play something I'd created. I would lie on my bed at night, staring up at the ceiling and daring to imagine what that might feel like.

And then suddenly all my dreams, all my choices, got taken away.

You always have a choice. Lucy's voice appears in my head, as it often tends to at moments when I'm feeling particularly sorry for myself. If only she were here now to show me what choices I actually have. What I don't understand, what makes me wake in the night panicked and gasping for breath, is that she was the lucky one. She was the one who was supposed to live a glorious life, not me. So what possible chance does someone like me actually have?

3.

I arrive back to the smell of grease and antiseptic that lingers in the communal hall. As always, there's a pile of junk mail on the front doormat: flyers for cleaners and yoga studios that I neither want nor can afford.

Kicking my front door shut, I shrug off my jacket and drop my bag on the floor, ignoring the parcel from my sister and going through to the small kitchen at the back of the flat. Flicking on the kettle, I busy myself with rinsing out a mug and hunting in the cupboard for some instant coffee. A quick look in the fridge tells me I'm out of milk, as well as pretty much everything else, so once again I'm going to have to sweet-talk Sam into fixing me a sandwich at work.

My eye creeps back to the hall, to the parcel that's still sitting there, waiting.

'You don't have to open it,' I tell myself as I pour boiling water into a mug and add two heaped spoons of coffee granules.

Except you do. This voice sounds distinctly like my sister's, only not as pure, like the recording of a recording, or simply the memory of someone I haven't spoken to for months. Someone I will never be able to speak to again. I don't want to open the parcel because it doesn't matter what's inside. Nothing could even begin to make up for her being gone.

But Lucy knew me. She knew that there was only so long I would be able to ignore a curiosity such as a parcel sent from beyond the grave.

I flick on the radio, scroll through the channels until I hit upon one that only plays songs from the nineties. A bouncy upbeat Britpop tune twists and curls through the air, making me think of dancing barefoot in the garden with the stereo turned up way too high. How many songs did we listen to during that long, languid summer? How many lyrics did we sing to the sky whilst we waited for Lucy to get back to who she was before?

Except she didn't; she changed, and I guess so did I. The whole trajectory of our lives was mapped out over the course of those months – a quiet, steely determination inserted itself inside her soul, pulling her away from me before I even realised it was happening.

Do I open it? Don't I? It's the same question that's been rattling around my mind ever since I came home one day and found the box outside my door. If only there was a way to know what was in there without having to open it.

Heads, I look, I think to myself as I reach into my pocket and take out the penny I found in the park, rubbing my thumb over the Queen's profile. *Tails, I don't*. With one quick flick, I toss the coin into the air, catch it, then slap it down on the counter.

Heads.

Best of three? I'm about to toss the coin again when the song on the radio changes. It used to be one of Lucy's favourites, a love ballad powered by the impressive (but slightly annoying) vocals of Celine Dion.

It's nothing more than a coincidence, surely? Yet it feels as if the past is conspiring against me, that the invisible threads from my life that I've managed to pull apart are now weaving their way back to me. First that stupid video of Tristan, then losing Flick because I helped her achieve her dream, and now another reminder of my sister.

Fine. I'll look. But just a peek, nothing more.

I turn off the radio before the song reaches its climax, then go out to the hall, pick up the parcel and bring it into the kitchen.

Slowly, tentatively even, I reach out and pull away a corner of the paper, then a little more. Piece by piece, the treasure inside is revealed. It's a box, roughly the size of a shoebox, along with a plain white envelope.

The box itself is black lacquered, inlaid with ivory flowers and with a golden dragon painted on the lid. Lifting it slowly from the counter I turn it around in search of an opening that I've already guessed won't exist. There are no hinges, no gaps, no obvious place in which to insert a key. It's a puzzle box, so very similar to one I had as a girl. That one came from a market town in France, close to where we used to holiday nearly every summer, and where they made the best ice cream known to man. This one looks old, really old, and I'm guessing from the style of the dragon that it was made in Japan.

Japan. The last place Lucy ever visited with Harry. A trip of a lifetime, they called it, with Lucy even taking a mini sabbatical from work because she wanted to be there when the cherry blossoms were in bloom. What she didn't tell us was that she already knew the tumour had grown back, that she wanted to get on a plane to visit the one place she'd always dreamt of visiting before the doctors refused to let her fly. What she didn't tell us was that she knew she was going to die.

Whatever is in that box was put there by her, or by Harry under her instruction, and then sent all the way from Oxford to London. Either way, she would have known full well how painful it would be to receive it. But why now? Why wait until she was gone before sending it?

I don't want to open the puzzle box. She must have considered the possibility that I might refuse to bow to her wishes, to stubbornly choose the other option. Just because she knew me better than anyone doesn't mean that she could have pre-empted how insanely annoying it is to be sent a box you don't want to open, and yet I really, really want to know what's inside.

I am standing on one side of a door, trying to figure out whether the knowledge of what's on the other side is worth the risk of peeping through the keyhole. Just like Pandora in that bloody story, except the only person who's likely to get hurt in this version is me.

I'm not going to open it. At least not yet, because I can't quite decide if I should.

Putting the box back down, I pick up the envelope, turning it over to find that side too is blank. Bringing it to my nose, I inhale deeply, wondering if there's any clue left behind as to who might have sealed it, but there's nothing there other than the blandness of paper. Slipping my finger under the seal, I pull it open and take out a pale blue notebook on the front of which is a Post-it note with only a handful of words written in black ink:

When you've opened the box, call me. Harry x

Harry. Lucy's adoring husband, who has clearly known about his wife's plan for weeks but said nothing. Why would he keep this from me? Why wait for me to open the box instead of telling me what Lucy left behind?

A quick flick through the notebook reveals nothing other than blank pages that I no longer have any idea how to fill. Lucy clearly thought otherwise, for why else would she send it to me, along with a box I'm pretty sure would be a bad idea to open. Because once I look, I can't unlook. Just as I now can't stop wondering what could possibly be inside that Lucy wants me to see.

Fine. I'll look. But if I can't open it, then I don't have to call him. I can go to work, forget that any of this ever happened. Just like all those nightmares, I can push it away, seal it in my own mental box and never think of it again.

But that dragon. Or, more specifically, its eyes, one of which is looking straight ahead, almost as if it can see me. The other is focused on something over my shoulder, and it could just be a mistake, but the rest of the box is so very precise, so perhaps it's actually deliberate.

I take out a knife, use the tip to press down on the wonky eye and – there – it gives way, just a little, but enough to make me press down again. There's a click and a pop and now that bastard's head is protruding out of the box, two black eyes staring at me as if to ask, what took you so long?

'Here goes nothing,' I say with a grin, and I look around, half expecting Lucy to be there, egging me on. Wrapping my fingers around the dragon's head, I turn it clockwise, bending my head close to listen for the second click that I know has to come, and then I feel rather than see the box split clean down the centre of the dragon's belly, showing me an opening that wasn't there a moment ago.

'Oh.' The word comes out more as a sigh than a sound, because inside the box is a hand-made card decorated with individual petals. I pick it up, my hand shaking because I remember this card. I remember where I was when I made it, along with all the others that we kept in a drawer in my father's study.

There's more. A sheet of paper, folded in two but through which I can see Lucy's neat, practised script, written in green ink. With a trembling hand, I unfold it, blinking through tears as I read my sister's final letter to me.

My darling Beth,

If you're reading this, it means I am gone. Although I bet you've left me on a shelf somewhere for weeks, months perhaps? Trying to decide whether or not it's a good idea to open me up and whether you want to know what it is I'm leaving behind.

What I want is for you to remember what happened. All of it, not just the parts you think you are to blame for. I want you to follow the clues I've left behind, just like the treasure hunts you loved as a girl. At the end lies a gift from me to you, to do with what you will.

I hope this helps in some way. I hope you decide to follow the clues, look back and remember the person you always deserved to be. But also remember it wasn't your fault, not what happened back then, nor what happened to me. You cannot change the past, Beth, but you can control your future.

Oh, and I want you to write it all down. Whatever it is that the clues make you think of, put it in the notebook I've sent. Don't be afraid of it, don't be afraid of who you used to be.

You once told me that you wrote because you had to, not because you wanted to. Does it matter then that you think you've forgotten how? Because, believe me, Beth, life can be cruel and unforgiving and surprise you in the worst possible way. You have time that I do not. And you have more inside you than you know, so please don't waste the life you have.

This is now. This is what you have, so live it, embrace it, and don't take a single moment for granted.

I love you, my beautiful hyacinth girl, and I will be with you always.

Lucy xxx

It's as if she has inserted a very long, very sharp object into my throat and is pushing it straight down towards my heart.

Putting the letter aside, I pick up the hand-made card, rubbing my fingertip across the petals and thinking back to the day we headed out in search of wildflowers. It is a day nobody in our family will ever likely forget, which is precisely why I know that Lucy wants me to remember it all over again.

Of all the cards, of all the memories, the words, the meaning, she had to go and choose this one.

But why? Everything changed that day. For better or worse I still don't really know. What is it you're trying to tell me, Lucy? What's the point of remembering when you yourself have just told me the past cannot be altered?

Dammit. She always did know exactly how to wind me up. Guess I should call Harry. Guess there's no going back now.

Easing apart the spine of the notebook, I'm overcome by a sense of déjà vu. And not just because there are several more notebooks identical to this filled with words and sitting on a shelf in my bedroom back home. It's the soft creak of spine, the feel of paper under my fingertips, the moment before the images spill from my mind and on to the page. It's all so familiar, which only makes it hurt to remember.

4.

Sixteen years ago . . .

Fat bees droned in lavender skies under which the two of us ran towards the river. It was one of those almost-summer days that held the promise of something more, and I remember hoping it would be a day we'd never forget.

Lucy let go of my hand, slipping between the trees to be covered by all that green.

'Lucy, wait,' I said, wondering if my legs would ever grow long enough to outrun her, or if I'd ever be able to remember all the things Mum kept expecting me to do. Like thinking before speaking, or taking off my shoes when I came home. But there were far more interesting things to think about back then, like learning new chords on the guitar, or what it was that had changed about my sister to make people look at her differently.

I asked Mum about it and she said I had no need to be jealous, that my turn would come soon enough. At the time it made no sense, but now I realise that Lucy had morphed from a pretty girl into a strikingly beautiful teenager with the sort of face you wanted to look at for longer than you should.

We were heading for a field beyond the river because Lucy wanted to collect wildflowers and use them to make cards, although she wouldn't admit who the cards were for. I had my suspicions, not least because she kept giggling on the phone with her friends, or staring out at nothing at all whenever I asked her a question. How different it all would have been if her first teenage crush was the only thing any of us had to worry about that summer.

Traipsing through the woods, I ripped up handfuls of ferns, tossing them over my shoulder and wishing we could go back to when Lucy was happy to play hide-and-seek, or help me look for fairies that might live in the trees. She'd even stopped listening to music and would come into whichever room I was in, yelling at me to turn the stereo down.

I came out at the narrowest part of the river, where we always used to cross, and that's when I saw her, down by the water's edge, hunched over and clutching at her head.

'Lucy?' I called out. 'What happened?'

She looked up at me, eyes half rolled back in their sockets and her fingers frantically tugging at her hair, as if she were trying to rip something out from the inside of her skull.

'What do I do?' I said, looking around me in the hope that one of our parents would magically appear. 'Lucy, please. Tell me what to do.'

She didn't reply, just sat there rocking back and forth, seeming so vulnerable and small. I remember being scared, properly scared, because Lucy always knew what to do and now it was up to me to figure it out without her.

'Where does it hurt?' I crouched down beside her and prised her hands away. In return, she began to moan, twisting her head from side to side and balling her hands into fists that she began pummelling against my chest.

'Kite, kite, kite,' she said, the words all twisted and turned around, like she was sucking on a sweet as she spoke.

'What kite?' I asked, holding her by the wrists and glancing up at the cloudless sky.

'Bike pulled up, tomato blue, GO AWAY.' She was staring at me, willing me to make sense of all the mismatched words.

'Lucy,' I said, suddenly aware that I should not under any circumstances panic, even though there was a whole great clot of it at the base of my throat, making it difficult to swallow. 'Lucy,' I said, hooking my arms under her armpits and helping her to her feet. 'I'm going to need you to walk, ok?'

As we slowly (really slowly, because she gasped with every single step) made our way back home, I remember thinking that this didn't seem like one of the migraines Lucy had been having, regular as the veritable clock, every month. Migraines that Mum told me were nothing to worry about and the doctor had said were just a symptom of hormonal changes. Chances were, she'd grow out of them soon enough.

I looked it up. Researched all the different ways in which people experience pain, including seeing sound and tasting colours, but none of what I'd learnt matched up to Lucy speaking in tongues and trying to pull her brain out of her eye sockets.

'It's ok,' I kept saying over and over, to myself as much as to Lucy. 'It's going to be ok.'

Needless to say, we didn't make it to the other side of the river, to where the wildflowers grew. Nor did Lucy end up sending a card to Thomas Hardy (I think she liked him just for his name), although we did sit and make all sorts of things together during those weird summer months that followed.

I still remember the smell of that hospital waiting room – antiseptic hidden under too many layers of perfume, all stitched together with a huge dollop of fear. There were tea- and coffee-making facilities and a TV in one corner playing repeats on MTV. I watched as Cher belted out a song whilst standing half naked on a battleship, surrounded by men in uniform. I hummed along to the melody, pressing my fingers against my thigh as I figured out the backing track and promised myself that I'd play it for my sister as soon as we got home.

Lucy was sitting next to me, calm as you like and sucking on a lemon drop from a packet that she'd been allowed to buy from a vending machine in the hospital foyer.

I also remember the look on the nurse's face when she came in to collect us. She looked from my parents to me, then Lucy, with a pathetic attempt at a smile. That's when I knew something was wrong. Really wrong. Wrong enough to make me grab Lucy's hand and try to stop her from getting up out of her chair. Because if she never got up, never went into the doctor's office to be told what the MRI she'd had only the day before had found inside her brain, then none of it would actually be true.

'Let go, Beth,' Lucy had said, pulling her arm away and rubbing at the small pink semicircles my nails had left on her skin. 'You have to let me go.'

'I think I'll stay here,' I replied, watching as first Lucy, then my parents, followed that stupid nurse out of the waiting room. I popped one of Lucy's sweets into my mouth, rolling it over my tongue, and silently told myself that every little thing was going to be all right.

5.

It's so surreal being back in Oxford. Part of me swore I never would, that I would deliberately avoid coming anywhere near the city, let alone stand outside the picture-perfect cottage that used to be Lucy's home.

The whole train journey out here I kept trying not to think of all the other times I'd sat in an identical carriage, surrounded by strangers but never feeling alone. Today, I never wanted the journey to end, wished I could somehow slow the passage of time, or will a tree to fall on to the tracks.

I haven't been here in what feels like forever. The last time was about four months before she died, and I couldn't find the courage to stay for more than the time it took her to tell me that all her luck had run out. After I left, Lucy called me, over and over, until eventually I picked up. We spoke nearly every day from then on, sent letters and emails and parcels filled with unimportant things. But I was completely incapable of being in the same space as her, had no desire whatsoever to look at her incredible face and wonder when the last time I would ever see it might be.

I used to tell myself it was so I could forever picture her the way she was, before. In reality, I think I was too scared, too weak, to be there for her, because I kept telling myself that it would be ok, that some kind of miracle would happen and she would be ok. So when

I finally found the nerve to call Harry and tell him I'd opened the box I was already terrified of what might happen next.

'There's something else,' he'd said from the other end of the phone. I was sitting, straddling the windowsill of my bedroom and smoking a cigarette from a very old, long-forgotten packet I'd unearthed from the inside pocket of my rucksack.

'I'm guessing you're not going to tell me over the phone,' I said, extinguishing the cigarette and dropping it into the flowerbed five floors below. I could almost hear the smile in his voice when he replied, and it made me sad and relieved all at once.

'Do you really think she'd make it that easy?'

'No,' I said, managing the smallest of smiles in return, because I suspected that my darling, annoying, smart and manipulative sister would have something more up her sleeve than a letter and a hand-made card. And yes, the fact it had been sent by Harry was also a not-so-subtle clue, but my mind has always been rather good at filtering out all the bad. It's like my secret weapon, one I have polished and perfected ever since the day we were told there was a tumour in my sister's brain roughly the size of a satsuma and it could in all likelihood kill her.

Which is precisely what it did do, despite the initial operation and subsequent years of check-ups. Along with all the reassurances that it hadn't grown back and Lucy was, as she always had been, going to be absolutely fine. But it was always there: the question, the fear. It was like living with a devil inside you, one that was sleeping, but you had no idea if and when it might awaken.

Lucy gave that devil a face. I smile at the memory of Mum discovering pages and pages of drawings all the same, featuring a caricature of an old man with spiky orange hair and a down-turned smile, each and every one with a thick red cross drawn across his face. She said it made it easier to believe the tumour was really gone.

It wasn't though. The doctors said from the very beginning it wasn't possible to cut it all out, because if they did Lucy might lose the ability to walk or talk, or even end up in a coma. Which in turn meant there was always the risk it might grow back, and of course there was no way of knowing which way the tumour would decide to grow (inward, as it happens, making it inoperable and ultimately fatal). Mum and Dad looked into all kinds of alternative treatments, including a hospital in Switzerland that had 'amazing' results at extracting whole tumours, but Lucy refused. Said it was her body and just because she was only fourteen it didn't mean anyone else had the right to decide what happened to her.

At some point she must have asked herself whether she had made the right decision. Removing more of the tumour might have meant she lived for longer, but what kind of life would it have been? Would she have been able to go back to school, to push and drive for all the successes she worked so hard for? Would she have ever met Harry and fallen madly in love? It's a question I turn over and over, usually when I can't sleep, because I have no idea which option would have been better, for me as well as her.

I bought a bag of satsumas with me the last time I visited. It had become a long-standing joke between Lucy and me (one that Mum despised, saying it was utterly tasteless). After the operation, I couldn't bring myself to eat satsumas, or any type of orange, as if the citrus fruits were somehow to blame for what happened to Lucy. Then one day, about a month after she came out of hospital, we were sitting in the back garden, arguing about whether Billie Holiday or Ella Fitzgerald was a better singer (which was a stupid argument as they're both incredible). All of a sudden Lucy got up, went into the kitchen and came out holding an orange.

'The look on your face,' she said, openly laughing at me and rolling the offending fruit between her palms. At that stage, her fine motor skills weren't back to normal and I knew she wanted to throw it at me but was worried about her aim.

'What?' I replied, all too aware of how I couldn't quite bring myself to look directly at the orange.

'Go on,' she said, holding the orange out and waving it in my face. 'I dare you.'

'Dare you back,' I said, slowly and deliberately using one finger to move her hand aside.

'Nuh-uh,' she said, giggling with delight as I walked away, and she began to follow me around the garden, nudging me every so often with the orange. 'I dared you first. Besides, eating an orange isn't going to make the tumour grow back.'

'It's not that,' I said, wondering how on earth she was able to see inside my brain, and wishing she'd been able to use that gift on herself, so that we could have caught the tumour earlier. 'I just don't like oranges any more.'

'Yeah, right,' Lucy said, reaching out to tap the orange against my bare arm. I flinched in response. 'Don't think I haven't noticed all the other weird stuff you've been doing.'

It wasn't weird. Not if it worked. Ok, so maybe the cracks in the pavement thing was a bit silly, not least because it wasn't that long since Lucy and I would pretend that if you stepped on the cracks you'd be eaten by crocodiles. But there was nothing wrong with knocking on wood or throwing salt over your shoulder, not if it protected you from the hands of fate. Lucy's tumour had proven that so much about life is down to luck, and I was going to do everything I could to make sure that Lucy's wouldn't ever be bad again.

For a minute or so we shuffled around the garden (her mobility was improving, but I wasn't about to run away, knowing full well she'd never catch me), and then I made a great show of relenting, with arms thrown above my head and a huge sigh of 'fine' as I took the orange and pierced its flesh with my thumbnail.

My guess is she'd known all along I would give in, just like I did with the parcel she sent me. Which is why I now find myself standing on the pavement outside their house, searching for that last bit of courage to actually knock on the front door.

'If you decide to run away, I promise not to tell,' Harry says, coming up from behind and making me jump.

'Jesus, Harry,' I say with a forced laugh. 'How to give a girl a heart attack.'

'Sorry,' he says with a genuine smile.

Harry is just as gorgeous as ever. But despite the perfect teeth, chiselled jaw and eyes you could get lost in, his usual bright and shiny is definitely gone, replaced by something I recognise all too well.

'Hold this, would you?' he asks, passing me a bag of shopping then fishing his keys out of his pocket. I glance in the bag to discover fresh bread, a pot of sun-dried tomatoes and something wrapped up in greaseproof paper. I wonder if it's for me, if he wants me to stay for lunch, and I don't quite know what to do with this simplest of gestures because I'm pretty sure I don't deserve his kindness.

'How are you holding up?' he asks, propping the door open with one foot and inviting me in.

I hover in the doorway, looking along the hall and out towards the garden, then kick off my shoes and leave my satchel by the stairs.

'I'm fine,' I lie, following Harry through to the kitchen and ignoring the sideways glance he sends my way.

'Tea?' he says, holding up the kettle, and I nod my response, then perch on one of the kitchen stools and watch as he busies himself with filling the teapot with fresh leaves and fetching milk from the fridge. It's such a simple thing, and also happens to be exactly what I was doing when I discovered that Lucy had died. It makes me furious, because she will never get to do any of the things we take for granted ever again.

The room is exactly as it has always been, but the absence of her seems to fill it. It takes me a while to figure it out, looking from the windowsill, busy with individual herb pots, to the fridge magnets Lucy has collected ever since we were kids. The fruit bowl is full (including a couple of oranges, one of which I pick up and begin to roll up and down the work surface), and the radio is, as ever, tuned to Classic FM.

That's when it hits me: it's not just Lucy herself who is missing but all the sounds and scents she created that would imprint themselves into the very air I was now expected to breathe. This is her home, but it no longer belongs to her, and the idea that she is slowly being erased from it all is enough to make me push away from the counter and go out to the garden.

'Beth?' Harry calls out as he follows me on to the patio, above which is a wisteria-covered pergola that I know he once spent a whole summer building.

'What is it?' he asks, resting a hand on my shoulder, and I resist the urge to shrug him off.

'I'm sorry,' I whisper, biting back tears.

'I know,' he sighs, and I hear the depth of his sadness in that one long breath. 'Me too.'

There are so many words I could say to try to explain why I stayed away. Or to somehow express what it really means to no longer have her here. But there is so much I don't know how to feel, let alone say, so instead I decide to forgo the sentimentalities altogether.

'Why am I here?' I turn to face him, noticing the dark circles under his eyes and day-old stubble on his chin. This has got to be just as painful for him as it is me. I know I do anything I possibly can to avoid talking or even thinking about Lucy, so God only knows why he agreed to do whatever it is she asked him to do.

Ok, so of course he agreed, she was dying, but that's hardly the point. He must know how careful we were with one another at the end. How our conversations and letters were filled with so many gaps that we assumed there would always be time to fill. I don't need to tell him just how broken Lucy's death has made me. What I don't understand is why he would let Lucy think that a trip down memory lane was going to be anything other than a complete waste of time.

Harry is looking at me in a way I can't put a name to, almost as if he really doesn't want to say whatever he is about to say but is worried about what will happen if he doesn't. I want to tell him it's ok, he can decide not to tell me because, other than the two of us, the only other person who knows about the puzzle box is dead, so we could easily pretend I never opened it in the first place.

'Before Lu died . . .' he says, then blows out all the air in his lungs and sits down on the back step. 'Before Lu died,' he tries again, sniffling loudly and clearing his throat, 'she asked me to help her with something.'

'Help her with what?'

'With you.'

'Sorry, what?' I ask, looking down at Harry, who is holding out a small glass bowl complete with a lid that he lifts to reveal a dozen or so sweets, each one different to the next. I spy a lemon drop, a sugar-dusted piece of Turkish delight and, of course, a butterscotch wrapped in paper.

'She used to keep this by the sofa,' I say, helping myself to the lemon drop and using my tongue to push it into my cheek. 'Mum made me go to the shop once a week so she never ran out.'

'Why didn't you take the butterscotch?' he asks, putting the lid back on and setting the bowl down beside him.

'No reason,' I say, sucking at the sweet and avoiding his eye. He's looking at me again in that strange way and it fills me with an urge to run all the way back to London, where I can pretend that everything is fine.

'Ok. Here's a question. What pulls you down and never lets go?'

'No idea,' I reply, watching as Harry helps himself to the butterscotch. I know this is another stupid clue; I can imagine the two of them sitting out here, laughing at their brilliance as they pieced each and every little detail together. It stings because, once upon a time, Lucy used to make up games with me.

'What did the card make you think of?' He heads back inside and I hear the clink of spoon against china before he returns with two mugs of tea.

'Nothing,' I say, blowing into the mug and thinking how ridiculous the answer is, especially when he just gave me some extra time to come up with a decent response. 'I mean, not nothing. Obviously. Just nothing in particular.'

'I see,' he says, taking a sip of tea and watching me over the rim. Clearly he knows this is bullshit and I'm surprised he's being so decent about it all and not grabbing hold of me and trying to shake out something, anything, that resembles an honest answer.

'But why did she call you hyacinth girl?'

I let go a small laugh because he knows precisely why. First it was a line in a poem; later it became the name of a song.

'Enough of the riddles, Harry,' I reply, spitting the sweet into my hand and dropping it into a nearby flowerpot. 'Can't you just tell me what she wants me to do?'

'I told you,' he says in a voice akin to an adult placating a child. 'She asked me to help fix you.'

'Fix me?' I laugh, but inside there's a nugget of dread about what he means exactly. 'There's nothing wrong with me.' I turn my head away so he can't see the lie behind the words.

'Course not, Beth. Your life is perfect.' He looks away and I want to peer inside his head, find out what he's really thinking about all this, about me.

'Don't be a prick, Harry. It doesn't suit you. Just give me whatever it is Lucy left and then I'll go and you won't have to be bothered or inconvenienced by me any more.'

He sends me a look, one that tells me he would rather be doing anything other than sitting here with me. 'Believe me, right now I wish I could. But I made a promise and I'm not about to break it just so you can skip the hard parts.'

It's insulting, when you think about it, the subtle dig behind his words. Because I have made countless promises over the years, pretty much none of which I've been able to keep. Apart from one, made the night before Lucy's operation, when she climbed into my bed and made me swear that we'd always tell one another the truth, no matter what.

I think she was terrified, not only of the odds linked to her survival but also of our parents becoming so overprotective that they wouldn't ever tell her the bad stuff. Which they did, smothering her with all their love, thinking it would keep her safe. They told us everything was going to be all right, but there was a part of me that knew it was a promise they couldn't keep. The tumour had still grown in the first place, they hadn't been able to protect Lucy from it, so how would they make sure it never came back?

But it's not Harry's promise to Lucy that is pissing me off. It's her not telling me herself, instead of using him to speak her wishes from beyond the grave. More than that, it's because she could have told me, if only I'd had the courage to actually spend time with her before she died.

Ultimately, it's too late and I have no way of going back and telling myself to realise that my fear was nothing compared to hers. This is what hurts most of all: the guilt of knowing it's my fault we didn't have the chance to make everything right before she died. Still, I'm not about to share any of this with Harry.

'Why do you think she sent you that particular card with hyacinth petals on the front?' If he's annoyed with me he doesn't show it, instead taking another sip of tea.

'I don't know, Harry. It was such a long time ago and, funnily enough, I try not to think about it.'

'Maybe you should.'

'Why?'

'Because Lucy wanted you to.'

And there's his ace, dealt so calmly but with the full knowledge that, even before she died, I would have walked through fire for my sister if that's what she asked me to do.

Even after she broke her promise to me, I still loved her more than anyone or anything. Which is ridiculous, I know, but I do remember having a conversation with her at some point about mind over matter. Something about how your mind (by which she meant my mind) is your own worst enemy; and she used the example of people walking over hot coals to prove her point.

Ok, enough. This isn't helping and Harry is now looking at me in a way that says he's expecting an answer to a riddle that my sister would have solved in a heartbeat. What was the question? Right, a card. A hand-made card with hyacinth petals stuck to the front and a clear reference to her favourite poem, by T. S. Eliot. A poem she first read when she was – what, fourteen? – in a book I borrowed from the library. A book she read cover to cover, again and again. Ok, now I get it. Or at least I think I do.

'Where's the book, Harry?' Lucy made me cycle all the way into town to buy her a copy. In fact I bought two, hid one under my pillow and read it in secret, because back then I thought I wanted to be just like her when I grew up.

'What book?'

43

'Seriously? I know you know. She based her entire thesis on that poem, a poem we both know she's been obsessed with ever since we were kids. So hand it over, pretty please, and then I will go.'

'It's not here.' There's half a smile on his face and I wish I knew what it meant. Is he pleased for me, or simply relieved that I won't be here for much longer?

'Then where?' Dammit, I know exactly where. Or rather where Lucy would have deliberately taken it in order to force me to do something else I have absolutely no desire to do. 'I'm not going home.'

Harry wipes his hand over his face in the same way Dad used to when he was disappointed in me but didn't want to hurt my feelings. 'Why not?'

I haven't been back to my childhood home since the argument with my mother. Too many memories bundled up with the stink of my mother's disappointment that the wrong sister died. I can still hear all those accusations, still feel all the hurt we threw at one another, exacerbated by the darkness caused by Lucy's death.

I should at least call and speak to Dad. I miss him and the way we would wake in the middle of the night to hear the other playing the piano. I used to sneak down the stairs to sit beside him and together we would play everything from Bach to Buddy Holly, with some experiments of our own chucked in for good measure.

'There's no point going back, and Mum probably won't even notice that I'm there.'

'That's a really shit thing to say.'

'Why?'

'Because she lost her too. We all did, Beth, and you don't get to have the monopoly on grief.'

'I was there the first time. I was the one who sat with her, read to her, plaited her hair and held her hand in the night when she was too scared to sleep. So don't tell me about grief or loss. I've been mourning her for years.'

'She adored you.'

'Then tell me, Harry!' I'm yelling now and fat, angry tears are streaming down my face. I try to swipe them away but they won't stop; why won't they stop? 'Tell me what the point of this stupid treasure hunt actually is?'

'She wants you to forgive yourself for what happened. To finally start living the life you're supposed to.'

Oh, great. This isn't what I was expecting. Or perhaps it is, because it is such a clever way to get me to listen to what Lucy has been saying for years and I have been casually dismissing.

'I'm not having this conversation.' I go back into the house, through the kitchen to the hall, where I pick up my satchel. Shoving my feet back into my shoes, I stare into the hallway mirror, at the wild fury in my eyes that I'm not entirely convinced is aimed only at Harry. My gaze moves across the wall, taking in all the photographs I have seen a thousand times before and resting on one taken at Lucy's matriculation ceremony, when she was formally accepted into Oxford University. It was a place where she flourished and soared and became happier than ever before. The two of us are looking at one another, smiles wide and faces filled with all the promise of youth.

It was the last photo taken before I discovered that even the bond between sisters is delicate enough to break. I wish I could go back, tell my teenage self that I had to forget it all, that I had to cling as tightly to my sister as I possibly could, because she'd be gone before she reached thirty. I hate that there's nothing I can do to change what happened. I hate that I allowed myself to stay so angry and disappointed with my life when she won't ever get to live hers to its proper end.

'I can't do this, Harry,' I say as he comes up behind me. I stifle a sob as I shoulder my satchel and open the door. 'I'm sorry.'

He reaches out a hand, tries to hold me back. 'When are you going to stop pretending that teaching piano and playing in a hotel bar makes you happy?'

'What would be the point?' I reply, shrugging him loose and setting off down the path. 'She'll still be dead.'

'If you change your mind . . .' he calls after me, and I want to scream at him to leave me alone, to stop caring because it's too late to change the past. 'I'll still be here for you, Beth. No matter what.'

Standing at the crossroads, I look right, towards the city centre, filled with exceptional students and a multitude of pubs that I could get drunk in. Instead, I turn left, back to the station; I can be back in London in under two hours, call Sam and ask for an extra shift.

Taking my phone out, I open up my favourite app in the vague hope that it might help me make sense of my current situation.

A strange letter or phone call could come your way today, and the information you receive may seem rather confusing. But today is not a good day to make any decisions.

Great, so rather than actually tell me anything of use, it would seem that all I'm supposed to do is nothing. Lucy was the one I used to turn to for advice, the one who always knew what I should do. Sometimes she used to tell me without me even realising I needed it.

It started when I was a gawky, nervous thirteen-year-old, with train-track braces and frizzy hair. Lucy was, of course, sleek and gorgeous and never had a single spot in her entire life. Mum didn't bother trying to make me more presentable – even before Lucy got sick I think she simply stopped trying to make me into something I was not. But Lucy was both persistent and persuasive, asking if she could practise her make-up techniques on me, or if we could try out a new hair masque together because it would be fun.

I hate this. I hate the fact she's gone and I'll never again be able to ask for her help, or sit up late at night watching a movie and eating far too much popcorn. What I hate most of all is that I wasted the time we had left.

As I arrive at the station, I feel my phone vibrate, announcing the arrival of a new text. Even before I put my hand in my pocket to check the screen I know who it's from.

She asked me to send you this, Harry has written, sent with an accompanying voice note. *Said it should help you remember when you used to have a dream.*

Sitting on the train, my head resting against the window and little puffs of my breath clouding the view, I feel the arrival of yet another text.

Hey babe, Got your number from Sam. You free for a drink later? Jack.

I start typing out a response, because yes, absolutely, I want nothing more than to get lost in his arms. Just before I hit 'send' I stop. I don't know why, or what it is that made me pause (although Natalie is definitely up there with all the reasons why it would be wrong), because rational thinking, processing the pros and cons of a situation, isn't something I would usually bother with. But today is clearly so very other, so very not normal, and definitely a day that I know, on some level, I need to remember, not deliberately try to forget.

I delete Jack's text, then open up the previous one from Harry. The voice note he's sent doesn't come with any kind of clue as to what it is Lucy wanted me to hear, and I am so very, very nervous as to what it could be.

Is it a song? It must be a song, which is nothing at all to worry about. But that's like saying it's just a kiss, or a look, or a second of time that won't mean anything at all when you're old and grey. Because Lucy won't ever grow old, or have kids, or be around to tell me off any more when I screw up all over again.

I miss you, I think for the millionth time today. Then I stick in my earphones and click on the link, closing my eyes and steeling myself for whatever memory she's about to send my way.

6.

Slamming the front door behind me, I dropped my school bag by the stairs and headed for the kitchen. There was a fruit cake cooling on the counter, the sweet scent of citrus softening my mood a little. I was about to help myself to a generous slice when I heard the soft chink of a cup being put down coming from the living room.

'Hey,' I said, lingering in the doorway.

'Hey,' Lucy replied, looking at me over her shoulder and then returning her attention to a repeat of Buffy the Vampire Slayer.

'There's cake in the kitchen,' I said, watching as Buffy stabbed yet another vampire through the heart.

'I know. Fetch me a slice?'

'But Mum said . . .' I replied, glancing behind me, because Mum told me every morning without fail that I was not to disturb my sister when she was resting. Which of course I ignored, because coming home from school to sit with Lucy was the best part of my day.

'I don't care what Mum said.' Lucy yawned, stretching her arms above her head to reveal a line of paler than pale stomach. 'She's driving me insane. Won't leave me alone for five minutes and refuses to let me do anything for myself.'

I listened through the quiet for the sound of Mum's annoyance. I'd become so very good at reading her mood since Lucy got sick – anything from the way she opened and shut a cupboard door to how long it took her to register my presence and eventually say hello.

'Ok, ok,' I said, heading back to the kitchen and taking two plates from the cupboard, then opening the fridge and taking out a can of Coke.

'That stuff will rot your insides,' Lucy called out from the other room, and I pulled a face, but opened the can anyway, then cut a thick slice of cake and sat down at the table. There was a small stack of papers at the far end, along with a copy of The Catcher in the Rye that I knew Lucy had been writing an essay on over the weekend.

I shouldn't have looked, but I could see the edge of a red circle on a page sticking out from Salinger's novel, and Lucy was in the living room so what was the harm in taking a peek? Before I could change my mind, my fingers had pulled the page free and I was staring down at a bright, red 'B' along with the words 'WHY do you think Holden is so afraid of change?' written underneath.

'Stop going through my stuff,' Lucy said, leaning against the door-frame and pointing at the table. 'And don't tell Mum.'

'What's wrong with a B?' I said, taking a large bite of cake and washing it down with Coke. I could feel the sugar fizzing against my teeth and wondered if Lucy was telling the truth about its rotting powers.

'Nothing,' Lucy said as she shuffled back into the living room and collapsed on to the sofa. 'Except a B won't get me into Oxford.'

'Ok,' I replied, thinking that if I ever got a B for my English essay, I'd be doing little laps of honour round the garden instead of worrying about university, which even for Lucy was an absolute age away. Why she was bothering with schoolwork when she had the perfect excuse not to do any was beyond me. But then again, even before the tumour, Lucy had always been determined to be the best at everything.

'I mean, I know you think it's silly,' Lucy said as I sat down next to her and passed her a plate and took another bite of my cake so I didn't have to answer. 'And it's just one essay.'

I nodded as she took a huge mouthful, closing her eyes at the warm, sugary deliciousness.

'Besides, Holden was an idiot. I mean, who wants everything to always stay the same?'

'Right,' I said, even though I had no idea what she was talking about.

'And it was selfish of him to try to save Jane because it wasn't even his choice to make.'

'So he didn't save her?'

'No. Well, sort of. But that's not the point.'

'Ok.' I was starting to wonder if there was in fact a point but knew better than to question Lucy when she'd had part of her brain cut out only weeks before.

'Sorry.' Lucy's head dropped back and there was a tear collecting in the corner of her eye that she quickly swept away. 'It's all just so . . .'

'I know,' I said, staring at the shaven patch of her skull, where a thick but actually rather neat six-inch row of surgical stitches glared out at me. 'It sucks. But I came third in a practice race for sports day, so it's not all bad.' I gave her a gentle poke in the ribs. 'Bet I could beat you now too.'

'Ha ha, very funny,' she said, bashing me with a cushion and then waggling her finger in the direction of the garden room. 'Come on then, play me something. Astound me.'

I laughed because it was the same thing our piano teacher used to say, right up to the point we decided I wasn't really suited to classical training.

I crept into the garden room and over to the piano, which was sitting proud and expectant in the bay window that overlooked the back lawn. It was a sleek black baby grand, a family heirloom that most people would fawn over and protect from all but the cleanest of fingers. But Dad had sat Lucy and me down before we could even speak let alone play and encouraged us to listen, to really listen to the music.

'Pull it deep inside you,' he said when we got old enough to understand the nuances of a piece. 'Feel the vibrations in your belly. Tell me what the music tastes like, what pictures it creates in your head.'

Lucy would always smile or shuffle on her seat, unsure what she should say. I, on the other hand, would race around the room, arms splayed and shouting about dragons soaring through thunderstorms or beetles dancing on sunbeams.

'It's a gift,' Dad would tell me when he came down in the middle of the night to find me playing a song that had woken me from my dreams. 'And gifts aren't meant to be wasted. So don't think this means you get to skip music practice.'

There's a photo of us somewhere, me no more than a babe in arms, gazing up at him as he played a lullaby. Music was so much a part of who Dad and I were. It stitched the world together in a way nothing else ever could, and taught me how to speak without words or simply lose myself inside a melody.

Eyes closed, I sat at the piano, trusting that my fingers would know what needed to be played.

'Oh please, not Simon & Garfunkel,' Lucy said, slipping on to the seat beside me, a little out of breath and somehow so much smaller, more childlike, than before.

'Then what?' I asked, watching as she pressed down with each finger in turn, slowly and with deliberate care. I had to look away, because there were so many things Lucy could no longer do, things she used to be brilliant at. If it had been me, I would have cursed and spat, raged and acted like a complete nightmare.

Not a single word of complaint ever left my sister's lips. That which would have crushed me only made her more determined than ever to succeed. When the doctors said it would take her months to be able to walk let alone run any distance again, she decided to do ten laps of the garden instead of the prescribed four. She would sit watching TV, a can of beans in each hand, doing hundreds of bicep curls, moving on to press-ups when she found the strength. She made me lend her my Dictaphone so that she could dictate all her schoolwork when holding a pen or staring at a blank page made her headaches worse. She did absolutely everything she could to make sure that the tumour wouldn't stop her from following her dream of being the very best version of herself she could possibly be.

Just before she went back to school, she got me to shave off all that hair, saying people were going to stare anyway, so might as well give them something to stare at. Mum had an absolute fit when she saw those platinum strands blowing through the rose bushes, even threatened to shave my hair off as well, as punishment I suppose for simply doing what my sister asked.

Lucy's hair grew back thicker and more lustrous than before, reborn and rejuvenated, just like the rest of her. Part of me was always jealous of the gift the tumour had ended up giving her. Part of me wished I had been the one to get sick.

'How about a bit of Dylan?' I asked, fiddling around with some chords as I searched my mind for the tune. Music filled the space around us, those perfect notes pulling at our hearts, and as I began to play Bob Dylan's soulful tune about the restorative power of love, Lucy rested her head on my shoulder. One hand curled around my forearm, squeezing gently so she could feel the movement of muscle under skin.

'I love it when you play,' she said, and in that moment I felt the kind of peace that you only ever get a handful of times, and only if you're smart enough to be paying attention. 'But I'd rather you played me one of your own.'

I smiled because she was my sister and therefore completely biased about my capabilities. She also knew I didn't have her courage, or her ability to not give a shit what other people thought about my music.

But she also had a hole in her head, could barely walk and had no idea if the tumour might one day grow back.

We all carried that knowledge inside us, hid it from one another, the thing we weren't allowed to ever really talk about. I heard Mum and Dad late at night, her crying, him trying to tell her it was all going to be ok. But nobody can ever be sure, can they? Which is why, when Lucy asked me to show her a piece of my soul, even though I was scared, I did it anyway.

Eyes closed, my fingers found the keys all by themselves. I took a long, slow breath and began to sing the lyrics I'd only finished writing over breakfast that morning.

> I walk with you,
> Through fields of lavender and blue.
> You take me to the river,
> We jump in one by one
> I will follow you for ever,
> But before we reach it,
> You'll be gone.

When the song came to an end I sat for a moment, unable to lift my head, to look at her face and discover if I'd made a fool of myself in front of the person whose opinion I cared about most of all.

'Beth,' she whispered, placing her fragile hand on top of mine. 'Beth,' she said again, and I turned my face to hers, saw that she was crying.

'I'm sorry,' I said, my own tears starting to fall. 'I didn't mean . . .'

'No, don't be sorry,' she said, smiling through her tears. 'It's beautiful.'

'I found a book,' I said, wiping the back of my hand over my nose, then glancing at the door as it was a habit I knew Mum disapproved of. 'In the library.'

Lucy rolled her eyes at me, but she was smiling so I didn't mind. 'What else would you find in the library?'

'It's by a man called T. S. Eliot. I don't know his full name, but he writes—'

'Poetry,' Lucy interrupted. 'I know, I've heard of him.'

'Well, anyway, when I started reading it, I swear, Lu, I swear I could hear an entire orchestra playing behind the words.'

Lucy bit down on her bottom lip, gazing past me with a veiled look in her eye. 'Mrs Patterson,' she said, shaking her head over and over. 'She's my English teacher and she's always telling us to listen to the rhythm of a poem. I never really got what she meant until now.'

'Really?' I said, grinning like a loon at the knowledge that I had somehow managed to teach my sister something instead of the other way around.

'The lyrics,' she said, gently pressing down on a couple of keys, and I mimicked her movement. 'They're from a poem?'

'I guess,' I said with a shrug. 'I mean, were they any good?'

'You mean you made them up?' Her eyes were wide, her face showing me all sorts of emotions, but I couldn't quite figure out what the sum of them meant. 'Bloody hell, Beth.' She exhaled the words and I giggled because we weren't supposed to swear.

Lucy shifted her weight on the stool, took hold of both my hands and squeezed them as hard as her body would allow. 'You need to write more,' she said, staring straight at me in a way that made me want to look away, but I didn't. 'Promise me you'll write some more?'

'Mum says music can't be anything more than a hobby.' My mother took great delight in reminding me that through hard work and sheer determination she had been the first in her family to earn a place at university. It wasn't something she ever had to remind my sister about.

'Then don't tell her.'

'I don't know, Lucy. She'd be kind of mad if she found out.'

'And just because Dad chose to stop touring it doesn't mean your dream can't come true.'

I bit down on my lip, feeling guilty somehow for having a dream so similar to my dad's. He gigged for years before meeting Mum. Touring all over Europe and playing keyboard for anyone who asked. But then Mum got pregnant and he came home, started teaching instead. It made me sad to think he had to give up doing what he loved.

'We all get to be extraordinary in some way,' Lucy went on, pressing down on the piano keys, slowly but firmly. 'And I think you've just found yours. One day you'll be standing on stage at Glastonbury, and I'll be in the crowd, cheering you on.'

I laughed. 'You and I both know I'd never perform in public.'

'Then fake it till you make it,' she said, bumping her shoulder against my own. 'Don't let the fear stop you from doing what you were born to do.'

I made countless trips to the library that summer, bringing back book after book of poetry – everyone from Plath to Dickinson with a whole load of Keats thrown into the mix. Lucy and I would sit, either on the sofa or stretched out on the back lawn, taking turns to read out loud.

When the books became too much, she would sit by my side at the piano and listen as I put my own words to music. I also started recording them on tiny cassette tapes that fitted inside a Dictaphone and kept them all in a box under my bed.

Perhaps, in a different kind of life, I could have been as extraordinary as she believed me to be. Problem was, long before Lucy died, someone else had already broken me into a million pieces, pieces that I've never been able to put back together into anything close to normal, let alone extraordinary.

7.

I don't bother going back to the flat. It's not like there's anything waiting for me there, besides which, I'm actually starving to the point where I think I might throw up if I don't eat.

Some days I simply forget to eat, others I gorge myself on pizza and endless packets of crisps. But I don't savour my food, not in the way Harry taught Lucy to. Their first date was a picnic down by the river, even though there was frost on the ground and the promise of snow lingering in the sky above. She told me how he'd made miniature quiches, sausage rolls stuffed with apple chutney and six different kinds of cake because he didn't yet know her favourite. Their house was forever filled with the scent of experimental cooking that was influenced by every possible culture and cuisine.

That was missing this morning. Another part of Lucy that is no longer there, and I guess it's because cooking for one, when Harry used to cook with so much love, must be rather loathsome.

'Hey,' I call out in turn to all the chefs and sous chefs, waiters and cleaning staff as I walk through the hotel kitchen, breathing in the familiar scent of roasting onions and spice. This place has been my home from home for the best part of five years. Always here when I needed some extra cash (which was pretty much all the time, as piano students have a tendency to come and go), or to convince myself that my life wasn't actually as sad and nondescript as I thought, because there's always drinks to be poured, meals to be served and tunes to be played for people whose names you'll never know.

'What are you doing here?' Sam says, glancing at me as I enter the bar, then going back to counting out the float for this evening's shift. There are several neat stacks of paper on the countertop, making me think of playing endless games of Monopoly with Lucy when she was at home, recuperating.

'Figured I'd come and give you a hand.' I go around the counter, trying to rid myself of the memory, along with all the others that keep popping up at unexpected moments.

Sam doesn't say anything, just watches as I hang up my bag and pull my hair into a ponytail. He's long since stopped asking me why I'd rather hang out with him than go home. I've even stopped asking myself, because then I might actually have to admit that pouring drinks for strangers is more appealing than a flat empty of anything other than the reminder of who I never managed to become.

'There was someone in here for you last night,' he says as I tie a crisp white apron around my waist.

'I know. You gave him my number.'

Sam shrugs off my request for an apology, scratching at the designer stubble on his chin and looking up as a group of twenty-somethings stumbles through from the lobby and half walk, half shove one another towards a table.

'Thought it might be good for you to go on a proper date.'

I ignore the dig at the state of my love life and help myself to a packet of peanuts and a pint of full-fat Coke. Even if I did want to go on a date with Jack, there's no way I can because of Natalie.

'If you're going to steal food,' he says with a nod towards the kitchen, 'at least go and get a proper meal.'

'Thanks, Dad.' I smile in response, because Sam is always trying to look out for me, like a kind but wayward uncle who seems to think that by telling me off every now and then it will miraculously transform me from vagabond to resilient. He's all about resilience, having spent most of the nineties working at a club in Ibiza, taking so many drugs that he himself admits the days blurred into months into years he can't quite remember.

'You don't need to worry about me,' I say, taking down a bottle of white rum from behind the bar along with half a dozen glasses and a metal jug.

'Just trying to look out for you, love,' Sam says, but I ignore the concern in his voice.

'Lucy is trying to teach me a lesson.' The truth is out before I've even had a chance to consider it, but perhaps that's what brought me back here tonight, the need to share my secret with someone who knows nothing about my past.

'Ok, now I'm really confused.'

I slice up wedges of lime, rubbing the sour flesh around the rim of each glass before dipping them in some sugar and filling them with ice.

'She sent me a puzzle box, like one I had as a kid. We used to make up riddles and treasure hunts for each other. Before. You know.'

'Before she got sick. The first time?'

'No.' I put a spoonful of the Mojito mix into each glass, add a generous splash of rum and top up with soda water. If anything, we did it even more that summer. Endless rounds of scavenger hunts and cryptic quizzes to stop Lucy from going insane with boredom. 'Anyways, she wants me to follow some kind of trail, at the end of which is a glorious prize, but I have no idea what it is.'

'And you're deciding not to because . . . ?' Sam may be a former DJ with a generous helping of middle-aged spread, but he's smart enough to know when I'm avoiding something.

I look at him. He's kind and puts up with all my shit. And I have nobody else to talk to right now whose opinion I actually care about.

'Because I'm pretty sure the next thing she wants me to find is at my parents',' I say, picking up the tray of drinks and taking them across to where my customers are waiting.

Of course she wants me to go back there, to heal wounds, salvage relationships and all that jazz. But I'm not ready to see them yet. I don't know if I'll ever be ready. Because there used to be four of us sitting around the kitchen table and sharing our lives with one another. Now we are only three and the absence of Lucy is something we will never be able to fix.

'But still,' he says when I come back to the bar. 'She must have done it for a good reason.'

'Lucy always had a reason.' Apparently none more so than now, but I'm not about to share my dead sister's need for fixing me with Sam, because he would wholeheartedly agree that it's probably time I reached out to the only real family I still have.

Sam and Lucy only ever met the once, a couple of years back, when I was pulling double shifts to try to save up enough money to go on holiday. Lucy was in town for a series of poetry lectures at one of the London universities (I hate to admit I can't remember which one), and she came to the bar unannounced.

I came through from the main restaurant, nearly tripping over myself at the sight of her sitting at the bar, chatting and laughing with Sam as if they'd known one another for years. It took her mere minutes to dazzle him, not only with her face but with her brilliance.

'You teach. At Oxford!' he exclaimed, mouth and eyes both widening as he realised just how much of a genius Lucy was.

'Well, not quite,' I heard her say as she took a sip of her drink (vodka, lime and soda, always heavy on the soda), watching me as I set down the plates at a nearby table. 'I've got to finish my PhD before they'll officially let me give lectures.'

'It means we have to start calling her Dr Franks and bow in her presence,' I said, giving Lucy's cheek a kiss then disappearing back to the safety of the kitchen.

After she'd left, Sam had commented on how it must have been wonderful to grow up with a sister like her. And it was, right up to the point she categorically proved that she was better than me at absolutely everything.

'You ok, sweetheart?' Sam says, placing his hand on my own, and I realise I'm crying.

'I'm fine,' I lie all over again. 'Why does everyone think I need saving?'

The TV screen behind the bar flickers, catching my eye. It's an advert for a new documentary series, one about the creatures that live in our oceans blue. I am not necessarily a lover of nature, but I know all sorts of random facts about animals. Mostly whales. For example, I know that the second-largest whale is the finback whale, and that a sperm whale emits a sonic boom through the depths of the ocean in order to track and kill its favourite food – the humble squid.

I know all this because I used to be friends with someone who was not only rather obsessive in their need for information but also had a very sweet tooth.

'Sam,' I call out as I go through the back door to where he's standing by the fire escape with one of the junior chefs, who looks like he hasn't slept in a year. 'Can I borrow your phone?'

'What's wrong with yours?' he asks, but hands his over anyway, then both men stub out their cigarettes and head back inside.

I lean against the wall as I listen to the ringtone calling through time and space, an invisible thread pulling me back to where I was only hours before.

'Hello?' Harry says, and I let out a sigh of relief that he picked up.

'It's me,' I say, tilting back my head and watching as a pigeon lands on the roof.

'Oh, hi,' Harry says, and I wonder where he is. I always asked Lucy, right up to the end, so I could picture her in the pub down by the river, or in the back garden rereading her favourite books.

'I figured it out.' I'm whispering, and the words feel as if they're being spoken by someone else.

'You did?'

'The sweets.' I don't know if I should laugh or cry or hit something now that I've put together the pieces of Lucy's puzzle in a completely different way, all because of a random fact about whales. 'You didn't ask because of Lucy.'

'And the riddle?'

'Gravity. Gravity comes down but never goes up.' It all makes perfect sense now. The riddle, the sweets. 'And it just so happened to be discovered by Sir Isaac Newton.'

'Lucy knew you'd figure it out.'

I smile, because Lucy would have figured it out in a heartbeat. But also because Mr Newton shares his name with my fact-obsessed friend who always carried a couple of butterscotch in his pockets because they were his favourite. Sweets that he shared with me the very first time we met.

'So, Isaac's in on this too?' I ask, picturing Isaac's face. I can't imagine he's agreed to this for any other reason than because Lucy asked him to. He always had a crush on her, even if he never admitted it. Mind you, everyone who met my sister had an annoying habit of falling for her.

'Only one way to find out,' Harry says. 'I'll text you his details.'

I hang up, stare down at the blank screen and wonder what on earth I'm supposed to say when I see him again. We met on the very first day of school, pulled together by a twist of fate, kept together by our mutual love of music. How different my adolescence would have been if he hadn't come up and spoken to me that morning.

8.

I was so excited about starting senior school that September. Most kids would count down the days until the beginning of the holidays, but my calendar had a huge red ring around the second of September. I'd rearranged my pencil case countless times (new, double-sided, with separate compartments for pens and pencils), decorated my satchel with hand-stitched flowers and had a rabbit's foot keyring hooked on to one of the straps for luck. I would even try on my uniform and stand in front of the mirror, imagining how totally and utterly awesome senior school was going to be.

That morning I was up with the birds, and I remember telling myself it was the first day of the rest of my life, which is stupid when you think about it, because every day is the first day of something. Downstairs, I busied myself with making fresh muffins, pancakes, bacon, eggs and anything else I could think of. When Lucy eventually came downstairs I was hot, sweaty and babbling with nervous excitement.

'I'm not hungry,' Lucy said when I asked what she wanted to eat.

'Nonsense,' Mum replied, piling high a plate with pancakes and strawberries. As she set it down in front of my sister, I saw her hand hover over Lucy's freshly shaven head. Lucy looked up at me, those *pale grey eyes magnified by the absence of hair. There was a smudge of mascara on her cheek and I wondered how many little things she and Mum had already argued about upstairs.*

'You ok?' I mouthed across at her, and she just shrugged in response, picking at her pancakes and staring out the window. I knew she was nervous about going back to reality, despite all her claims of abject misery due to being stuck at home for so long. But I also knew that she had no need to worry. The tumour was gone and there was nothing to indicate that she had even been sick at all, apart from the scar and the shaven head. Besides, we would still be together. We might not be in the same class, or even year group, but we would meet for lunch every day and I would seamlessly slot into her group of friends. I would look after Lucy, and she would look after me.

We drove to school that morning, Mum insistent and claiming it was tradition. After a few weeks, once Mum was back at work and Dad was left in charge of getting us up and out of the house each morning, we would cycle to and from school, taking off our helmets as soon as we rounded the first bend.

Before long, Lucy asked if I minded her going on ahead, or told me not to wait for her after school because I was old enough not to need a babysitter. But that first morning, sitting in the car with the radio blasting out Stevie Wonder (one of Dad's faves), I really did believe that senior school would be nothing short of magical.

'So that's the tumour girl.'

A boy came to stand next to me and together we watched as Lucy became engulfed in a crowd of friends and well-wishers, all clamouring for a look at her scar and giving her all the attention she secretly craved. She didn't look back, not even once, and I tried not to feel nervous about doing this without her.

'She made me shave her head.' I looked over at him, taking in the messy hair and eyes as rich and glossy as conkers.

'For attention?' he asked, reaching into his pocket and staring over to where an older boy, tall and handsome in an all too obvious way, had draped his arm oh-so-casually over Lucy's shoulder and bent his head to whisper something in her ear. It made Lucy giggle and I felt a short thrust of jealousy deep in my belly that made me fist my hands.

'That's my brother, Thomas,' he said, producing two sweets wrapped in white paper from his pocket and offering one to me. 'Looks like we have something in common.'

'Thanks.' Unwrapping the sweet, I smiled when I realised it was butterscotch.

'I'm Isaac,' he said, popping his own sweet into his mouth and grinning at me. That smile changed his face in an instant from average to extraordinary and I found myself unable to look away. There was a tiny scar above his left eyebrow and he had a line of moles on one side of his jaw.

'If you added one more' – I reached out to press my fingertip to the mole that sat just below his ear – 'it would make the Plough constellation. I'm Beth, by the way.'

If he thought it weird that I was touching him, he didn't show it, instead holding my gaze and looking at me in a way nobody ever had before. It was like he was trying to see inside my head, figure out what made me do and say the things I did.

'You like astronomy?'

'Not really.' Which wasn't a complete lie. I mean, Dad had a telescope that he'd pull out on random occasions. He taught me the names of all the constellations and told me that even if we were on opposite sides of the world we could both look up and see the same stars.

More recently, it was astrology rather than astronomy I'd developed an interest in. I checked my horoscope in the newspaper every morning, Lucy's too. She teased me about it, said that the alignment of the planets *wasn't going to determine whether or not you were going to have a bad day. But it was like a need, a compulsion, because if I'd checked them before, if I'd had some kind of sign, then maybe I could have stopped Lucy from getting sick in the first place.*

None of which I was about to admit to a complete stranger.

'Do you know what form you're in?' he asked, and I rummaged through my satchel for the letter that had arrived a few weeks before.

'7LC.' I held my breath and crossed my fingers for luck.

'Me too,' he said, and relief flooded through me. Because keeping him close, establishing the fragmented beginnings of a friendship, was suddenly and irrevocably the most important thing I had to do. 'What's your favourite subject?'

'Music, I guess.'

'Same! What do you play?'

'I play the piano,' I said, wishing it was something less nerdy. 'And I'm learning guitar . . .' I paused, wanting to share something more with him, but afraid of what he might think. 'I also write my own stuff.' The words tumbled over one another as I spoke and I immediately wished I hadn't said anything because, apart from Lucy, nobody else knew.

'Really?' His tone was more curious than derisory. Later, I would discover that he had a penchant for seventies rock and could play the guitar in such a way that made it sound as if the instrument was singing. 'What sort of stuff?'

'Nothing in particular. Mainly whatever wakes me up in the middle of the night.'

'Play for me sometime?'

'Maybe.' I looked down at my feet to hide the blush I could feel on my cheeks. The idea of playing for him was terrifying but also made my insides curl up with delight.

The school bell called out across the playground, the sound making me think of a fire alarm and causing the same sort of mad frenzy as everyone started piling in through the main doors. I noticed Lucy being spoken to by a teacher, ushered to the front of the line with Thomas, who was dutifully carrying her bag.

'Seems like tumours make you popular.' The two of us hung back, and I found myself feeling overwhelmed instead of excited because nothing was going the way I had imagined it.

'I don't think I'll ever be popular,' I said, wishing I could turn around and run home, run all the way back through space and time to when Lucy first came out of hospital, so I could be cocooned with her all over again.

'Popularity is decidedly over-rated,' Isaac said, handing me one more sweet. 'Leave your sister to it.'

I took the sweet with the shadow of a smile, thinking that perhaps today could be the beginning of something special after all.

9.

I hate hospitals. I mean, I get it, nobody loves hospitals, but so much of my life was shaped by the times I had to be in one it's like my body has an involuntary physical reaction as soon as I inhale the cloying scent of antiseptic.

I look down at the crumpled piece of paper I'm holding, on which I scribbled the name of both the hospital and the department Harry told me Isaac now works in.

You can do this, I tell myself as I go across to the reception desk and ask for directions to the paediatric wards.

You can do this. I repeat the words like a mantra as the lift doors close and I instinctively hold my breath. I used to do it all the time in the bath, counting the seconds and waiting for the pressure to build behind my eyes, then the beginnings of a burn deep in my lungs. I'd also do it in the car, or whilst waiting in the queue at the post office with Dad, or sitting at the kitchen table, waiting for someone to ask me about my day.

It started off as a dare of sorts to stop me thinking about all the things that were wrong with my life, all the teasing and staring and not being picked for team sports. The game grew and developed when Lucy got sick into one involving words, numbers and specific people. For example, if Lucy was asleep when I got to her room, then I had to hold my breath for a full minute, but if she was awake and eating breakfast I only needed to do it for ten seconds before saying hello.

I knew it wouldn't change anything, that voluntarily depriving my lungs of oxygen would in no way make Lucy better, or stop the kids at school making fun of me, but a part of me believed that if I did follow the rules then nothing really bad would happen. Either way, it's one of those peculiar habits of mine that still pops up unannounced, usually when I'm nervous.

There's no need to be nervous though, is there? Isaac was my best friend, the person I told each and every one of my dirty little secrets to for all of my formative teenage years. We knew one another in as intimate a way as is possible, without all the physical, sexual stuff that always makes being friends with a guy so awkward.

I loved him, I relied on him, but that was all such a long time ago and neither of us are the geeky eleven-year-olds who forged an unlikely allegiance on the first day of school.

Coming out of the lift, I turn left, then left again and through a set of double doors. It hits me immediately, such an overwhelming sense of déjà vu that it's strong enough to make me lean against the wall and close my eyes, waiting for the world to stop spinning.

Lucy hated being in hospital. She hated having the nurses wash her and accompany her to the bathroom (she'd actually screamed at one who dared suggest it would be easier to keep the catheter in her bladder once she was discharged from ICU). Most of all, she hated being on the children's ward, with all the overly cheerful posters, crying toddlers and the endless loop of cartoons on every TV screen.

It may not be the same hospital she had to stay in for just over a month, but everything about this ward is making me want to turn around and run. They were supposed to save her. They said she was better, that she could go home and, eventually, live a normal life.

But turns out doctors aren't magicians; they don't always make the bad stuff disappear.

'Can I help you?'

I open my eyes to find someone watching me. A junior nurse behind the reception desk, her uniform a little tight around the hips and her cheeks as rosy as a newborn's.

'I'm looking for Isaac – sorry, Dr Hardy,' I say with what I hope is a friendly enough smile.

'And you are?' She's eyeing me with suspicion, plus a hint of possessiveness, and I wonder if Isaac is aware of the crush she has on him.

'Beth,' I reply. 'Beth Franks.'

At this she frowns, looks along the corridor then back at me.

'I see. He said you might be coming.' Her eyes dart all over my face, then the full length of me, and I'm relieved to be dressed in jeans and a hoodie rather than the full-on glam I use for work.

'Wait here,' she says, picking up a clipboard and setting off down the corridor. I flinch at the familiar squeak of plastic soles on linoleum flooring, lean my head against the wall and close my eyes to try and block out all the memories of being on a hospital ward.

'Are you ok?' I open my eyes to see a little lad standing in a doorway watching me. One of his hands is clasped around a metal pole on which a plastic bag filled with clear liquid is attached. There's a tube running from the bag down to a catheter on the back of his hand and he's dressed in only a pair of Spiderman pants.

'I'm fine,' I say, nodding at the book he's also holding. 'What are you reading?'

'*Danny, the Champion of the World.*' He holds it up so I can see the cover and I wonder if Isaac gave it to him, because it used to be his favourite when he was a kid.

'It's a good book,' I say, taking in the dark shadows under his eyes and the greyness of his skin. 'But I think *Matilda* is even better.'

'Don't listen to her.' I look up to see Isaac coming down the corridor towards us. He looks the same as he did when we were young – messy hair that curls over the collar of his lab coat, mismatched socks and trousers that are an inch too short.

'Danny is by far the best hero ever. But you need to go back to bed, Freddie,' he says, crouching down in front of the boy. 'Got to get you better so you can go home.'

I watch as he takes the book from Freddie, then leads him by the hand through another set of doors. Freddie twists his head around to me, and just before the door swings shut I poke out my tongue at him, making him giggle.

It reminds me of when Lucy was in hospital, lying in bed with tubes coming out of various parts of her body and a plethora of machines monitoring her even whilst she slept. There was a nurse called Deborah who was all brusque efficiency, a fake competence driven by a need to impress. She used to tell me off for sitting on the end of Lucy's bed or talking too loudly or bringing inappropriate snacks. I asked her how any kind of snack could be deemed inappropriate, because surely snacks are designed to be both rewarding and appropriate? I was rewarded with a giggle from Lucy and Deborah snitching to my parents, but I didn't care, because I had made Lucy smile, even if only for a moment.

'Why don't we go to the cafeteria?' Isaac says as he comes back through the doors and steers me in the direction of the lifts. 'I'll buy you a coffee and we can talk.'

'Ok,' I reply, even though the last thing I want to do is talk. Or drink coffee. Or answer questions about how I am and what it is that Lucy has asked Isaac to do.

'I'm sorry about Lucy,' Isaac says as soon as the lift doors close.

'It's ok.' I sniff loudly and step away. The space between us feels odd, disturbed somehow, and I want to wipe it away.

'Still. Can't be easy coming back to a hospital.'

71

I'd forgotten this about him. His directness has always been, in my opinion, one of his best qualities. It's refreshing to have someone actually talk about Lucy's death, not wriggle around it with pathetic attempts at compassion.

The lift doors open and I follow him along another corridor, this one with floor-to-ceiling windows on one side, an inner courtyard beyond the glass. I wait as Isaac holds open a door for a man pushing a wheelchair in which a woman sits cradling a tiny, wrinkled baby. Her face is all puffy and she looks like she hasn't slept in weeks, but the way she is gazing down at her child is enough to make a lump appear in the back of my throat.

'Congratulations,' I say, and the woman glances at me, then returns all that attention to where it belongs.

'Lucy would have been an amazing mother,' Isaac says as he steers me in the direction of the cafeteria. There he goes again, saying all the things that nobody else dares to, and I don't know if I should be crying or laughing right now.

Lucy and Harry wanted children, but they also wanted careers and a house and to travel all over the world before having a baby. They only started trying the year before she died, and even though the doctors all told her otherwise, Lucy was convinced she'd left it too late, that it was the tumour's fault she couldn't conceive.

'I can't decide whether or not it's better she didn't get pregnant.' I stand beside Isaac, looking but not really seeing all the pastries and sandwiches laid out on the counter.

'I think it would have made it even harder for her, knowing she'd never see her child grow up.'

I stifle a sob, covering my mouth as if somehow this could push all the hurt back in. Is it selfish of me to have wished for a niece or a nephew, purely so a part of Lucy would always exist? I'd never thought of how utterly hideous it would have been for Lucy to have a baby and then have to say goodbye.

'Why don't you find us somewhere to sit?' Isaac says, passing me a paper napkin and pointing across the room. I do as I'm told, blowing my nose as I weave between the tables, and barely anyone looks up as I pass. I guess it's hardly unusual for someone to be crying in a place like this.

Taking a seat over by the window, I'm struck all over again by how similar hospital cafeterias are to airports. Both are a curious mixture of joy and despair, saying goodbye or reuniting with loved ones through tears and tissues and hands that reach out for one more touch.

Isaac slides into the seat next to mine and passes me a cup of coffee, along with a tuna sandwich.

'Figured you'd be hungry.'

'First time I've seen you in your work clothes,' I say, taking a large bite. 'It's funny.' Except it's not. It's sad, because there's so much of his life I thought I would be a part of, but instead he's been living it without me.

Loosening his tie, he undoes the top button of his shirt then runs both hands through his hair. It's a gesture I recognise as one that he does when he feels awkward or nervous, or usually both, and suddenly that lump is back in my throat.

'You're avoiding the subject.'

'Aren't you?' I sip my coffee and then wish I hadn't, as it really is disgusting.

'No, I'm trying to find the right moment to bring up the subject of Lucy's request.' He clasps his hands together and bounces them off the edge of the table whilst watching to see how I react. I want to ask if it's something they taught him at medical school – make a statement, don't break eye contact, wait for the patient to confess that actually they smoke forty a day and never do any exercise.

'But clearly that's not going to happen, so I'd best get on with it as I still have patients to see.'

'Lives to save, miracles to perform. Sorry,' I say when he lays his head on his hands and kicks the table leg, sluicing both our coffees over the surface.

'I knew this was a mistake,' he says, lifting his head to look at me then glancing at his watch. 'I knew you wouldn't take it seriously.'

'I will. I will.' I reach for his hand, pretending not to be hurt when he slides it away. 'I promise. Cross my heart and all that.' I sit up straight, swipe over my heart and give him a mock salute.

'Don't do that.'

'Do what?' I ask, taking another bite of my sandwich and thinking it could do with some more mayo.

'Cover up whatever it is you're really feeling.'

'I'm not.'

'You are. Never used to.'

There's so much inside the silence between the words. So many things we've never spoken about and probably should have, once upon a time.

'Why did Lucy send me to you?'

'You tell me.'

'No idea.' Which in itself is a lie because I know she's doing this for a specific reason. I know she's deliberately making me remember what happened between Isaac and me.

We both know the exact moment I changed. It's the big, fuck-off elephant in the room that's hanging between us like a balloon one of us will eventually have to pop.

'This has nothing to do with Tristan.'

'If you say so.' He takes another sip of his coffee, watching me over the rim, and I want to swipe it away, tell him to talk to me, really talk to me, the way we used to when we were kids, rather than this psychoanalytical bollocks.

'It was years ago,' I say, pulling my hair free from its ponytail and fluffing it from underneath, setting free the scent of the honeysuckle conditioner that I have used ever since Lucy told me it would transform my hair (it did; the frizz was gone in an instant, replaced with glossy curls that made all the jibes about having pubes on my head disappear too).

'And yet he's still responsible for what happened.'

'Can we please not have this argument again?' Isaac was wary of Tristan from the very start. Aside from them being practically polar opposites in looks, character and pretty much everything else, Isaac's bullshit radar has always been on point. But I was blinded and stubborn and convinced myself that my infatuation with Tristan wouldn't affect any other part of my life.

'Why?' He looks at me in the exact same way he did back in my parents' kitchen when SuperKing were playing on the radio and we both said things we have never been able to move on from. And even if we could, if Lucy thinks she has the power to put Isaac and me back together again, it could never be the same. We're too different, irrevocably changed from who we used to be.

Besides, even if we did kiss and make up, what on earth would we talk about? I know practically nothing about his career, his life, other than the snippets passed along from my mother, and I'm pretty certain he can't relate to anything about mine.

'Because' – I sigh, folding up the wrapper of my sandwich into ever smaller squares – 'if Tristan was the reason I screwed up my life, then by default the second he was no longer in it, everything should have gone back to normal.'

'Except it was too late by then.' He'd tried warning me, tried helping me, but I still managed to ruin my future all by myself. 'You'd already decided he was your only option.'

'But it's not too late now?' My phone vibrates in my pocket and I resist the urge to look.

'I don't know, Beth,' Isaac says with an exaggerated sigh, glancing again at his watch. 'Lucy left that part up to you.'

It's obvious he doesn't want to be here with me, and it hurts in a way I never expected it to. Stupid, really, to think that I could come here and have everything go back to the way it was before. Delusional even, because we haven't been part of one another's lives, not really, for close to ten years. He played by the rules, graduated with honours, is now a junior doctor working double shifts, and I know he will always put his patients first. Isaac became exactly the person he always wanted to be, someone his parents could be proud of.

Being here, seeing his success, only highlights how little of that there is in my own life. I used to tell myself my luck would change, that something would happen to make all the mistakes, all the bad choices, no longer matter. But since Lucy died, I can't help but think there's little point in trying, because at any moment it can all be swept away.

'Can't you just give me whatever it is she gave you and then I can go?' I hold out my hand and meet his gaze, imagining all those cogs and wheels inside his brilliant mind trying to decide what the best option might be. Always weighing up the pros and cons, just like Lucy.

'I don't actually have it with me,' he says eventually, reaching into his pocket and pulling out his phone. 'Just a picture.' He slides the phone over to me, revealing a photo of the puzzle box I bought at a market in France.

'Is it at yours?' I use my thumb and forefinger to zoom in on the photo.

'No,' Isaac says, reaching for his phone. 'Lucy said you'd know where it is.'

Not this again. I know exactly where it will be: on a shelf in my bedroom, back at my childhood home. It would seem that Lucy is indeed trying to manipulate me into going to the one place she knows I really, really don't want to go.

'I'm not going home, Isaac.'

'Why not? So you can keep hiding from the people who actually care about you?'

Mum always liked Isaac. It wasn't uncommon for me to come home and find the two of them sitting in the kitchen sharing a slice of lemon cake (never fruit; Isaac said raisins were just decrepit grapes) and talking about all the wonderful things he was going to do with his life. It was another thing about him that I both admired and hated: his ability to talk to grown-ups, really talk to them, and not just because it was polite.

Secretly I think Mum hoped we would end up together, that Isaac would somehow, through osmosis or sheer willpower, manage to change me into the sort of person she thought I should be.

'I have people,' I say.

'Yeah, right,' Isaac replies, draining his coffee and tossing the cup in a nearby bin. 'But I guarantee not a single one of them knows anything about the real you.'

'Why are you helping me?'

'No idea. Call it one last selfless act of kindness.'

'You once told me there's no such thing as a selfless act.' There were so many conversations, so many ideas passed between us whilst stretched out on the living room floor, watching movies and sharing an enormous bowl of popcorn. How many nights did we spend in my room, writing songs and questioning absolutely everything about our lives in a way that only the young and carefree can? He helped make me who I am, or at least who I was.

He stands, shoves his hands in his pockets and looks over at the exit. 'Yeah, well, maybe there is when the person you're trying to help is too bloody stubborn to admit that she needs it.'

I stare down at the tabletop, running my fingertip over the stains and cracks and desperately trying to think of something that will make him stay.

'I'm sorry.' The words are no more than a whisper and I don't dare look up at him, to see all that pity etched over his face, because that would most definitely make me cry and I don't want him to see me cry, not over this. Not over how pathetic everyone thinks I have become.

'I know, but they're just words, Beth. Go home, don't go home, right now I'm close to not giving a shit.'

'Why are you really doing this, Isaac?'

'You were my best friend, Beth. That's not something I took lightly.'

'But I did?' I did, I took him for granted, assumed he'd be there no matter what.

'We used to walk home together every day after school. Sit up half the night listening to music, writing songs and telling ourselves that it meant something.'

It meant everything to me. *He* meant everything to me, but his dream was never about the music, he simply went along with it to keep me happy. Deep down I knew he was waiting for something better to come along.

'And then you decided to hook up with Jessica Cartwright.' It still stings, how easily he grew up, moved on, leaving me flailing about with no clue as to how I was supposed to fit in.

He looks at me a while, perhaps searching his mind for the memory of a day when something shifted between us. And all because he knew how to be a teenager, to fit in, and I didn't.

'Why didn't you come to Peter's party?'

He asked me to go with him and I very nearly did. But then I discovered something in Lucy's room and secreted it away.

'I wasn't very good at parties back then.'

'I thought you'd at least show up.'

'Why?'

'Because I asked you to.'

'What does it matter?' I say with a scoff. 'It's not as if one night can change your entire life.' But we both know that's not true; we both know how the one party I actually went to ended up changing everything.

He smiles, but only a little, suggesting that there might be some sadness muddled in with all that pity, and I feel the lump in my throat swell as I try to swallow it away.

'Go home, Beth. Open the bloody box.'

'Why?'

'Because your sister wants you to.'

I watch him walk away, think of all the times we said goodbye to one another at the crossroads. What would have happened if I had gone to the party and snogged Peter, or another boy from school? One decision – go to a party, steal from your sister, play the piano for a stranger – each and every one has a knock-on effect that can only be pieced together when it's too late to go back and change anything.

She knew, I think to myself. Lucy must have known what's in the puzzle box she has tasked Isaac with leading me back to. But why does she care, and what on earth does any of it have to do with Isaac?

Reaching into my satchel, I take out the notebook Lucy sent me and open it to a clean page.

10.

Twelve years ago . . .

'Hey,' Isaac said as I walked across the playing fields to where he was waiting, just like he did every day after school.

'Hey,' I replied, taking the can of Coke he was offering and heading in the direction of the woods. Isaac followed and, as we passed by the cricket pavilion, we both turned our heads to see Lucy and Thomas, firmly locked in an embrace.

'God,' I said, making a puking sound. 'It's so gross the way they keep pawing at one another.'

'Jealous?' Isaac replied with a smirk. 'They do more than kissing, you know.'

'Whatever, Isaac.' It wasn't the answer I expected. I also had no desire to tell him that Thomas wasn't the only boy Lucy had been swapping bodily fluids with. Only the week before she'd woken me up in the middle of the night by tapping at my window.

'Where have you been?' I asked as she climbed in from the conservatory roof, all long limbs and painted toes.

'Nowhere,' she replied with a wink, but as she padded across the floor I caught the scent of something that didn't belong to her.

'Does Thomas know?' I whispered, and she paused in the doorway, an unfamiliar look on her face.

'You can't tell Isaac,' she said, then slipped back to her room, her secret safe with me. I lay back down on my bed, holding tight to the knowledge that she still trusted me, still wanted to confide in me.

'Fancy a bit of Stevie?' Isaac asked now, taking his iPod out of his bag and handing me one of the earphones. We walked along, the chord dangling between us, and I listened to 'Superstition' as Isaac played air guitar, even though I'd heard him play that hypnotic opening dozens of times before.

'Lucy's not having sex with Thomas,' I said as the song finished, taking out the earphone and looking straight ahead in the hope that Isaac wouldn't guess I'd been working up the nerve to talk about this ever since he put the idea in my head.

'Course she is.' We were still walking in sync, the soft scuff of his heels the only sound, and I tried to figure out how he knew this when I apparently had absolutely no clue what was going on in my sister's life any more.

It seemed as if Lucy was constantly running towards something that wasn't there, as if she was afraid to do anything at less than full throttle. I remember thinking how exhausting it must be for her, constantly trying to improve herself. I also remember wondering if she would have been quite so determined if she'd never got sick.

'How do you know about Lucy and Thomas?' I asked Isaac at the same time as I realised that Lucy wasn't actually confiding in me about anything important after all.

'Thomas told me.' Just like that. As if it were no more unusual than trying on a new pair of shoes for the first time, and I wanted to know why Isaac got to know something about Lucy that I didn't.

'Boys are so lame,' I said, bumping my hip against his when really what I wanted to do was ask how he could be so casual, so flippant, about something that was clearly a very big deal.

'Gee, thanks.'

'Not you. You don't count.'

'Thanks again.'

'You know what I mean. If I even say hello to a boy, he assumes I want him to stick his tongue down my throat.' Everyone was doing it, literally everyone, apart from me and Isaac. Or maybe he was but just didn't tell me because he knew I would ask him a million questions about it. Like, how do you know who puts their tongue in first?

'What's wrong with kissing someone?' He was looking at me, another question hiding behind his words.

'I don't know. It's weird. Everything used to make sense and now it doesn't.' I kicked at a pebble on the pavement, sending it bouncing into the road, where it came to land in a pothole filled with dust and pollen. 'I mean, I don't understand why everyone's so fixated on Peter's party this weekend.'

'You're not going?' Isaac said as he tugged on my elbow, making me stop and turn around.

'Not invited. Are you?' I searched his face for an answer, scared that he'd been going to all the parties without me.

'Might be fun,' he said with a shrug and a sniff.

I responded with an explosive, one-beat 'ha'. 'Sure, if your definition of fun is taking part in some sort of animalistic mating ritual where the males grunt and fight and the females are supposed to be impressed.' I had absolutely zero desire to go to a party if there was even a chance that Lucy might be there. Because all it would do was highlight once again how easily she fit in, and I didn't.

He rolled his eyes at me, actually rolled them, and shook his head before crossing the road, not bothering to see if I was following.

'What's the matter?'

'Just come to the party, Beth,' Isaac said with a small laugh, then he ran both his hands through his hair and stared up at the sky. 'You might surprise yourself and actually enjoy it.'

I looked up to see small dots of colour appear all over his neck. 'Don't be ridiculous,' I said, resisting the urge to reach out and press my fingertip against each pink circle on his skin.

'I'm just saying,' he said, blowing out all the air in his mouth and looking down at the ground. 'It would be kind of nice if I didn't have to go alone.'

'Why?' Although I could already guess, and the suspicion of it hurt only a little less than the actuality of him admitting it to me.

'You know Jessica Cartwright?'

'Doesn't everyone?' She was blonde, pretty and annoyingly popular. She was also a class A bitch who everyone was terrified of offending for fear they'd end up on the receiving end of her wrath. 'Please tell me you don't fancy her.'

'What's wrong with that?'

'She's like a demonic Barbie. All boobs and no brain.'

'That's not entirely true.'

'What do you guys even have in common? Tell me one single thing that's interesting about her?'

He laughed, a small individual sound that not only failed to cover up his embarrassment but also served to highlight my own. I would never be like Jessica or Lucy or any of the other girls with all their prettiness, and it hurt to think that even Isaac wasn't able to resist the pull of beauty.

'There's more than one kind of beautiful,' he said, as if reading my mind, then drew me in for a hug, and I breathed in the scent of him. It was different to before, less sweet but still unique, and I leant my head against his chest, thinking that it wasn't so long ago we were the same height.

So much had changed in such a short amount of time and I was struggling to keep up with all the nuances of being a teenager that everyone else seemed to have no problem at all understanding. Isaac made me feel safe, like I actually belonged somewhere, but it seemed that even he was slipping away, leaving me trailing behind with nobody else to turn to.

Planting a kiss against my head, he stepped away. 'For a musical genius you can actually be kind of stupid sometimes.'

'Says the boy with a photographic memory.' I grinned up at him, aware that something had shifted between us, but I didn't know what. I wanted to go to Peter's party, but only because Isaac was going. Everything else was too much.

'Wanna hang out tomorrow?' he said, stretching his arms over his head to reveal a band of skin and a line of hair snaking down from his belly button that made me blush and look away. 'I've been working on a new riff. Thought it might go with those lyrics you showed me.'

'Sure,' I replied, my mind already wondering what Isaac might have come up with.

'And I think you should come with me to Peter's party. Live a little. You never know, you might find someone to crush on.' Grinning, he walked away from me backwards, then raised his hand and turned towards home.

We spent all of the following afternoon going back and forth over a handful of notes, adding in layers from both a keyboard and Isaac's guitar until we could play it without thinking. It was a song about fear, about not being ready for whatever life would throw at you next.

Afterwards I went home, tried on a little black dress 'borrowed' from Lucy's wardrobe and styled with a pair of DM boots and too much mascara. Standing in front of the mirror, all I could see was a little girl playing dress-up, pretending to know how to be fourteen. I went across the landing to Lucy's room to ask for her help, but my sister had already gone, out into the world that was so much easier for her to live in than it was for me.

Tiptoeing across the carpet, I hovered in front of her bed. There was a magazine open to a page about which boy you were most compatible with, depending on your star sign. Lucy had drawn a heart next to Aries, which just so happened to be the most compatible sign for her as a Sagittarius. Problem was, I knew for a fact that Thomas's birthday was in June.

With a quick glance back to the door, I went across to her desk and opened each of the drawers in turn, discovering nothing more than textbooks and the stub of a cinema ticket. Looking up, I saw her jewellery box, next to a row of CDs she never listened to.

Taking it down, I opened the lid, then promptly shut it again when the ballerina began to spin and the tinny sound of 'The Dance of the Sugar Plum Fairy' from The Nutcracker spilled out. I waited, listening for footsteps coming up the stairs, but all was quiet. Mum and Dad were in the living room watching TV and Lucy was gone. So what was the harm in having another look?

If I hadn't looked, if I hadn't discovered not only a Polaroid picture of Lucy snogging a boy from the year above but also a condom, wrapped up in foil, maybe I wouldn't have taken it. But the sight of the necklace Thomas had given Lucy for her birthday – a perfect gold heart hanging from a chain that she wore around her neck every single day – was enough to make me want to throw the damn box against the wall.

Sitting on the end of Lucy's bed, I held the necklace in my palm. It didn't seem fair that someone liked her enough to give her such a gift, only for her to sneak out with another boy. It was also enormously unfair that the only reason I was even contemplating going to a party was because Isaac needed a wingman, not because anyone actually wanted me there.

What hurt most of all was that Lucy was slipping away from me, too quickly for me to reach out and pull her back.

It was so easy to slip the necklace inside my pocket, to squeeze it tight and make a wish that one day someone would love me too.

As I stood, the magazine slipped to the floor. I picked it up, lay it open on the duvet at the right page. My eye travelled across and down to my own star sign, skimmed over the words to where it announced that my perfect match, my soulmate, was a Pisces. Isaac was a Pisces, but the idea of him ever thinking about me the way he clearly thought about Jessica Cartwright was so ridiculous that it made me run from Lucy's room and back to my own. I hid the necklace inside my puzzle box, underneath a strip of photographs Isaac and I had had taken in a booth on the pier when we went on a day trip to Brighton and nearly threw up on the Wurlitzers.

I never made it to Peter's party, but Isaac did. And on the following Monday I listened and smiled when he told me how not only had 'loads' of booze been smuggled in, but he'd snogged Jessica behind a tree in the back garden. I hated myself for not being happy for him, but I hated Jessica even more for being the sort of girl my best friend fancied.

11.

Even before Lucy died, there was always an excuse to be found as to why I couldn't visit my parents. Usually, it was the false pretence of being too busy, not having enough time. (In reality, I had so much time my days stretched like a baggy jumper I could never fill). The one who brought us together was Lucy, convincing me that Sunday lunch back home or a BBQ for Dad's birthday was a good idea, might be fun even.

I hated those days more and more as the years went by. Sitting around the kitchen table, or stretched out like a lazy cat on the lawn, I would smile and nod as Lucy answered all of Mum's questions, filling the sky with all her achievements like bright and shiny stars that twinkled with her brilliance. Sometimes it felt like she was ticking off a list, racing to get to the finish line before the clock struck midnight. It also made me fearful that at some point Lucy would run out of time.

On the train journey down here, I made a list of the clues and corresponding memories I have so far, hoping they might provide me with the final answer, the pot of gold at the end of Lucy's rainbow. But there are so many links and ideas and possibilities, because as a child (and particularly as a teenager), everything matters. Each and every part of your day is loaded with importance and meaning – from how you style your hair to whether the girl who kissed your best friend would steal him away from you.

She didn't, mainly because she'd snogged at least two other boys that night, including Peter. Isaac pretended not to care, but I caught him looking at Jessica for weeks afterwards. I both loved and loathed the fact he was miserable, but I was mainly thankful that I got to keep him after all.

I attended one of Lucy's lectures, just the once. I told myself it was because I had nothing better to do, but secretly I wanted to know if she was actually any good at her job. The short answer was absolutely, because Lucy always made certain that anything she set her mind to would have a positive outcome. Which is painfully ironic given what was in that brilliant mind eventually killed her.

During that lecture, she spoke about the journey a reader is taken on during the course of a novel or a poem, and that there is always a specific structure to any kind of story, put there for a reason. She told her students that someone she knew would read the last chapter of a novel first (at which point she looked at me with a smirk), claiming that if the ending was disappointing there was no point in reading the rest of the book. She then went on to argue that the ending of any story can only be understood when considered alongside what came before, that an ending doesn't truly exist unless there is also a beginning and a middle.

What Lucy didn't know is that the real reason I always read the end of a book first is because I only wanted to read ones that had happy endings. I needed a fairy tale, a happy-ever-after, even though I knew that stories didn't always work out that way.

Is this what she's trying to tell me? That in order to understand whatever it is she's leading me towards, I first need to go back to the beginning, read the story all over again?

Standing in the driveway of my childhood home, I look up at the house, willing it to give me a clue as to what is waiting for me inside. There are so many memories stored inside those walls. Like fireflies in a jar, all fighting to get out. I wish I could throw some of them away, keep only those that don't hurt so much. But they all hurt, even the good ones.

Should I ring the doorbell or use my key? I imagine Mum in there somewhere, standing at a window and watching as I pace up and down the drive. Just as I find the nerve to go up to the door and ring the bell, I hear it. Soft notes from a piano that curl around from the back of the house, along the side passage and up over the fence. It's jazz, Ella Fitzgerald to be precise, the sort of song Dad always played when he was trying to rid his mind of something.

Time spins back as I open the front door and head towards the sound of my father playing, the past whispering in my ear. So many summer evenings were spent outside, lying on our backs and waiting for a shooting star, or picking daisies and making them into chains that were wilted when morning came. There were picnics and BBQs, parties and water fights with friends, and it's all so familiar it hurts. All of it was accompanied by the sound of a song being played on the stereo or the piano or the iPods Lucy and I would take on holiday with us so that there was always music, and it strikes me now that perhaps we were all afraid of the silence.

Dad doesn't look up as I step into the room and kick off my shoes. Nor does he stop playing, simply shifts along the piano stool to make space for me. I lean my head on his shoulder and watch his fingers running up and down the keys, then reach out my hand and add a few notes to the melody.

It's like slipping on an old coat, one you'd forgotten about but still fits perfectly. Music has always calmed me, stilled the chaos of my mind and replaced it with a gentle sort of understanding. It's like another language, one I cannot speak but which makes perfect sense.

When I was researching migraines, before Lucy's diagnosis, and came across those reports of people tasting colours or seeing sounds, it struck me as being the exact same way I felt about music. Not the music you hear on the radio, or even listening to Dad play, but rather the sort that lives inside me, waiting to get out. I once described it to Dad as a tiny creature, fizzing with light and colour and feeling. He smiled and told me it was the sort of creature that hated being kept in a cage.

'This is a nice surprise,' he says when the tune comes to an end. He kisses the top of my head, lets his mouth rest there a moment, and it fills me with so many emotions that I don't know what to do with.

Moving away from his touch, I go into the kitchen, flick the kettle on to boil and take the teapot over to the sink for a rinse. Dad's hovering in the doorway, one leg tucked behind the other, and he looks lost, like he's not sure what to do any more.

'I went to see Harry,' I say, adding fresh leaves to the pot and peering in the cake tin, only to find it empty.

Dad comes into the kitchen and opens a cupboard, taking out a store-bought lemon cake in plastic wrapping. I don't think we ever had store-bought cake growing up. Baking was Mum's 'thing', an obsession she was actually rather good at. Every Sunday without fail the house would be bathed in delicious aromas of sugar, almonds, stewed fruit and rum. She and Lucy would spend hours together weighing and measuring, lining tins ready for blind baking, stirring and whisking eggs into pristine peaks, all whilst listening to Classic FM. Dad and I preferred to taste rather than bake, neither of us ever able to follow a recipe without chucking in something extra.

'How is Harry?' Dad asks, unwrapping the cake and cutting two generous slices.

'Bearing up,' I reply, the words completely and utterly wrong, because none of us seems capable of actually saying what we mean. I'm also more than a little distracted by the fact Dad clearly knows nothing about the real reason I'm here, and now I have no clue how I'm supposed to casually slip into conversation that I think there's something in the house Lucy wanted me to collect.

My mind seems to be unravelling bit by bit because I don't quite know what I will do if I leave here empty-handed. Stupid as it may sound, I was sort of looking forward to seeing what came next, because Lucy's clues have given my day a small sense of purpose.

The kettle boils and, as I pour the steaming water into the pot, I'm aware of someone coming down the stairs and into the kitchen. I turn around and my entire body tightens at the sight of my mother.

'Elizabeth,' she says, her voice thin and cold. She looks terrible. Her hair is lank, her cheeks hollow, and there's no real colour to her skin. She's dressed in an old cotton dress that hangs dejectedly from her stick-thin frame. Overall, I get the impression that her grief is peeling her apart, one layer at a time. But even with all that grief, she is still beautiful, in the exact same way as Lucy.

This is another reason I didn't want to come home. Because Mum is a walking, talking reminder of how my sister would have looked if she ever had the chance to reach middle age. I can't imagine how hard it is for her, to look in the mirror every day and see the same thing.

'Mum,' I reply, taking down an extra cup.

'I'm having a G&T,' she says, going over to the fridge with a dismissive wave. 'Care to join me?'

I dart a look at Dad, who is staring at his feet and making no effort to stop Mum from taking out tonic and some pre-sliced lemon. I watch as she retrieves a near empty bottle of gin from the larder and pours the entire contents into a glass, topping up with a splash of tonic and then taking a large sip.

'Mum?' I say, taking a step towards her then thinking better of it because if she's drinking at two in the afternoon (and by the looks of it, this is not a one-time occurrence), then she is going to be rather prickly.

'I'm assuming that you can be trusted not to throw anything at me this time?' Mum says as she takes another sip, watching me over the rim of her glass.

'I was aiming for the bin.' Which we all know is a blatant lie, but I'm not about to admit that I might have been in the wrong. Nor do I really want a rematch of the argument we had last time I was here.

'Were you putting it there along with all your long-lost hopes and dreams?'

Ok, so it would seem that Mum is more than willing to go another round, and I am so close to yelling at her all over again that maybe, just maybe, if she'd been as supportive of my future as she was of Lucy's, then I wouldn't have had to keep so much of my life a secret from her.

'Miriam,' Dad says without raising his gaze.

'Oh, come off it, James. We're far beyond the point of pretending everything is going to be all right.' She gives me a half-hearted smile then walks back out of the kitchen and up the stairs. A few seconds later there's the sound of a door being slammed, making Dad and me flinch simultaneously.

'She didn't mean it,' Dad says.

'Yes, she did.'

'Go wait in the garden room,' he says, one hand on my waist and steering me towards the door. 'I'll bring the tea through in a bit.'

The room I go into is largely unchanged, including the same green sofa where Lucy spent so much time convalescing. There's a low coffee table we used for puzzles and board games, various house plants that seem to be just about clinging on to life, and a vintage bird cage standing by the door that opens out on to the garden. At one point it was filled with origami cranes and crystals hung on strings that would turn in the breeze and cast tiny rainbows on the tiled floor. Now it's empty save for a spider's web, in the centre of which is a blue fly all wrapped up and ready to be eaten.

So much more seems to be missing, and not just from this room; the whole house feels like it's lost, without purpose. A bit like a stuffed toy put up high on a shelf when the child no longer wants to play. Is this all because Lucy and I grew up, or has it become exacerbated by her death? It all feels so claustrophobic, like the walls are closing in around me.

How much of a home is made up of the things that fill it? How does a house become more than bricks and mortar and a view? How much of the home is lost, redundant, when there are no people, or love, left to keep it alive?

I think of my flat, buried in the middle of London and full of stuff I have no real attachment to. If there was a fire, I don't know what, if anything, I would choose to save. Which is pathetic, or perhaps just sad, because if there's nothing in there worth saving, what does that say about me, about the life I am supposedly living?

What would I save from this house, this room? I was so quick to leave everything behind, to take few reminders with me, almost as if I was trying to make a point. Now I'm desperately hoping that at least some evidence I once lived here still exists.

I perch on the end of the sofa and look up at the row of book-cases that line the wall behind. There's a shelf filled with old records, several more with all the books Lucy and I read and reread over the years, and various nonsensical knick-knacks. But it's not any of these things that make me stand and go behind the sofa, reach out my hand as if towards a spindle, afraid I might get pricked.

My hand moves back and forth until it eventually decides to make contact with a small wooden box. My puzzle box, to be precise, bought as a souvenir from a French market when I was only six years old. Mum had tried to convince me it was a waste of money, that I should perhaps buy a bracelet or bag like Lucy. I had to have it, though, loved the idea of being able to hide something inside, a secret or a wish that belonged just to me.

'Here we go,' Dad says, setting down the tray and proceeding to pour out two mugs of tea, adding milk and sugar to both.

'Where did you get this?' I ask, turning the box over and over, checking for any scratches or imperfections.

'Hmm, what?' Dad says, taking a bite of lemon cake, then putting his plate back down.

'The puzzle box, Dad. Where did you find it?'

'Oh, that,' he says, slurping his tea and sinking into the sofa. Then he gets back up and goes to stand by the window. 'Lucy brought it round.' His words are small and shaky. I should go over to him, give him a hug or something, but it's too much. I don't know how to start sharing my grief with him, how I could explain it, or justify it, because I may have lost my sister, but he lost his child.

'When?' I ask the question that immediately sparks a whole load more, because the answer might help me figure out how long ago Lucy started planning this whole charade. It might also tell me how many letters and emails and conversations we exchanged without her deciding to help me, fix me – whatever she's trying to do – in some other way than this.

'Does it matter?' I hear the weariness in his voice and wonder how many nights he's actually been able to sleep. I can picture him, alone in the darkest hours, sitting at the piano or watching old movies whilst cradling a tumbler of whiskey, and it hurts all the way down to my bones to think of him living in this house with Mum, yet somehow all alone.

'I guess not.' It does matter to me, but only because there's so much more here than just a box. Why this box? Why now? Why did she take it from here, only to bring it back again? The biggest question though, the one that keeps circling my mind, is why did Lucy not want my parents to know about the treasure trail she's leading me along?

'I should go,' I say, glancing into the hall and wondering if Mum might put in another appearance before I leave.

'She just needs . . .' Dad says, and I look back at him. We hold one another's gaze, neither of us brave enough to close the gap between us or give voice to the reason why there's a gap at all.

We both know what Mum needs, what we all need but will never have. The absence of Lucy hangs around like an unwanted guest nobody knows how to get rid of.

'Do you mind if I take this?' I ask, holding up the box and forcing myself not to think about what I will do if there isn't actually anything inside.

'Not at all,' Dad says with another slurp of his tea, and I'm hit with the memory of sitting on his lap as a child, dunking digestive biscuits into his tea and him not caring a bit when all the crumbs fell to the bottom of the cup. 'She asked me to give it to you. Next time you came.'

'She did?' I don't know what to do with this information. I wish I could go back in time and be part of that conversation. There's so much I wish I could have been a part of, but hindsight does very little other than show you just how easy it is for one bad decision to screw up the rest of your life.

'And a book,' he says, looking around the room as if this will somehow procure what it is he's searching for. 'Poetry, I think, but it wasn't in her room, nor in here, so I'll have to have another look.'

A poetry book. A specific poetry book that I am certain contains the poem about a hyacinth girl and which must, surely, have something else hidden away inside those pages? There must be something other than Eliot's own words, because otherwise all I'd have to do is go and borrow a copy from the library.

'Thank you,' I say, although it doesn't feel like enough, or the right words to convey just how much I am thankful to him for.

'Promise me you'll come back for it?'

'Promise.' The word tastes bitter in my mouth and I take a sip of tea to swallow it all away.

'At some point you need to make up with your mother.' He's looking at me now with so much concern, and I have to bite down on the inside of my cheek to stop myself crying. 'Lucy wouldn't want you to stay angry with one another.'

'I miss her, Dad. I miss her all the time.' Shit. Now I am crying. And he's put down his mug and is coming towards me and wrapping me up in his arms and, oh god, now I'm sobbing because he smells of home.

'I know. We all do,' he says, and I realise he's crying too, which only makes me sob all the more, great heaving, wretched breaths that do absolutely nothing to make me feel any better. I can feel his chest rise and fall, hear the wobble in his own breath as he lets me go and we step apart. 'Can you stay a while? Talk to Mum, perhaps? She's generally more placid in the afternoons.'

I would love nothing more than to stay here with him. To play piano and eat bland lemon cake and drink endless cups of sugary tea. But it's too soon, it's too much for him to have to bear the weight of me as well as his own sorrow.

'I start work in an hour,' I say with an attempt at a smile.

'At the hotel?' he asks, and I nod my reply. 'I see.' He goes back to the piano and runs his fingers up and down the keys before turning and fixing me with a look.

'Regret is nothing more than a waste of time, pickle,' he says, and I draw breath at the sound of the nickname he used to call me.

'I don't regret giving up music because it gave me you and your sister.'

'But it was your dream.'

'And dreams change, Beth. Yours can too.'

I don't know what to say because it feels like I've failed him all over again. It feels as if I'll never be able to do anything to make him proud of me, because I never managed to finish what he himself once started.

'Bye, Dad,' I say, placing a kiss on his cheek, and head for the hall.

'Love you,' he calls after me, but I don't look back as I open the front door.

'Me too,' I whisper as I walk away.

At the bottom of the road I turn right, head for the river. I could do this walk in my sleep, tell you what month it is just from the scents and sounds that follow me as I go – bluebells, cowslip and a few straggling snowdrops that will soon be replaced by common violets and wild garlic that Dad always asked me to pick. There're also swifts and swallows, returned from their winter migration, and the soft cackle of a cuckoo somewhere nearby. I pause at the great elm tree, step closer but don't touch the initials Lucy and I carved there so long ago. It makes me think of a Plath poem, one I read over and over when my heart felt shattered beyond repair.

I know the bottom – I say the opening words to myself. This feels like the bottom right now, with Lucy gone and my parents too far away for me to reach. Pain is such a peculiar thing. A cut is something you can see, the slash of skin and flesh showing the blood that flows within. But loss or sorrow, grief and despair, they all manifest themselves in sneakier ways, ways that can't be fixed with a plaster and a kiss.

I'm at the river's edge, watching as a couple of sand martins chase insects across the ever-flowing water and wishing I could figure out a way to keep going. How am I supposed to carry on when Lucy, darling Lucy, who worked and cared and always tried her absolute hardest, is gone? Where's the sense in taking her, but leaving me behind with nothing to do but mourn?

Barefoot, I step into the wet, gasping as the chill creeps around my ankles then shoots all the way up my spine, and I laugh at how alive I suddenly feel. I look both ways along the river, first to the bend and dip that creates a miniature waterfall, where Lucy and I would cast off Pooh sticks, then run along the bank in search of the winner. Looking east, I follow the current as it builds then slows where the river grows wide and deep. My eye travels a little further, to where a rope hangs from the branch of an outstretched tree.

I used to swing from that rope, and I wish I could remember the exact feeling you got in the moment between letting go and crashing into the water. It was something akin to expectant bliss, back when all I had to worry about was how many hours it was until bedtime.

I used to be fearless, confident, a sassy little girl who believed in herself and the world around her. I would think nothing of jumping into a river or rollerblading down a hill or playing a song that I'd heard in the rain. Then the world took everything I thought I knew and replaced it with the knowledge that none of us are safe, no matter how many times you knock on wood or hold your breath and count to one hundred.

Lucy's diagnosis changed me as much as it did her, but nobody ever realised because she was always the priority.

'Oh, Lucy,' I sigh, wading back to the riverbank and wiping my chilled feet on the grass. 'I wish you would just tell me what I'm supposed to do.'

Sitting on the ground, I pull on my socks and boots then take out the puzzle box from my bag. It's all too easy to open – once you know which panel to slide, the box reveals itself in all its glory. Inside is the necklace I once stole from her, along with a pebble with a hole through its centre, a dead bumblebee and the rabbit's foot keyring I used to carry around for luck. There's also the photographs of Isaac and me, him wearing sunglasses and looking impossibly cool, whilst I was pulling my mouth apart with my fingers and sticking out my tongue.

Underneath it all is a photograph of Lucy and me. We were in Portugal, the last family holiday before Lucy disappeared off to Oxford, and the last summer before I learnt just how utterly wretched love can be.

It means she knew I'd taken her necklace, despite me protesting otherwise when she asked. When did she find out – years ago or only when she opened the box to add something of her own?

Turning the photo over, I see that on the back, she's written me another riddle.

What do all of these have in common?
A diving board, a flamenco dancer and a bottle
of wine?

She's taking me back, step by step and piece by piece, forcing me to remember. I don't want to; all I've ever done is tell myself not to think about that time of my life – specifically to do whatever I can not to think about Tristan. It would be like ripping out the stitches from Lucy's skull and having her brain ooze all over the floor. Except these stitches are invisible, somewhere inside me, buried under years of denial and pretence, and I can't go back there, I just can't.

If I add all the clues together, if I follow them to where she wants me to go, surely she must know there's a real risk I would be completely undone?

The only person who truly understands me is Isaac, because he was there before, during and after. Which is precisely the reason Lucy has sent me back to him.

I glance over my shoulder in the direction of my childhood home. She didn't tell our parents of her madcap plan, couldn't tell them, because it would be too much for all of us to cope with.

There is no one else. I have nobody else to ask for help and I feel so ashamed and wretched because Isaac was right. My friends don't really know me, I've made sure of that. But I still don't know if I'm brave enough to ask for his help.

A lone magpie swoops down to land on the other side of the river, head cocked and looking in my direction.

One for sorrow, I think, giving the bird a quick salute as I get to my feet. I'm surrounded by sorrow; it's like a leaden weight I cannot put down.

Two for joy. Another magpie lands next to its mate. Then two more, and my mind skips through the rhyme – *three for a girl, four for a boy*. Is it a sign? Or nothing more than four black-and-white birds pecking at the ground in search of food?

If Isaac were here, he'd laugh at my silly superstitions, just like he did when we were kids. He once told me that superstitions were like religion – people used them to provide comfort in an inexplicable world, but that scientific reason negated the need for such beliefs. I seem to remember calling him a philistine, claiming that there was nothing wrong in putting your faith in the unknown. In turn, he said I liked to believe in a higher power because it meant I could shirk responsibility for my actions. At which point I stormed off, because he was infuriating when he was right.

Taking out my phone, I scroll through my contacts, my thumb hovering over the name of the person I know I need to call. But calling would mean speaking and I don't think I have it in me to do so without crying.

Hey, I text as I set off back through the woods, waiting for a signal to appear. *Was wondering if you had time to meet? No worries if you're busy. Beth x.* Then I delete the '*x*', thinking it's too much. Or is it rude to simply sign off with only my name? But I have to put my name down because what if he didn't keep my number? What if he doesn't want to see me now that he's done as Lucy asked? For goodness' sake, Beth, stop overthinking it and just send the damn message.

A few minutes more and a reply lights up the screen.

How about dinner?

I stop walking, stare up at the sky. This is it. This is the moment that will make me decide which path to take. This is the moment that Lucy had no way of controlling, which means she's trusting me to make the right choice.

That would be great

I press 'send' and hold my breath, counting all the way up to one hundred as I wait for his reply.

I'll pick you up tomorrow.

I look back at the photo of Lucy and me, flip it over to reread the clues that are all referencing one specific night during that holiday – a night when we talked about the future and how enormous it all seemed.

12.

Eleven years ago . . .

Lucy and I were lying out under the stars on a flat roof that we'd climbed on to from the bedroom we were sharing whilst on holiday. The apartment was part of a complex and we were situated on the third floor – 'The penthouse!' Dad had declared as we climbed the white-washed staircase to our door. There were a dozen or so buildings in all, with a communal pool and within walking distance of the beach. We were also given access to its sister hotel, located a stone's throw away, with two rectangular blocks jutting into the cerulean sky and a series of nightly entertainment to keep its guests happy.

On the evening in question, Mum had dragged us all along to watch a performance of traditional dancing, accompanied by sweet and salty paella and gallons of (highly potent) sangria. She sat as far away from me as our small table would allow, every so often sending me furious glares to make sure I knew she was still annoyed with me due to an incident earlier in the day.

The communal pool had been closed for cleaning, so Lucy and I had wandered across to the hotel to use theirs. There was so much sun cream clinging to the surface of the water that no light could get through, which meant both that you couldn't see the bottom and it was doubtful anyone had been in to clean it for weeks. But it was sticky and hot and we totally didn't think about all the diseases lurking in the water, so we took it in turns to leap off the diving board, giving each other scores out of ten and Lucy ignoring all the boys who whistled for her attention.

Each time I went under, I closed my eyes and held my breath, waiting for my feet to find the bottom, and then pushed as hard as I could to get back out into the clean air. On my last jump my foot went down but didn't come back up. I tugged, only to discover that it was wedged inside a hole. Eyes open, I looked up, peering through the murky water but unable to see anyone on the other side. Which meant that anyone looking down wouldn't be able to see me either. I should have panicked, but instead I told myself that if my foot had gone into the hole, then there was no reason why it shouldn't come back out again. Pointing my toes, I gave my foot one last wrench then kicked back to the surface.

Lucy was by the side of the pool, frantic and screaming, then she spotted me and leapt into the water, grabbed me by the arm and tried to pull me back to safety.

'I'm fine,' I said, climbing out of the pool and squeezing out my hair.

'You're not fine,' she said through jagged breaths. 'You nearly died, and look, you're bleeding.'

I was bleeding, quite profusely in fact, from a gash all the way along my ankle and down to my little toe, but otherwise I really was ok. I was also secretly enjoying the fact that for once it was Lucy worrying about me instead of the other way around. Part of me delighted in the knowledge that finally she might understand the kind of fear we'd had to live through because of her.

The other part of me was thinking about how I hadn't been scared, that the possibility of drowning in that pool hadn't even crossed my mind. Which was kind of weird given how often I tried to stop anything bad from happening to Lucy.

When Mum heard what happened, she told us off for being stupid enough to willingly jump into a pool when you couldn't see the bottom. Dad, on the other hand, told me that one of these days my luck was bound to run out, then returned his attention to the copy of The Da Vinci Code he was reading.

On the evening in question, we were sitting together at dinner, stuffing our faces with saffron-infused rice and watching as Mum and Dad proceeded to get absolutely plastered. Three glasses in and Mum was out of her seat, hitching her skirt and winking at the waiter (who was about twelve and kept dropping things whenever he came near our table). Mum's inability to hold her drink meant she didn't notice Lucy helping herself to more, as well as passing several glasses along to me.

A few hours in we tired of the terrible music, drunken parents and kids running around half naked throwing food at each other. Making our excuses, we staggered back to the apartment, arms looped together and laughing about things that weren't even remotely funny. I can't remember whose idea it was to climb out on to the roof. I do remember I was the one who stole a bottle of rosé from the fridge, convincing myself Mum wouldn't notice (she did, but Lucy took the blame for that one as Mum with a hangover was not a pretty sight).

Passing the bottle between us and staring up at the darkening sky, it was the closest I'd felt to Lucy in years. We were having a game of sorts, one that we first came up with when Lucy was recovering from her operation. One of us would recite a line from a book or a song, or even a film, and the other would try to name it. The forfeit began with taking another sip from the bottle, but when we ran out it swiftly turned into truth or dare.

'I think I need to break up with Thomas,' Lucy said after failing to identify the opening lyric to Aretha's 'A Rose is Still a Rose'.

'Why?' There were so many other things I wanted to say, and I nearly did, until I realised she was crying.

'I mean, it's probably for the best.'

I stayed quiet, not trusting myself to remain impartial about their relationship and all the extra people who had been in it over the years.

'And I don't need any distractions.'

At this I rolled over and crawled to the edge of the roof, watching as a couple embraced in a doorway and thinking that Lucy seemed to enjoy precisely the kind of distraction she thought she could do without, just not from her current boyfriend.

'I have to focus on my studies, not mope about pining for someone on the other side of the world.' Thomas was already in New Zealand for a gap year – a ski season on the South Island before heading back to Europe to do another season in the Alps. Quite why they decided not to break up before he left was beyond me, but I had a feeling it was because Lucy couldn't bring herself to do it in person.

The couple down below seemed to be melting together, his hand sneaking up her skirt, and I bit down on my lip, waiting to see just how far they would go. I rubbed my fingertips over my lips, wondering for the millionth time what it might feel like to have someone kiss them.

'Are you nervous about Oxford?' I said, turning back to face her, because pining for a long-lost lover I'd never even met was pointless.

'A bit.'

'You'll have them all bowing down and worshipping you in no time.'

She gave me half a smile, then let go an elongated sigh. 'Sometimes I scare myself, how obsessive I can be.'

'Now there's an understatement.'

'Stop it.' She swatted at my arm. 'I'm trying to have a moment.'

'Sorry,' I said with a grin. 'Moment away.'

'I want a big life,' Lucy said, staring off into the distance. 'A meaningful life. One that people remember. And I'm jealous because I think you're the one who's going to get it, not me.'

I ignored the compliment, mainly because the dream I had was so wild and enormous and terrifying and in all likelihood never going to happen. Unless Isaac suddenly turned around and decided he wanted to be a singer in a band instead of a doctor, I had pretty much zero chance of ever getting my songs heard by anyone other than him.

'I made a promise to myself,' she said. 'Right before they took me in for surgery. To never settle for second best, because I have no idea how much time I still have.'

'The tumour won't come back.' I hoped this sounded more convincing than I felt. Because it was there all the time, the knowledge that the next scan might reveal precisely what we'd all been trying to ignore for years. 'You're going to have an amazing life. And when we're both old and grey, I'll annoy you constantly by reminding you just how right I am.'

'Even if it doesn't come back,' Lucy said through a sigh, 'it changed me. Made me scared of wasting even a second.'

I wanted to ask her if that's what all the boys were about. Did they help her forget what the doctors told her every single time she went in for her annual scan: that just because the tumour hadn't grown in years, it didn't mean it wouldn't? I wanted to ask her if a kiss could really make the rest of the world fade away, even if only for a moment.

For a while we just lay there, looking at one another, perhaps trying to commit the moment to memory. It all felt so familiar, but also strange, and it made me sad to think of her going away, starting a new life without me.

I turned to look up at the sky, at the thousands of stars winking back at us.

'It's like there's a whole galaxy of angels up there,' I said, the beginnings of a song appearing in my mind. 'And each of those stars is one of them, linked to one of us. They're all up there, watching over us as we stumble through the maze of living.' I liked to think that Lucy had her own angel, one who would look after her no matter what.

'Promise me,' she said, searching for my eyes in the moonlight. 'Promise me you'll keep writing.'

'But what's the point if nobody ever hears them? Dad always says music is meant to be shared, but I can't sing, Lucy. I can't stand up on stage and perform something I've written. I'd make a fool of myself.' The idea of exposing my innermost thoughts to anyone other than Isaac or my sister was sickening, because once the songs were out there, I had no way of taking them back.

'Dreams aren't meant to be easy,' she said through a yawn. 'If they were, they wouldn't mean as much.'

A month later and she was gone. The back of her Mini piled high with suitcases, books and boxes of CDs (I snuck in some Stones and Joplin to take the edge off all that Chopin). As she started the engine, the sound of Fleetwood Mac poured out of the stereo and she laughed at the bittersweet perfection of those lyrics, shouting out that she'd try not to get lost as she went her own way. I can still picture her face, so open and excited at the prospect of starting the next chapter of her life, one that she'd been working towards for years. I had no doubt she would come back to us even brighter and better than before. What I didn't know was if there would be any room in her new world for me.

13.

When Isaac comes to collect me from my flat, I laugh as I climb in the passenger side of his Golf (the same one he'd had at school, complete with cassette deck and faux leather seats that you'd get stuck to in the summer) and say I'm surprised the car is still working, given how ancient it is. In response he looks me up and down and asks if I'm dressed like a Stones groupie for a reason. I say something banal about there being a seventies fashion revival, don't you know, then turn my face away so he can't see the blush rising up from my neck.

Truth is, I spent the best part of an hour trying to figure out what to wear to have dinner with my former best friend. The result is a burgundy mini dress paired with over-the-knee suede boots and a fringed jacket. I'd rough-dried my hair and added an extra coat of mascara whilst peering into the mirror, the whole time telling myself I had nothing to worry about, it was just Isaac.

Except his flat turns out to be a terraced house in Kennington that once belonged to his great-uncle. Four storeys of pale brick, with a glossy black door, railings to match and within walking distance of the Oval, which is precisely why his cricket-mad uncle had bought it.

'Hope you're hungry,' Isaac says as he opens the front door and moves aside to allow me in.

It's like stepping into another world – from the outside every house on the street looks the same – nondescript – and at one point I imagine there was little difference between what lay beyond all those front doors. Now, I expect that each and every house is like reaching your hand into a lucky dip at the fair with no idea what you're going to get.

I don't know what I was expecting, but it certainly wasn't parquet flooring, white walls and stone-grey woodwork and doors. Overhead hangs an enormous light, clear and perfectly spherical, and there is a narrow console table against the wall, behind which hangs a black lacquered mirror.

'Mum did it,' Isaac says by way of explanation, relieving me of my jacket and hanging it up.

'That was good of her,' I say, peering along the hall to where I can see another room, presumably the kitchen, given the smell of roasting onions and garlic that is seeping out, along with music and unfamiliar voices. Isaac hadn't said anything about flatmates or friends and, even though I should have asked, it annoys me that he didn't think it was worth mentioning and now I don't feel prepared for this at all. It's all so grown-up and refined and it really, really doesn't seem like the sort of place I should be having dinner in.

'Do you want the tour?'

Isaac is talking to me, but all I can focus on is the bead of sweat that's collected at the back of my neck and how, when I glance at my reflection in the mirror, I'm painfully aware of my mascara-smudged cheeks and the small stain on the front of my dress.

'Isaac.' I try to speak, to tell him this is a mistake, but my mouth is dry, my palms feel clammy and there's a far-off ringing inside my head. I can think of nothing better than walking back out on to the street and heading for the pub that we passed on our way here. Problem is, Lucy sent me to Isaac for a reason, and he agreed to help. He tried to help me before, but I pushed him away, and if I walk away now, I seriously doubt he will ever speak to me again.

'Why don't we have dinner first? Then I'll show you around.'

I try to smile in acknowledgement, but my face seems to have forgotten how, so I simply nod and follow.

The kitchen is an extension to the back of the house, with the same parquet flooring and a mixture of grey and white cabinetry. The roof is glass, with black steel beams, and the whole of the back wall is a sliding glass door that's open to a patio garden beyond. On the stove is a bright-orange pot, from which thin ribbons of steam are escaping. There's a fruit bowl, a bread board and an enormous vase of lilies on the marble-topped island, and the dining table is laid for four. It is at one end of this table that two people are sitting, close enough to make me realise they are a couple, and both of them looking directly at me.

'Hi,' the woman says as she extends her hand in greeting. 'I'm Margot.' Her voice is throaty, as if she smokes forty Gauloises a day, and I'm immediately transported back to a badly lit bar where underage girls wear too much make-up and not enough clothes.

'Are you French?' She definitely looks French, or like a French version of Audrey Hepburn, with a sleek bob, red lips and a tiny little body.

'No,' she says with a laugh, revealing a set of perfectly straight, whiter-than-white teeth. 'My mum liked old movies.'

'I'm Nathan,' the other stranger says as he finishes rolling a cigarette and taps one end on the table. 'Do you smoke?'

'Not really.'

'Good for you,' he says with a mock salute. 'Filthy habit.'

I watch him unfold from the chair, my eye travelling ever upward as he stands, then ducks his head as he goes through the open doors and out to the patio.

'Six foot seven,' he calls back as he lights his cigarette. 'And yes, the view from up here is rather marvellous.'

'Are you hungry?' Margot asks as she stands, and I guess her to be no taller than five eight, which immediately makes my mind meander off to all sorts of inappropriate places, because even in heels they wouldn't fit together, surely? 'I made chilli, so I hope you don't mind a bit of heat?'

'No, that's fine. Thank you.' I hear myself say the words, but this all still feels too normal for me and I don't know how I'm supposed to behave. I honestly can't remember the last time I had dinner at someone's house, and it's so intimate, the way Margot and Isaac move around the space together – opening and closing cupboards, taking out a bottle of chilled wine from the fridge, setting down a bowl of wild rice and another of chilli that I can already taste.

I should be helping, or at least have thought to bring a gift to say thank you, but I'm pretty sure I'd get in the way or drop something, and a bunch of decrepit carnations from the corner shop wouldn't belong in a place such as this. I don't say anything else, just take a seat at the table and watch as Isaac spoons out an enormous portion that he sets down in front of me.

'Wine?' Margot asks, lifting the bottle in invitation, and I say yes, because a glass (or two), would be the perfect way to take the edge off my nerves. Then I sense Isaac beside me, and the room seems to be getting smaller by the second. The desire to run is back, but I push it away, filling my mouth with a spoonful of chilli to stop myself from doing or saying anything stupid.

'Jesus,' I say, taking a long sip of water, and then reach for some bread. 'This is hot.'

Margot and Isaac both laugh, no doubt at the sight of me with tears streaming down my face and shoving bits of bread in my mouth, but it's enough to break the tension and I find myself laughing too, relaxing into the moment and looking from Isaac to Margot and then Nathan as he comes back to the table.

I sit and listen and eat (after a few more spoonfuls your tongue sort of gets numb so the chilli doesn't seem as fierce), and it's a weird sort of feeling, one I'd nearly forgotten, that of being included.

'Isaac says you work in hospitality?' Nathan says, helping himself to a gargantuan portion of chilli.

I give a small laugh and sit back in my chair. 'Isaac's being too generous,' I say. 'I teach piano and also play at a hotel bar.'

'But you know each other from school?' Margot asks, and I can imagine her trying to connect the dots between brilliant surgeon and part-time musician. 'Isaac says you used to write music.'

'She was by far the most talented person in the whole school,' Isaac says, and I wince at the word 'was'.

'What happened?' Margot says, then puts her hand to her mouth. 'Sorry. Forgive me, I'm horrifically nosy.'

'Occupational hazard.' Nathan plants a kiss on Margot's head and, when I frown, he shields the side of his face with one hand and says in a stage whisper, 'She's training to be a shrink.'

I laugh at the non-existent joke because it's the polite thing to do, but seriously, Isaac lives with a psychiatrist? I feel all exposed and awkward and could brush the question aside, but she's looking at me in a way that suggests she won't give up so easily and I figure what the hell.

'I fell for the wrong person.'

Isaac clears his throat and another look passes between him and Margot, but I have no idea what this one means. Does she know? Has he told her about what happened with Tristan?

'And?' Margot persists.

I sigh and puff out my cheeks and look around the room because it's the question everyone (including myself) has been asking, over and over, but there's no real answer, or at least not a good enough one to explain all the years I have clearly wasted. Because

112

who does that, right? Who just gives up and walks away instead of brushing themselves off and trying again?

'And nothing,' I say, taking a long sip of wine and refusing to meet Isaac's eye. 'I realised it wasn't meant to be. Some people are simply luckier than others.'

'There's no such thing as luck,' Isaac says, and I want to laugh or scream or do something to convey just how infuriating it is to hear this from someone whose life has turned out exactly the way he planned.

'Tell that to Lucy,' I say, my voice catching on her name.

'Shit, sorry,' Isaac says, and the shift in the room is sudden and fierce. 'That's not what I meant.'

'It's fine,' I say all too brightly, smiling across the table and blinking back tears. 'Actually, no, it's not fine. It's unbelievably shit, but she's gone and that's that. The point is she was brilliant, and I wasn't.'

'That's not true,' Isaac says, scraping back his chair and turning to face me.

'Yes, it is,' I reply, blowing my nose into a napkin and then wishing I hadn't because they're linen not paper, and yet again I feel so very out of place. 'She wouldn't have given up. But she also wouldn't ever have been stupid enough to throw it all away in the first place. Lucy was always so much better than me, and so it makes no sense that I'm the one still here. I'm sorry,' I say, pushing back my chair as I stand. 'I didn't mean to ruin dinner. Especially when you've all been so welcoming. Perhaps I should leave.'

'No, stay,' Margot says, and Nathan nods in agreement. 'It's my fault. I shouldn't pry.'

I look over at Isaac and there are a million more questions and apologies and things I should say, but I have no idea where to begin. That's when I realise how much I've missed him and how badly I need his help, so when he starts clearing the table, stacking plates and taking them over to the sink, I'm terrified he's going to tell me that yes, I should go.

'Leave that,' Margot says, nudging Isaac aside with her hip and rolling up her sleeves. 'Give Beth the grand tour.' She looks over her shoulder at me, sends me a genuine smile, and I allow myself to hope that maybe we could learn to be friends.

I follow Isaac up the stairs, only half listening as he points out various rooms. The first floor is divided into two, with a living room at the front of the house, a bedroom at the rear and a bathroom in between. Another floor up and there are only two doors, one of which is ajar to reveal an enormous bedroom, with floor-to-ceiling windows and a guitar propped up against a chair in the corner.

'I'm guessing this is you?' I ask, wanting to step inside and see what else remains of the Isaac I used to know. Are there shelves filled with old records, half-finished scale models of classic cars and a pet iguana living in a terrarium somewhere? Does he still have a *Star Wars* poster on the wall, or has everything been upgraded to suit this new version of him that I don't quite recognise?

He goes into his room, and I'm about to follow when my eye lands on one of the pictures that line the walls. It's a photo of the two of us, sitting on the ground back to back, my head tilted towards the camera and his in profile. He's playing the guitar and we're both barefoot, dressed in clothes that would only make sense in the summer. His hair is long, longer than I ever remember it being, whilst mine is fashioned into a plait that drapes over one shoulder, woven through with golden beads that I have no recollection of ever buying.

'When was this?' I ask, and he stops, turns around to see what it is I'm pointing at.

He smiles, but only with half of his mouth, suggesting the memory I've shown him is bitter-sweet. 'Thomas's eighteenth,' he says. 'Do you not remember?'

'No, I do. I do,' I say, as all the memories of that night reappear in my mind. 'I just had no idea this photo even existed.' I remember a group of us, mostly Isaac's extended family, but also a few people from school and, of course, Lucy, sitting at a long trestle table on the patio, eating Mexican food and drinking beer straight from the bottle.

'Do you still play?' I ask as I turn away from the photo and follow Isaac into his bedroom.

'Sometimes,' he says, picking up his guitar and perching on the end of his bed. A second later he's picking out a tune, one that I used to sing along to, and I suspect this is precisely what he's trying to get me to do.

I step past him and across to the far wall, which is lined with bookcases. He does indeed still have every single one of the records we used to sit and listen to as kids, but the sound system is now Bose. His hand stills on the guitar and I register the absence of sound, feel it somewhere deep inside me, somewhere I don't want to go.

Instead, I look to the wall where a framed print of Robert Plant is hanging. It was taken when Led Zeppelin were performing at Earls Court in 1975. I know this because I was the one who gave it to Isaac on his sixteenth birthday. Next to it is a page of sheet music for 'Kashmir', his favourite song of all. It's so complicated, all those notes looking like ants crawling across a page, but Isaac could read music better than any book. I want to ask him if he can still play it, even though I'm pretty sure he remembers it perfectly, every single note.

I also want to ask if he ever found that again, what we had? Because I miss it, all of it, and it makes me feel so wretched to think that I took music away from him, replacing it with a great big hole where our friendship used to be.

'Is it weird, living with a couple?' I ask, anything to steer my mind away from memories I have kept locked away.

He shrugs, looks back towards the landing as Margot's laughter floats all the way up from the kitchen. 'I've known Margot since college.'

How well, exactly? Was Margot ever more than a friend? I'm struck by another image, this one of the two of them in his bed, all limbs and tongues and soft groans, which makes me weirdly jealous. My thoughts must be written all over my face because he chuckles. 'Not like that,' he says, then blushes and shifts uneasily on the bed.

'Besides,' he goes on, looking directly at me now, and I feel my own skin start to flush. 'I like having people around.'

This is true. He always hated being by himself. When his parents went away for the weekend and Thomas disappeared off with Lucy to various parties, more often than not Isaac would throw stones at my bedroom window until I opened it wide to let him in.

'Did you speak to your parents?' he asks, those long fingers of his pressing down on the guitar strings and sending me back in time as the opening bars of Stevie Wonder's 'Superstition' crosses the space between us.

'Sort of,' I reply, clearing my throat and picking up a small hardback copy of *The Hare and the Tortoise* from the bedside table. As I do so, a sheet of paper falls out and on to the floor. Bending down to retrieve it, I notice four small drawings, along with the words *What's the connection?* written in Lucy's looping script.

'That's for you,' Isaac says.

I sit down on the bed next to him and flick through the book, then look again at the drawings. There's a violin, a train, a fish and the cartoon face of a boy with a lightning bolt on his forehead.

'Harry Potter,' Isaac says, picking out the theme tune on his guitar then changing back to another Stevie Wonder song. 'No idea what he's got to do with either a violin or a fish though.'

For a moment I don't say anything, just sit and listen to him play, my mind following along with the words. If he had the book here, does that mean he only invited me for dinner because Lucy asked him to? Is her death the only reason he's even talking to me, making him feel obligated to carry out her request?

'Do you think she drew this too?' I say, pointing to one of the pages, where someone has drawn in a dog chasing the hare as it runs away from the tortoise.

Isaac stops playing to look at me. 'No idea. But I have a feeling the book's about Tristan.'

'How so?' I ask, turning the page in search of any more clues and swallowing away the sense of dread that keeps coming back whenever anyone mentions Tristan's name.

'You only met him because of Lucy.'

I look over at him as I think back to how this can be true. 'Because Lucy had a summer fling with his brother.'

'And where did they meet?'

'At the Hare & Tortoise.'

'Precisely.' He flashes me a grin and my stomach does a quick flip in response.

'There has to be more to it,' I say, looking back down at the book, then the sheet of paper, anything to avoid his eye and the way that smile just made me feel.

'Why?'

'Because it's too random, too easy to miss. And Lucy wouldn't give me something without there being a specific reason.'

'That reminds me,' he says, holding up one finger then disappearing from the room. I hear a door being opened and shut, along with the sound of things being moved around and Isaac muttering to himself about being sure he'd put it right there. A second later and there's a dull thud, followed by a yell and a quiet 'fuck that hurt', then he's back in the room, rubbing at his head and holding out a blue spiral-bound notebook with doodles all over the cover.

It's the same type of notebook I always used. I had stacks of them on the shelves in my room, next to poetry books and records and framed photos of me with my only real friend. This, however, is a very specific notebook, inside which I wrote my favourite song of all, one I have thought about pretty much every single day for eight years.

'Where did you get this?' Except I already know. Just like everything else, Lucy has conspired to send me back a very poignant piece of my past, given to me by the only other person I should have trusted to see inside my soul.

My hand shakes as I take it from him, the sound of the world becoming muffled as I open the cover.

'Oh, shit. I think I was supposed to give you a clue first. Something about a baby goose.'

'A gosling?'

'That's the one.'

'Seriously?' I say with a laugh as I connect the dots between a bird and a notebook. 'That's her clue? Ryan Gosling?'

'It's a good film.'

'You've seen *The Notebook*?' It was one of Lucy's favourites; I once watched it with her and I swear she couldn't see the screen she was crying so much.

'Do you still write?' Isaac asks, pointing at the notebook, and I realise one of the pages is marked with a yellow Post-it note.

'If I said yes, would you believe me?' I open the book at the marked page and click my tongue when I see what's written there in my own messy script.

'I always loved that one,' he says, coming to stand beside me, and I resist the urge to lean into him, to have him enfold me in a hug.

'Me too,' I say, my eyes skimming along the lines of words, a poem of sorts that I set to music, and now I remember singing it at the bottom of his parents' garden, with my head resting on his shoulder as someone captured the moment on film.

Isaac glances at his watch and stifles a yawn. 'Sorry, I was on nights all week. Need to play catch-up on my sleep.'

'I should get going,' I say. 'Thank you for dinner, Isaac. I had a lovely time.'

'A lovely time?' he says with another grin, and I cover my face with my hands. 'Since when have you been so polite?'

'Since I've forgotten how to be around you.'

His smile drops, replaced by a look that I don't have a name for, and I wish I knew a way to break the tension between us, to stitch together all the years we've been apart.

'Ever since Lucy contacted me,' he says, putting his guitar back on the stand, 'I've been having random conversations with you in my head. Actually no,' he goes on, running his hands through his hair, 'I've been having random conversations with you for years.'

'Me too,' I say, swallowing away the lump in my throat because I would talk to him all the time. Whenever something weird or wonderful happened, whenever a certain song came on the radio or I stumbled across an awesome new band, I would turn around, or pick up my phone, expecting to be able to tell him. The feeling that followed is one I've never really been able to find a name for – the best I've ever come up with is sorrow, but it's so much more.

It's also the exact same feeling I now have whenever I think of all the conversations I missed with Lucy over the years, conversations that never happened because I was too wrapped up in my own self-pity to close the gap between us.

Lucy has given me a second chance with Isaac, one that I wasn't ever able to give myself. Wiping away a tear, I take a very long, slow inhale before saying the only two words that really matter. 'I'm sorry.'

He doesn't reply at first, and I hold my breath, terrified that he's not going to forgive me, even after all this time.

'I know,' he says with a sigh.

'I'm sorry for what I said. For blaming you.'

'Look,' he says, sitting down on the bed, hands clasped together and resting on his knees. 'I'll admit what you did was totally and utterly shit.'

'I'm sorry.' Suddenly these words are nowhere near enough. I've always been able to live (at times only just) with the pain I had to endure, but the knowledge that I'd probably done it to him, to my best friend, is something I've always tried to ignore. But now I have to accept it, own it and somehow make amends.

'I was lucky, in a way,' he says. 'Because I had uni, a chance to move on, or at least I told myself that's what I was doing. But you . . .' He looks up at me, and I go across to the window, turn my face away, because I can't stand the pity behind his eyes.

'I gave up.' It seemed like the only option at the time. But I know that if I hadn't pushed Isaac away, if I'd shared my grief with him, he would have helped me through the darkness. If I'd let him be my friend, I wouldn't have wasted so many years with him, and perhaps with Lucy too.

'You drifted off course.'

I wipe my nose with the back of my hand, laughing at his kindness. 'Bit of an understatement.'

'Do you think . . .' he says as he stands and crosses the room to stand next to me. 'Do you think Lucy is asking you to set the record straight? To tell the truth about what happened?'

'I don't know, Isaac. I still don't have a clue how Tristan got hold of it in the first place.'

Back home, I go into my room and take out the two puzzle boxes, put them next to one another on top of the bed. Running my fingertips around each lid, I imagine Lucy doing the same thing. I think of her deciding which clues to leave me, and where. Then I allow myself a smile because she would have thought through each and every last detail, right down to getting Isaac to hand over the notebook that's tucked inside my bag, waiting for me to open it.

Easing apart the spine, I start from the very beginning, rereading words I scribbled down years ago. Sitting inside one of the pages is a ticket to Glastonbury. Isaac and I were supposed to go after finishing our A Levels, but I never made it; just one more bad decision I have no way of undoing. Everything that happened that summer, everything that went wrong, is because of the song that's written on the next page of this book.

I still remember the night I wrote it. I still remember lying on my childhood bed, having not even taken off my boots, and scribbling the words that appeared in my mind so suddenly and without warning. It's a song I wrote before I really understood what love meant, and what it could do to a heart that was too open and willing.

14.

The Hare & Tortoise pub was on the outskirts of town, tucked away at the end of a country lane and backing on to a medieval churchyard. It wasn't much to look at from the outside, but cross the threshold and it was like stepping into a labyrinth, with a U-shaped bar and plenty of nooks and crannies where teenagers would lurk, cradling ill-gotten pints or feeling one another up under the table.

I was supposed to be meeting Isaac there to celebrate the end of AS Levels and the beginning of summer. Ever since that kiss with Jessica, he'd been assimilating himself into the 'cool crowd', which was precisely the reason I didn't want to go.

I was late, even by my standards, thanks in part to Lucy taking ages in the bathroom (definite disadvantage to having her back from Oxford for the summer), but mainly because I'd spent the entire walk to the pub trying to figure out the right words to fit the melody that had been following me around for days. However, if I'd turned up on time, then maybe I wouldn't have left early, and then I wouldn't have had a certain conversation with my very best friend.

When I arrived at the pub, my head was full of music and madness, my body weaving through the crowd in search of Isaac, but my mind only half paying attention. So when I walked through the conservatory to the garden, I didn't register who it was sitting in the corner, head bent close to the person who would inadvertently change my entire future.

'You're late,' Isaac said, handing me a drink as I put down my bag and sat on the bench next to him. Jessica was sitting on his other side, drawing heavily on a cigarette and attempting to blow smoke circles, but looking more like a child pretending to be a dragon than the sex goddess she was aiming for.

'Sorry,' I said, wafting the smoke away from my face and taking a sip of warm, flat cider.

'You'll never guess who's here,' Jessica said, leaning around Isaac to stare at me. As always, it sounded like a test rather than simply a question. The two of us were never going to be friends, I knew from the outset there would be no sleepovers or pampering sessions, no shopping trips or secrets shared. But she tolerated my presence at parties and social events, which turned out to be mutually beneficial – I could pretend to my parents that I had some semblance of a life and she could use my weirdness to highlight her perfection.

'Who?' I said as I looked around.

'Damian King,' Jessica said with a smile that told us she'd already claimed him for herself.

Damian had joined school at the beginning of the year and immediately had all the girls in a tither due to the fact he bore more than a passing resemblance to Tom Cruise, only taller. Problem was, he was going steady with a girl from his old school named Tallulah.

According to the fountain of gossip that was Jessica, Damian dumped Tallulah the day after her final AS exam ('How noble of him to wait before breaking her heart,' Isaac had said), and was coming to the pub that night with a single purpose, to find a new girlfriend.

Jessica was convinced she would be the one to win the prize, but secretly I hoped it might just be me. It was ridiculous and naive and heavily laced with the teenage romanticism that came from reading too much poetry, but a girl could dream, right? Besides, I'd heard his brother was in a band, so maybe we could bond over a mutual love for music?

'Didn't know Lucy was back,' Peter said as he returned from the bar with a tray-load of drinks.

'Short terms at Oxford,' I replied. 'Why?' I continued, but my head was already turning in the direction of the conservatory. 'Is she here?'

'God, your sister is annoyingly gorgeous,' Jessica said as she leant across me to stare at Lucy and Damian, who were sitting with heads bent close together and ignoring everyone around them. 'You'd think she'd leave at least one hot guy for the rest of us. Or rather, for me,' she said, looking me up and down.

I felt the blush rising up from my chest as I stood, fumbling under the bench for my bag and getting my foot caught through the strap.

'Beth, wait up,' Isaac said as I pushed my way through the crowds that seemed to be multiplying and spilling on to the street like ants from a disturbed nest.

'You didn't have to follow me,' I said, hitching my bag on to my shoulder and striding off into the night. 'I'm perfectly capable of walking myself home.'

'I know,' he said, falling in step beside me.

'I can't believe she'd do that.'

'Do what?' he asked, looking back over his shoulder.

'Steal him from Jessica.'

'Who are we talking about?'

'Lucy. And Damian.'

'Ah.' We walked on, and I was glad of his quiet presence. 'But how would Lucy even know that Jessica was after Damian?'

'That's not the point.'

'Are you going to tell me what is? Wait, do you fancy him?'

'No,' I said, punching him on the arm, and when he responded with a mock 'ow' I punched him again then climbed over a stile into *a poppy field and lay down. He came to lie next to me and I tried not to think about how incredibly romantic it would be in different circumstances. 'But even if I did, it wouldn't matter. He'd never fancy me back.'*

'You don't know that,' he said. It was kind, but it also hurt because it was a lie. I hated being the only girl never to have been kissed (which wasn't entirely true, but it certainly felt that way).

'I want someone to know each and every part of me,' I said, staring up at the sky and picking out all the constellations Dad once taught me. 'To count all the moles on my skin and not think it's weird that I can pick things up with my toes or that I like to spread peanut butter on raw carrots.'

'Or eat tuna straight from the tin.' I heard him searching his pockets for something and a moment later there was the sound of a lighter, followed by a small golden circle of flame that appeared at the end of a pre-rolled joint. 'Want some?' he asked, coughing as he spoke and holding the illicit cone out for me. I hesitated a moment, then shook my head, no, and he took another drag before blowing a perfect smoke ring into the sky. I watched it disperse into the night, thought of tiny little insects getting stoned then eaten by the swallows and swifts I could see darting above our heads.

I turned my head to look at Isaac, at the line of his nose in profile and the scar above his eyebrow. I remember thinking it would be so much easier if we fancied each other. But could we ever be more than friends, even if we wanted to?

'I've been thinking,' I said, rolling on to my side and propping my head up with one hand.

'Sounds dangerous.'

I gave his shoulder a poke. 'Just listen, would you?'

'I'm all ears,' he replied, using a finger to waggle the ear closest to me.

'Everything in life only exists because you make a choice about something.'

'Is this about you or Lucy?' Even when stoned, he was remarkably astute. Both he and Lucy were planners, with their futures all neatly mapped out after careful consideration and digestion. I, on the other hand, couldn't make up my mind about whether or not I should even go to university, let alone which one or which course to take.

'Both?'

'You could just not choose. Accept whatever shit gets thrown at you.'

'Exactly.' I picked one of the poppies surrounding us, pulling off its petals one by one. 'The entire trajectory of our lives can be traced back to a single choice.'

'Can't choose love though,' he said with a sigh, resting his hands on his stomach and closing his eyes.

'Why not? You can choose whether or not to let someone kiss you.'

'But you can't force someone to love you in return.'

The conversation had shifted, albeit unwittingly, and I watched him a moment, wishing I could see inside that thick skull of his and rummage around through all the things he still wouldn't tell me.

'Who is she?'

'Who what she?' he said, half opening one eye to stare at me, then promptly shutting it again.

'Come on,' I said with a childish whine. 'I promise not to tell. As long as it's not my sister, I won't judge.' Please, dear Lord, let it be anyone other than her.

Isaac smiled. A long, languid smile that turned into a small laugh the moment before he started singing.

'It's funny how you never fall for the girls who want to love you,' he sang.

'Since when are you a Smiths fan?' I asked, staring back at him and trying to figure out the look on his face, which wasn't exactly easy, given he was stoned out of his tree. Was it Lucy? Of course, it would be her; everyone she ever met fell in love with her.

'Not the Smiths,' he said, his face creasing in concentration as he racked his brain for the name of the band, even though he'd muddled the lyrics.

'Oh, my God,' I said, sitting up and rummaging in my bag for a pen, but the best I had was an old lip-liner I'd stolen from Lucy and never used.

'What?' Isaac sat up and began looking back and forth, eyes wide and paranoid.

'Do you have any paper?' I asked, upending my bag and shaking out its contents.

'No, why? Hey,' he complained as I grabbed his arm and turned it over to expose the soft, hairless crease of his elbow and began to write down the words that had suddenly appeared in my mind.

Isaac didn't move, just sat there and waited for me to finish.

'Why didn't you use your own arm?' he asked, tilting his head to try and read in the half-light.

'Yours is longer,' I said, then I got to my feet and skipped back towards the road, waving goodbye over my shoulder without looking back.

I went home and rewrote the entire song, sitting up long after I heard Lucy creeping up the stairs, no doubt flushed with kisses. Isaac came round the very next day, helped me fix the chorus, and we recorded it on the Dictaphone Dad had given me years before. That song means more to me than any of the others I wrote, either before or after, and it was also the reason why Lucy started calling me Hyacinth Girl.

15.

Two weeks. Doesn't sound like much. Stretch it out to days, then hours or more than one million seconds, and time takes on another meaning. It's been two weeks since I opened the box Lucy sent me, since I discovered the first clue about a song I wish I'd never written.

The thing I can't wrap my head around is that Lucy didn't know I was there the night she met Damian. And she could have had no possible way of knowing that was the night I wrote 'Hyacinth Girl'. But it can't be a coincidence, surely? Then again, it can't only be about that song; why else would she remind me about the night on a rooftop in Portugal and Isaac's favourite sweet? It doesn't make sense, and this is why I am going slowly insane with frustration at not being able to figure out the connection between a violin, a train, Harry Potter and a fish.

Ok, so the train and Harry Potter is obviously King's Cross station, which is close to Regent's Canal, but that's no more than a tenuous link to a fish. The violin is what's thrown me. There are no theatres or music halls or academies nearby, and I can't think of any famous violinists that have a link to Harry Potter or a train.

Each night, I lie everything out on my bed, trying to see the links, the patterns, whatever it is that Lucy wanted me to see, but they're just things, they're not her.

I still dream of Lucy. I still wake in the middle of the night dazed and confused and looking around the room as if I expect her to be there. The pain is still with me too, mean and nasty and catching me off-guard, making it hard to breathe or stand or do anything at all.

Just the other day, I was in the supermarket when a woman walked past, and I looked up in expectation. It wasn't her face or her hair, or even her voice that threw me, made the edges of my vision blur and the air catch inside my lungs. It was her perfume, the same perfume Lucy had worn for years, a subtle mixture of violet and lemon that made you turn to follow the scent. When I sank to the floor and stuck my head between my knees, nobody realised why, nor did they notice how hard I was pressing my nails into my palms in an effort to stop myself crying.

'You daydreaming again?' Sam asks as he comes in from the bar to find me leaning against the kitchen counter.

'Sort of,' I reply as I pick up my coffee mug and rinse it out in the sink, because in precisely four minutes my shift is due to end and Isaac is coming to pick me up and drive us out to listen to Flick play in her last ever school recital.

'*Fancy going to a concert Thursday night?*' I'd said in my message, telling myself he would be working or out having a life so I wouldn't be disappointed when he turned me down. As soon as I hit 'send' those two little ticks turned blue and I held my breath as I saw the speech bubble appear, along with the grey dots which told me he was already responding.

'*As long as it's not Justin Bieber,*' he'd replied, and I smiled, because it was exactly the sort of thing he would have said when we were younger.

'Hey,' Isaac says, and it makes me jump because I was checking the clock instead of the door.

'Don't do anything I wouldn't do,' Sam says with a wink as I pick up the same satchel I've had since I was sixteen.

'Any luck with the violin?' Isaac asks as we head outside.

'It's driving me insane,' I say, blinking against the light and following him to his car.

'I brought snacks,' I say once we're on the move, rummaging in my bag for some pretzels and a can of ginger beer.

'Just don't make a mess,' Isaac says, darting me a look as he pulls up at the lights.

I shove a handful of pretzels into my mouth then hold the packet out to him. His car, his flat, no doubt his office (does he have an office? I wonder), are all spotlessly clean. I used to wind him up, deliberately move things on his desk or jump on his bed to mess up the duvet. He seems in a good enough mood today, but probably best not to deliberately annoy him by dropping crumbs on the floor of his beloved Golf.

'There are some old tapes in the glove compartment.' He leans across and bangs on the corner of the dashboard, making the flap pop open, then has to swerve to avoid a cyclist coming the other way.

'Watch the road,' I say, and he flicks my arm. 'When was the last time you actually bought any music?' I ask, searching through his meagre collection and then smiling as I find an old mixtape I once made for him.

'Perfect,' he says with a grin as I hold up the tape in question.

There is a click and a whir as I slide the cassette into the car's stereo, then a pause after I hit 'play' before the opening bars of 'American Idiot' spill from the speakers, filling the small space with bass notes that I can feel all the way down to my toes. Immediately I am transported back to being seventeen, listening to music loud enough to make the books on my shelves dance.

'You ok?'

'I just wish . . .' I say, but I've no idea what it is I should wish for, because what I really want isn't possible.

'I know,' he says, reaching across and giving my hand a squeeze.

I rest my head back and close my eyes, unsure what to say. With anyone else, I would have filled all the gaps in conversation with endless words, anything to avoid the silence. But being with Isaac is like coming home or putting down a heavy bag after a long walk, and I realise it's been such a long time since I've allowed myself to just be.

Flick's school is a Gothic monstrosity on the outskirts of London, with floodlit tennis courts, electric gates and a position on the list of the top thirty schools in the country. The car park and surrounding streets are lined with expensive cars from which designer-clad parents and perfectly preened offspring emerge. I fiddle with the fabric of my dress as we walk down the tree-lined drive, wishing I'd made more of an effort with my hair.

'You look fine,' Isaac says as we approach the entrance, and I flinch at the word, not least because I doubt the woman standing at the front door has ever been described as 'fine' in her life.

'Name?' she says with a too-bright smile, her eyes sweeping over us both like a bouncer at a nightclub.

'Elizabeth Franks,' I reply, taking in the line-free face, whippet-thin waist and diamond earrings.

'Ah yes, Felicity's teacher,' she says, handing us each a ticket and glossy brochure and pointing us in the direction of the auditorium.

'Do all your students attend schools that cost more than most people make in a year?' Isaac asks as we walk into an oval-shaped room with a vaulted ceiling and a stage that wouldn't look out of place in a London theatre.

'Overachievers help pay the rent,' I say, looking around the room and thinking of how I still need to start gathering up a few more students to compensate for losing Flick.

'Beth!'

I turn at the sound of my name, see Flick cross the room with her mother in tow.

'You made it,' she says, enveloping me in a hug and then standing back when she catches sight of Isaac.

'Elizabeth,' Mrs Miller says, extending her hand in greeting. 'Lovely of you to join us. I see you brought a guest?'

'Isaac, this is Mrs Miller, Felicity's mother.' I notice Felicity stealing glances at Isaac and I wish I'd had the nerve to call her Flick in front of her mother.

'I hear you're starting at the Royal Academy in September?' Isaac directs the question at Flick, and I could kiss him for making her feel important.

'I can't wait,' she replies with a grin. 'But it's all down to Beth. I couldn't have done it without her.'

'Well, I don't know about that,' Mrs Miller says with a stilted laugh. 'Genetics certainly helped.'

'Felicity really is exceptional,' I say, giving her arm a squeeze. 'I'll be sorry to lose her.'

'I have to go get ready,' Flick says. 'Wish me luck?'

'Good luck,' Mrs Miller says, and I flinch, even though it's music, not *Macbeth*.

'Break a leg,' I call after her as the sound of a ringtone cuts through the air. Isaac pulls out his phone and switches it to silent.

'Sorry,' he says, glancing at the screen. 'I need to take this.'

He heads for the door and I resist the urge to go after him, because I have no idea what to say to Flick's mother, or anyone else in this room actually.

'How do you two know each other?' Mrs Miller asks.

'School,' I say, rocking back and forth on my heels.

'And what does he do?'

'He's a doctor. Well, surgeon,' I reply, noticing the new-found interest on her face. 'Or at least he will be once he's finished his residency.'

'And the two of you are . . . ?'

'Just friends.'

'I see. Well, in that case I may have to ask you to keep him on hold for Felicity,' she says with a trill to her voice. 'Handsome and a doctor. Such a wonderful combination.'

The lights in the auditorium flash and I offer up a silent prayer of thanks as people start taking their seats.

'Enjoy the concert,' Mrs Miller says, heading towards the front row.

I check my ticket, and it seems Isaac and I are in the bleachers. Which is fine, but it only serves as a reminder of how I am forever destined to stay in the background of life.

A couple of years ago, Lucy was invited to give a speech at the Leavers' Assembly of our old school. I only know because Mum told me about it, saying how inspiring it must have been for the pupils to see what it was possible to achieve through hard work and perseverance. It felt like a dig, but then most of the conversations I have with my mother inevitably end up with her asking if I've given any thought to doing something else, something more, with my life.

I think again of the argument we had when she accused me of wasting my life, of living without purpose, and I in turn blamed her for never supporting my dreams. The truth hurts in so many ways, not least because I know that even now Mum hates the fact I can't be more like my sister.

As the room quietens and the headmaster (I presume that's who he is, given he's wearing a cap and gown, for pity's sake), takes to the stage, I spot Isaac hovering at the other side of the room, nose to the air as he seeks me out. I raise my hand and he does so in return.

Isaac is the sort of person who would get invited back to give speeches, or not be ashamed to attend a school reunion because if people were to ask him what he's been up to for the past eight years he wouldn't have to shrug and say, 'Nothing much.'

'Sorry about that,' he says, slipping into the seat next to me and taking off his jacket. His arm brushes against mine as he does so and I feel a shiver run up my spine. 'You cold?' he asks, and I shake my head, no, pretending to read through the brochure as I try to sort through everything that I'm feeling right now.

'Flick's just before the break,' I say, scanning the list of performers. 'So we can sneak out early if you get bored.'

'Why would I get bored?' he says. 'Although if they bring out the recorders then I'm off.'

'Do you remember that girl in our class?' I say through a laugh. 'Rebecca Fitz-something,'

'Oh God, yes,' he says, eyes wide and head nodding in agreement. 'NHS glasses, dressed like a teacher, carried books with her at all times.'

'She had a whole collection of recorders. One of them was almost as big as her.'

'I wonder what happened to her,' he says, taking a packet of butterscotch sweets from his pocket and offering me one.

It's such a simple gesture, one that used to be so familiar, but it makes my throat constrict because I ache for everything that's missing between us. All those years when he could have been a part of my life, time that I cannot get back.

He's watching me, about to say something, when the first student steps on to the stage and the audience breaks into a round of polite applause.

'Wake me up when it's over.' He shifts down in his seat and closes his eyes, so I whack him with my brochure. 'Ow,' he says, but he's smiling and then the couple behind us start making shushing sounds and he waggles his finger at me.

Stop it. I mouth the words at him, wiping at my eye and trying not to giggle.

The next twenty minutes are spent sitting and listening and clapping as half a dozen students take their turn in the spotlight. A couple of them are pretty good, but not enough to stop Isaac from yawning, and suddenly I feel foolish, outdated even, for bringing him here. Wouldn't he rather be out at a bar or a party with people our own age, swapping details about their lives over cocktails and pressing close to one another on the dance floor?

It strikes me then that I don't even know if he has a girlfriend. I heard he broke up with Kate shortly after Lucy's wedding (another phone call from Mum, this one informing me that Isaac was single and so maybe I should get back in touch?), but other than that I know absolutely nothing about his love life.

'Isaac?' I say, and he turns his face to mine at the same time as Flick walks up on stage, and all my attention moves to her.

The entire auditorium falls silent, as if we all know that something amazing is about to happen. I watch Flick, see the way she curls her fingers into a fist and then lets them out, one by one. There's a pause, right in the moment before she starts playing, and I sit forward on my seat, hold my breath and then let it go as she fills the room with music.

It's a classical piece, a waltz that people will recognise even if they can't name the composer, and it's perfect for demonstrating just how good a pianist Flick has become.

When she stops playing, there's a split second before we all begin to clap, and Isaac leans across to whisper in my ear a single word, 'Wow', and it makes me proud and yet somehow sad because he used to tell me I was amazing. I miss that. I miss knowing that I did something other people thought was worthy of praise.

As the applause dies down, I'm about to ask Isaac if he wants to go or stay for the second half when Flick starts to speak.

'This next piece is the one I performed for my audition at the Royal Academy,' she says, and I lean back in my seat, because she didn't tell me she was going to play it. 'It's an original song, one I wrote with the help and guidance of my incredible teacher, Beth Franks.'

Great, now she's gesturing towards me and all those heads are turning to look. There's a flush on my face and chest, I can feel the heat radiating from my skin and, oh crap, I think I might just pass out.

'Relax,' Isaac says, placing one hand on my knee and making me startle. 'It's not you up there.'

I manage to smile in response, then try to focus on the stage.

There's no sheet music, she's playing from memory, but more than that, she's in the music, making it a part of her rather than simply hitting the right notes.

That's where the real talent is. My dad's voice pops into my head. He taught me that music has the power to change a person's mood, that the very best musicians would capture your attention not from what they played but how they played.

I wish he was here, to be able to witness that the lessons he taught me have been passed along. Or is it best he doesn't see how close the apple has fallen to the tree? Does he really not regret giving up gigging and staying home to teach? Will I ever stop regretting the choices I've made?

The irony is, Mum wouldn't have minded if I ended up teaching if that's what I set out to do in the first place. As long as I followed a clear path towards something attainable, she would have been more than happy to help steer me on my way.

The applause this time is bigger, louder, longer, and then everyone is on their feet as Flick takes a bow, the most enormous smile on her face as she waves up at me.

'Do you mind if we go?' Isaac says, getting out of his seat.

'No, that's fine,' I say, grabbing my bag and following him out the door. 'Is everything all right?' I ask as we walk through the main entrance, and he stops so suddenly I bump into the back of him.

'It's just . . .' he says, turning round to face me. There's a slight twitch to one eye and he's tapping his foot on the ground, which means he needs to say something but doesn't know how I'm going to react.

'Just what?'

'You're doing it again.'

'Doing what again?'

'Giving away your music.'

'Giving away?' I say with a snort of laughter. 'I'm not giving it away, Isaac, I'm helping her.'

'Which is the exact same thing you said about Tristan.'

'That was different.'

'Different how, Beth?' he says, voice raised and hands on hips. 'Because from where I'm standing it looks like you're still letting people use your talent for their own personal gain.'

'She's my student.'

'Who probably wouldn't have stood out from the competition if it weren't for you teaching her about how music needs a soul.' Ok, he's shouting now, and there are a few people gathered in the doorway, clutching champagne flutes and looking our way. 'Anyone can play a pretty tune, but not all of us have the sort of talent that makes people feel something.'

'She's really good,' I say, a fake smile on my face as I nod over at the people who are still watching, and no doubt listening.

'So are you. Or at least you were. And it kills me you're not willing to use that talent to your own advantage, instead of just helping other people,' he says, waving his arm in the direction of the school.

'I tried, Isaac, ok?' I squeeze my fingernails into my palm as I screw my eyes tight shut, because I am so tired of this conversation. I am so tired of being told that it's simple, Beth, all you have to do is pick up a pen and write some songs, just like you used to. But I'm not that person any more, and I have no idea how I'm supposed to find any kind of inspiration in my so-called life.

'Then try again.'

I want to agree with him. I want nothing more than to shake off the fear that I missed out on the only opportunity I was ever going to get.

'I'm scared,' I say, the words no more than a whisper. 'I'm scared of letting her down.'

'Beth,' he says in a voice that's soft and low, making my insides tighten.

'Yes?' I say, watching as the wind ruffles his too-long hair and making me think of the boy he used to be.

Whatever he is about to say or do is interrupted by several large drops of rain that fall on to his nose and then several more that slink down the back of my neck, making me shiver. A moment later and there's a deep vibration of thunder, along with enough rain to make it seem as if someone has upended a bucket over our heads.

'Come on,' he says, grabbing my hand, and we sprint across the playing field, splatters of grass springing up with every step and sticking to my legs.

'Hang on,' I say, letting go of his hand as we reach the line of trees by the back fence.

'You all right?' He stops, turns round to see me doubled over and clutching at my side.

'Fine,' I say, remembering how he always used to come first in cross-country back at school. 'Been a while since I went for a run.' It's been a while since I've done anything even remotely resembling exercise, apart from sex. I want to ask him when the last time he had sex was, but that would be inappropriate and I need to not say every tiny little thing that comes into my head, and oh God, now I'm picturing him in a way that I never have before. Well, maybe once or twice, but not like this.

'Hurry up,' I shout, then shoot through the trees and across the road, skidding and banging my hip against the car bonnet. Isaac wrestles with the lock, swinging the door wide and ushering me in, then runs around to the other side. The car wobbles as he slams shut his door, and we sit, panting and fogging up the windows but unable to do anything other than stare at one another.

It would be so easy to reach out my hand, to wipe away the raindrops on his eyelashes, or press my palm flat against his chest to see if his heart is racing just as fast as mine. It would be simple enough to peel off my sodden clothes, watch him do the same, have him cover my damp skin with kisses and pretend that it wouldn't in fact be a terrible idea to let him.

All of a sudden there's a loud bang from above and I swear my heart skipped at least two beats. We both turn at the sound, Isaac rolling down his steamed-up window to reveal the bearded face of a man wearing a bright-yellow rain jacket and shouting at us for blocking his drive.

The journey home is quiet, other than the heater turned up full blast and the constant swish of the wiper blades as we head back into town. The silence is filled with sideways glances, mouths that open then shut, having decided it would be better not to talk about what nearly happened.

Problem is, I can't get the sight of him out of my mind, or how I felt in the precise moment before I was certain he was going to kiss me. I also can't help but think about the very first time a boy didn't kiss me, and how completely and utterly undone he made me, sending me spiralling out of control.

16.

Nine years ago . . .

It was one of those parties that imprints itself on your memory before it's even happened. The end of the beginning, or the beginning of the end, depending on how you might remember it one day.

Everyone was going, according to Isaac, who claimed it was our last chance to let loose before the leaden weight of A Levels forced us to actually take school seriously.

I remember Lucy helping me get ready that evening. She did my make-up and convinced me to wear my hair down whilst we listened to Foo Fighters on repeat. She even gave me a pair of her earrings: two tiny shooting stars that caught the light, making me wish they were a sign of something still to come.

'Cover for me tonight,' she said, taking another sip from a bottle of vodka that I knew she kept hidden in the bottom drawer of her wardrobe.

'You're a fully-fledged adult,' I said in reply, shaking my head when she offered me the bottle. 'Why does it matter if you don't come home?'

'You know what Mum's like,' she said, leaning close to the mirror as she filled in her lips with red. 'Always checking on me, asking if everything is ok. It's suffocating. I can't wait to get back to Oxford and be able to live without her peering over my shoulder the whole time.'

'She worries, that's all,' I said, although she was right; Mum became over-protective to the point of obsession whenever Lucy came home. If she knew the full extent of what Lucy really got up to both at home and at university, I think she'd probably have had a heart attack.

'I'm fine,' Lucy said, slipping into a pair of stilettoes then changing her mind and opting for flats. 'At some point she has to accept that we're all going to die.'

'Luce,' I said, meeting her eye.

'Ok, ok, we're not supposed to joke about death, I know,' she said, picking up the bottle and taking two generous sips. 'But just because every single scan has confirmed the tumour hasn't grown, that doesn't mean the next one won't. I refuse to be afraid of it, Beth. I can't spend my life assuming the worst is going to happen.'

'I guess.' Although the tumour was the reason why Lucy pushed herself to always be better – she'd told me as much that night on the roof in Portugal. If anything, I'd have said she was more terrified than the rest of us by the idea that she might not have as much time as she wanted. 'But maybe don't drink the entire bottle before we even get to the party.'

'Lighten up, would you?' she said as she headed for the door. 'Otherwise you're going to die a virgin.'

The party was at Damian's, his parents away on an adventure of their own, giving their boys free rein of the house. Lucy walked straight through the front door and promptly disappeared into the throng of bodies that were filling every room. Everywhere I looked there were people – sprawled across sofas, downing shots in the kitchen, or leaping off the diving board and into the pool out back.

The house was vast, but the garden seemed to stretch into forever. There were lights and lanterns leading you along paths to a tennis court (floodlit, of course), a summer house and a pond filled with bright orange fish. I was about to turn around, go home, when I heard it, the soft call of a song being played on an acoustic guitar. I followed the sound like a rat the piper, stepping through a small archway cut into a jasmine bush, the scent of which stuck to my skin.

Half a dozen people were sitting on oversized bean bags dotted around a central firepit listening to Isaac sing. He was in an egg-shaped chair, which was suspended from an iron frame that rocked back and forth in time with the music. I could smell marijuana and pine, and when I peered into the fire I saw a few cones glowing deep and bright.

There was a girl at Isaac's feet, drawing heavily on the joint in her hand and gazing up at him in such a pathetically obvious way. I wanted to go and sit next to him, but I also knew this was Isaac's preferred method of flirtation – far easier to sing to a girl about love than actually speak to her.

'Hey,' Isaac said when he saw me. His fingers stilled on the guitar and all those eyes turned to see the reason why.

'I should have known you'd be hiding in the woods,' I said as he came over to give me a hug, and I smiled at his familiar touch. I also saw the way that girl was looking at me, with slanted eyes and sulky lips, and I was about to whisper to Isaac about bunny boilers when something, or rather someone, made me turn my head to see.

I still don't know what it was, the pop of a beer bottle being opened, the scuff of a boot against the ground, or maybe it was the scent of him, subtle and easy to miss unless you got close. But the very second before I saw his face, before I felt my whole body tighten as his eyes found mine, I remember being absolutely terrified.

'Damian was right,' he said, lighting a cigarette, the thin flame exaggerating the angles of his face. 'You look nothing like your sister.'

Everything else slipped away, as if there were a haze surrounding him, forcing me to focus on him and him alone.

'You say that like it's a bad thing,' I heard myself say, but the words sounded distant and strange, as if spoken from the other end of a long tunnel.

'Just an observation,' he said, taking another drag of his cigarette, one eye squinting, but both of them fixed on me.

There was a rustle from the bushes before Lucy and Damian stumbled into the circle, arms wrapped so tight around the other there was no light left in between.

'Hello, Tristan,' she said in a voice laden with sarcasm and booze, looking from him to me and back again.

So this was the infamous Tristan. Damian's older brother, fresh out of art school and lead singer of an up-and-coming band with a reputation colourful enough to make me blush. Lucy had told me all about the after-parties, the groupies and all that rock and roll fuelled by arrogance, ambition and a healthy injection of cash from Daddy dearest.

Tristan was the most intoxicating person I had ever met. It wasn't just his face, the hair, or even those eyes, but more the way he seemed so completely at ease with himself, a certain type of confidence that made you want to get to know him. Nothing had prepared me – not Tina or Stevie or even Keats – for how I would feel in that moment, and I doubt I could have stopped it, controlled it, even if I'd wanted to try.

'I'm heading in for more beer,' Tristan said, at the same time as Lucy skipped over to pick up Isaac's guitar then held it out to me.

'Sing something,' she said with a lopsided smile, and I felt my cheeks flush pink, because Tristan had paused in the archway, his head half turned towards me.

'I can't,' I said, noticing how large her pupils had become, making me wonder what else she had indulged in apart from too much vodka.

'Please, Beth. Isaac will help, won't you?' she said, going over and planting a kiss on his cheek. He blushed and I felt angrier than ever before about how my sister always managed to make everyone do her bidding.

'How about "Hyacinth Girl"?' Isaac said, picking out the opening notes and looking at me in expectation.

'I'll be right back,' I replied with a wave of my hand, not listening as my sister asked me to hang on a sec, she wanted to talk to me. I know now that if I had, everything, absolutely everything, would be different.

I ran all the way back to the house, through the kitchen and into the hall. Reaching out for the front-door handle, I stopped, looking left into another living room, bigger even than the one that had been turned into a dance floor. In the bay window was a huge, glossy grand piano, its lid open and waiting.

I pulled out the stool and sat down, my fingers hovering above the keys as I glanced over my shoulder. Not that anyone would be able to hear anything over the persistent beat of drum and bass that was pouring from every speaker in the house.

Lucy hadn't done anything wrong and yet I still felt humiliated. She knew, and Isaac knew, that I couldn't sing one of my own songs in front of a group of strangers, no matter how badly I wished that I could.

How do you become confident? Is it something you can learn? Or is it, like height and eye colour, dependent on genetics? Lucy wouldn't stay shy if she didn't want to be. She would figure out a way to overcome the crippling fear of not being good enough.

It felt like I was running out of time. One more year before Isaac would head off for university, so where did that leave me? He could sing, he played guitar like a pro, but as much as he loved music it wasn't something he ever wanted to do as anything more than a hobby.

I had no idea how to get to the next stage of my life, how to make something out of the songs that followed me around, snuck into my dreams and demanded to be played.

Of all the songs I'd written, 'Hyacinth Girl' felt special, and not just because I wrote it after lying in a field of poppies with my best friend and talking about wanting someone to love me. It was about the absence of love and how I yearned for it. I ached for it like an addict does their next fix.

I knocked twice on the wood for luck, a silly superstition inherited from my father, then pressed my fingers down on the keys, finding the opening chords to the song without even trying. I began to sing, safe in the knowledge that no one was listening.

'Did you write that?'

I spun around, heart in my throat as I saw Tristan standing in the doorway watching me. I nodded in response as he crossed the room and sat down on the stool, close enough for me to feel the heat of his skin.

'Sing it again,' he said. 'For me.' It wasn't a question, and I would soon learn that he never had to ask me anything; I just did whatever he wanted.

There was a voice somewhere inside my head telling me this was a very bad idea indeed. But I didn't care, or at least I told myself that there was no harm in being there, alone, with someone who made the entire world around him fall away.

'Are you and that guy Isaac, like, together?' he asked when I'd played right past the end of the final chord.

I shook my head, no.

'But you write with him?'

'Sometimes,' I said, sitting on my hands and not wanting to admit how much Isaac had worked with me not just on 'Hyacinth Girl' but all the other songs since we'd met. 'Mostly he just helps me figure out chords and stuff.'

Tristan raked his hands through his hair and looked at me like nobody else ever had before. It made me excited and nervous all at once and I held my breath, scared and hopeful as to what he might say or do.

'Has anyone ever told you,' he said, 'how amazing you are?'

I shook my head again, the compliment making speech impossible.

If it were possible to capture a moment, to bottle it, seal it tight and take it out every so often, release the cork and drink it one sip at a time, I would choose that one. No matter what happened next, I would give anything to relive that illicit desire again and again and again.

'My band's meeting here for practice tomorrow,' he said, and it felt like he'd put the words inside my mouth for me to taste. 'You should come along.'

The idea of becoming part of a band, with him, was intoxicating and terrifying and all the other things I have ever felt in my entire life. I knew it was one of those pivotal decisions in life that would change everything, and I couldn't wait for it to start.

'Oh, and Beth,' he said, getting up from the stool and reaching out to tuck a strand of hair behind my ear, 'bring some more of your songs. I'd love to play them with you.'

17.

Isaac's housemates have a standing date – every Friday night, whoever is around makes a point of being home to eat, and they take it in turns to cook. It reminds me of Isaac's parents, who were anything but strict yet insisted that the four of them sit down every Sunday lunchtime without fail to share a roast. Their rule was no phones, no television, no distractions whatsoever, and it meant that they all ended up talking to one another rather than swapping piecemeal information in passing.

Taking the pan off the stove, I give it a gentle stir, then go across and turn up the radio on the counter. For some reason I offered to cook tonight, and I'm already regretting it, not least because I don't know if Nathan will even fit in my tiny flat.

I've been agonising over it all week, watching endless episodes of *MasterChef* and trawling through Spitalfields Market in search of inspiration. I've set the table, made a jug of Pimm's, put fresh flowers in a vase and even remembered the napkins. There's Persian chicken with turmeric and lime, a cucumber and herb salad and then saffron doughnuts with pistachio cream for dessert. Part of me can't quite believe that I've managed to pull it together, especially as my usual diet consists of frozen pizza and Pot Noodle. Another part of me still thinks that this is actually all happening to somebody else.

I've also been trying not to think about Isaac and that almost-kiss. I didn't imagine it, did I? Because I keep trying to remember it in every tiny little detail and then asking myself if any of what I'm feeling is actually real or only as a result of his kindness. Maybe all I've done is some kind of transference; a patient/doctor type thing where I'm so thankful for him being back in my life that I've twisted the emotions into something more.

It feels like a lifetime ago since I woke up in that stranger's bed, then went home and finally opened the gift from my sister. Every morning I wake, surprised to find the world still spinning, that everything still functions, including me, without her.

I don't know what Lucy expected to happen, how she thought she might shape my life through this strange quest, but I'm struggling to figure out what I'm supposed to do next. Is this all she wanted me to do: open a couple of puzzle boxes, follow the handful of clues and somehow stumble across a whole new way of living?

There has to be a reason why she sent me to Isaac, something more than rekindling a friendship that I so readily tossed aside. All I know is that my life can't go back to the messy imperfection it was before, but nor is there any obvious way forward, something good enough to live up to my sister's expectations of me.

The sound of the doorbell makes my heart skip a beat and I glance around the room, trying not to think how it might look in comparison to Isaac's pristine home, then go out to the hall and open the door.

'Hey,' Isaac says as he comes into the flat and drops his bag on the floor. 'Sorry I'm a bit late.' I see him looking at all the photos on the wall before following me into the kitchen, which now feels oppressively small.

He rolls up his sleeves as he looks around the room as if he too can't quite believe what he's seeing. 'You did all this?' He's standing by the table and peering at all the food on offer. 'Smells amazing.'

'Hope you're hungry,' I say, busying myself with wiping down the surfaces, even though I did that already.

'Nathan's going to be late.' He goes across to the fridge and takes out a beer. He doesn't need to ask; he never needed to ask because I spent just as much time eating dinner with his family as with my own. We used to go to one another's houses and open the fridge without asking. It was seamless and straightforward, but this is different; we're not kids any more and so much has changed.

'You still read these things?' he asks, pointing to a magazine on the counter, open to this month's horoscopes, which claim my life is about to hit a crossroads. They also claim that Isaac is at risk of an upset with a partner, which I have been doing my best not to think about.

'It's just a bit of fun.' I shove the magazine into a drawer, ignoring the smirk on his face. 'Should we wait for Margot?'

'Can do,' he says, taking out his phone as it pings with the arrival of a new message. 'Except she's apparently at a networking event she forgot about.' He puts the phone on the counter and looks over at me and I wonder if he's thinking the same thing: that we've been set up.

'Oh,' is all I manage to say as I head for the table, and I'm sure he can hear how loud my heart is beating.

'How was your day?' he asks, sitting down and pouring us each a drink. The fact he's making small talk and refusing to meet my eye suggests he's feeling just as nervous, or perhaps embarrassed, as I am.

'Fine.' I ladle out a portion of chicken and pass it to him. 'You?'

'Long,' he replies, taking a forkful of food and then making appreciative noises and looking up at me with a raised brow. 'This is really good.'

'You don't have to say it like that.' I'm pouting but, inside, I'm grinning because I've done something to surprise him, and not in a bad way, which feels utterly divine.

'Seriously, I'm impressed.' He takes another forkful and I marvel at the simplicity of it all. At how food can be like a sort of alchemy, a magical process that transforms not only the food itself but the mood of the people you share it with.

'I cycled up to King's Cross the other day,' I say, a little too loudly and far too brightly.

'To spot trains?'

My response is to throw my napkin at him, and he ducks out of the way. 'To see if it would help me figure out the clue. I ended up playing the piano that's there.' I sat there for nearly an hour, my fingers finding the melodies, blurring them together and making me forget about everything else. A little girl came up to me, tapped me on my arm and then handed me a pound coin.

'Do you sing?' she asked me, and I looked into her face, so honest and open and completely unaware of life's atrocities.

'Only on special occasions,' I replied.

'It's my birthday next month,' she said, hopping from foot to foot, and I looked over her shoulder to where her mother was waiting. It made me ache for the family Lucy would never have, for her child who would never be born.

'Tell you what,' I said, patting the stool and waiting for her to sit. 'Why don't I teach you how to play "Happy Birthday"?'

'The chap next door to me has a piano,' Isaac says, bringing my attention back to the room, and him. 'I could talk to him, if you like?' He's still filling his mouth with food, has gone back in for a second helping. Meanwhile I seem to be incapable of eating anything at all, even though I'm starving and my stomach is growling its annoyance.

'Maybe.' I push my food around my plate, thinking of how Mum hated it when I did this, even when she'd made liver and bacon with onion gravy, the smell of which always made me retch.

'Or you could always go back and play the one at home.'

Why does he always do that? I do wish he wasn't quite so good at peering inside my mind and figuring out what I'm thinking about or worrying about, or deliberately not saying.

'It's not mine.' Even though I played it every single day for years, it never really belonged to me. That piano is as much a part of my father as the bones inside his body. Every single one of those keys bears the imprint of his fingertips and all the music he taught me to love.

'Does he know about the clues Lucy's sent you?'

'Sort of. I said I'd found my old notebook and he asked me which one.' And then we spoke a little about how we used to sit up late into the night swapping ideas for melodies and listening to old records for inspiration. And then I said I had to go, because the memories were making me cry and I am so fed up with crying.

'The night I met Tristan . . .' I say, watching Isaac's face to see how he's going to react. If he's surprised, he doesn't show it, and I want to ask if he's been thinking about it too. Does he remember me stumbling out of that room with my hair standing out at odd angles and a flush across my chest? Does he remember asking me what had happened, grabbing my arms and forcing me to look him in the eye? I whispered, 'Nothing', and that single word was enough to make me push him away, go into the kitchen and start downing shots of tequila.

'What about it?'

'He heard me playing "Hyacinth Girl".'

'Makes sense.' He shrugs, but I know he's not feeling as nonchalant as he'd have me believe. There's so much more we need to talk about, especially the song that started it all, but I'm scared that if we do, one of us will end up broken, again.

'I wish I'd never written that stupid song,' I say, picking up my half-finished plate of food and taking it to the sink.

'Don't say that.'

'Why not?' I scrape the wasted food into the bin and rinse the plate under the tap before putting it in the dishwasher. It's a habit left over from childhood, from a mother who became obsessive about germs and cleaning after her elder daughter got sick. 'If it hadn't been for that song . . .' I say, turning to look around the room, at the handful of possessions I own.

'You still have time.' He stands and I hold my breath as he walks towards me and sets his plate down on the worktop. 'We're all just trying to figure out what the hell we're supposed to be doing and pretending to be happy.'

'You're not happy?' The idea of Isaac not being happy makes me all sorts of sad, but also confused, because if someone like him can't be happy, then what does that say about my chances?

'Sort of. Maybe. I guess not.'

It feels like opening a drawer and discovering something new, even though it was there all along.

'I've been working on something.' I wasn't expecting to share this little secret with him, but it's there and it feels a little exciting to have confessed it to him.

'You have?'

I have, and it's been surprising to discover how much better my day feels if I've spent at least part of it immersed in music. That's why I sat down at that piano in King's Cross station: my fingers were itching to feel the music, my mind desperate to have the chords resonate through my skin.

'Do you still have your guitar?' he asks, and I nod. 'Sing it for me?'

'Ok,' I reply. 'Although I'm a little out of practice.' I go next door and pick up my guitar from where it's propped up against the far wall, then stop, glancing over my shoulder and trying to decide if this is a good idea.

I don't know if the nerves I'm feeling are because of him or the song. I look out of the window to the communal garden below, thinking of all the nights the two of us would sit together, one of us singing and the other following along on guitar. Perhaps that's the way it was supposed to be; perhaps by choosing Tristan I set off a chain of events that should never have happened.

I take the guitar, strum out a couple of chords as I go back into the kitchen. Then I lean against the counter, close my eyes and start to sing. The song is about Lucy, about wishing you could go back and start again. It's simple and way too optimistic and there's something missing from the chorus, but still Isaac sits and listens and, when I open my eyes, he's looking at me like he sees me, the real me.

He stands up and steps toward me, and my body tightens the closer he gets, like a belt around my ribs, making it hard to breathe. It feels like the evening has been made up of a sequence of events all leading in one direction, at the end of which is either a staircase or a deep, deep hole.

I hold my breath as he comes right up to me, so close I can smell the lime on his mouth.

'Beth,' he says, and I tilt my head up in expectation, but then he's stepping away and looking at me in a completely different way than only seconds before.

'What?' I ask, the word coming out all spiky and sharp, because I'm actually annoyed that he didn't kiss me, again. He didn't kiss me and now I feel small and ridiculous and just like I did as a teenager when I so badly wanted a boy to kiss me but no one ever did.

'The key change,' he says, taking the guitar from my hands and then replaying the chorus.

'What about it?'

'It's the exact same one as in "Hyacinth Girl". The original version.' He looks at me, a million things behind those dark brown eyes. 'I can't believe I'm about to say this,' he says, putting down the guitar.

'Don't,' I reply, because I already know what he's about to say. I've known all along there was one piece of the puzzle I'd have to do by myself. It's a piece Lucy has been suggesting from the very beginning but which I have done my best to ignore.

'You need to talk to Tristan.'

'I can't.' My hands are shaking, my whole body is shaking with the feeling of what I might do or say if I was ever again in the same space as Tristan King.

'It's the only way you'll ever be able to move on.'

'You mean closure and all that bullshit?'

'I mean realising that it wasn't your fault. And that you deserve to love someone who will also love you back.'

I have no idea what to say or think about the suggestion behind his words and so I start clearing away the rest of the plates, putting them in the sink even though they're clean. Then I turn on the radio, anything to drown out the ringing in my ears.

'Have you really never had a serious relationship?'

'Not really,' I say, the fact he somehow knows the dire state of my love life making my cheeks burn. 'I am as unlucky in love as I am with everything else.'

'Those walls you've built do a great job of protecting you.'

'Has Margot been giving you psychology lessons?' I ask, turning on the tap, aware that he's come up behind me because I can feel his breath on the back of my neck.

'They may stop anyone from getting in and hurting you,' he says, turning me around and cupping my face with both hands. 'But they also stop anyone from being allowed to love you.'

I seem to be vibrating, like a glass whose sound is only released when touched in a very precise way. And then he kisses me before I have time to react. All the months and years we were together,

155

then apart, were filled with an intensity that passes from his lips to my own and it's like everything I have ever felt before is bland and untrue. It's a feeling I never realised I possessed until now, which is both terrifying and wonderful at the same time.

'Beth,' he whispers as he kisses the tears that I didn't even realise were falling, and then his mouth is back on mine and my hands are in his hair and his arms come around my waist and it feels like I could never get close enough to him. All of a sudden, he pulls away, steps back and runs both hands through that mane of his.

'Sorry,' he says, staring at the floor. 'Shouldn't have done that.'

'Why?' I say, biting down the burning sense of disappointment because, wow, that kiss was . . . that kiss was intense and delicious and suddenly it feels like all I have ever wanted was for him to kiss me. 'Are you seeing someone?' Please say no, please say no.

'Sort of.'

Shit.

'I mean, yes. You remember Kate?'

Bollocks. 'I thought you broke up?'

'We did,' he says, a look of surprise on his face, and no doubt he's wondering how I know. 'But then she called and asked if we could try again.'

'Does she know about what Lucy asked you to do?'

'Sort of.'

'But not about us.'

'There is no us.'

That hurt. Like a slap to the face, or rather ego. A not-so-subtle reminder that I don't have the right to know all the intimate details of his life.

Before I can reply, the song changes on the radio and we both turn our heads towards the sound of Nina Simone singing a song that I once played to Tristan, then taught him how to turn a jazz piece into something more suited to his vocal style.

'What are the odds?' I say with a small, shrill laugh, and Isaac looks back at me, his expression tight, when only moments ago it was soft and warm. I want to tell him it's ok, it's going to be ok, but it feels like the universe is constantly reminding me of the one person I never wanted to think about again.

'It's just a song,' he says. And he's right, except it's also a song that SuperKing added to their set list because of me. It's a song that acted as an invitation for me to become part of the band and set off a course of events that changed everything.

'Actually no, it's not,' he says, puffing out his cheeks and staring up at the ceiling. 'Do you remember that night at the Half Moon?' He's looking directly at me now and I find myself frozen on the spot, unable to move because of course I know which night he's talking about. I remember all the nights and all the days and all the moments I've ever spent with him.

'I thought that perhaps you . . .' he starts, and I want him to go on. I want to know if he felt it too.

I need to know if I was a complete and utter fool not to have taken a risk on him back then, instead of focusing on the person standing on stage. I always assumed we were just friends, that he fancied my sister and Jessica and all the other girls who weren't me.

'You know what,' he says. 'It doesn't matter any more.'

Except it does, and there's this horrible feeling in the pit of my stomach that I'm about to lose him all over again.

'Isaac, I . . .' I take one step towards him.

'I can't,' he says, hands raised and backing away. 'I know you think this is what you want, but I need you to be sure.'

'I am sure.'

'Talk to Tristan,' he says, shouldering his bag and opening the front door. 'You have to want to change, Beth, not just hope someone will do it for you.'

I should go after him, say something to make him stay. Instead, I pick up the half-finished bottle of beer I bought just for him with money I don't have to spare and take a sip. Going over to the window, I wait for him to come out of the doorway five floors below. He crosses the street without looking back, just like he did on the night we were talking about, the first time I made no effort to stop him walking away.

18.

Nine years ago . . .

'*I do wish you'd stop going through my stuff,*' Lucy said, leaning against my bedroom doorframe, arms folded and giving off a notable air of superiority.

She was wearing a peacock-blue satin dressing gown over shorts and a t-shirt, no doubt having spent her day lounging on the patio, drinking herbal tea and reading Virginia Woolf. The whole summer had been like a bad impersonation of Brideshead Revisited, and for the first time I wasn't sad that she was packing up her things, ready to return for another illustrious year at Oxford.

'*I do wish you'd remember to knock before entering,*' I said in deliberately plummy vowels, plaiting my hair and shoving the mini-skirt I'd taken from her room into my bag.

'*Where are you going?*' she asked, eyes narrowed as she peered a little closer at my face.

'*Isaac's,*' I replied, grabbing a notepad and pushing past her, heading for the stairs. '*We're helping one another study.*'

'*Bollocks.*' Lucy laughed as she followed me down and into the kitchen, watching as I took a muffin from the tin. '*You're wearing far too much mascara for a study session. Unless*' — she licked the side of her lips and raised one eyebrow — '*unless you and Isaac are finally shagging?*'

'As if,' I said, slipping out the back door and through the garage to fetch my bike.

'Have you really never . . . ?' She left the question open and I chose not to finish it, because everyone always assumed there was more going on between Isaac and me than just friendship. It would seem that once you reached a certain age, it was deemed impossible to be friends with someone of the opposite sex without wanting to rip their clothes off.

'Tell Mum I might end up staying over,' I said as I wheeled my bike on to the drive then kicked off and down the hill.

'Whatever,' I heard Lucy say as she went back inside. No doubt she wouldn't bother to pass on the message. She was too preoccupied with spending her last precious moments with Damian to worry about her little sister.

'Hurry up!' Isaac waved his arm at me, standing on the platform with one foot inside the train as the guard blew his whistle.

'Thanks,' I said as I jumped on board and the doors slid closed behind us. 'Lucy was asking too many questions.'

'Do you think she'd snitch?'

'Possibly,' I said, shrugging off my cardigan and unplaiting my hair. 'She's all pious and self-righteous at the moment. Pissed off about having to leave her summer lover.'

'Damian seems to think he's going up to visit her before Christmas.' Isaac took a hip flask from his jacket and unscrewed the lid before taking a sip.

'Damian's delusional,' I replied, holding out my hand for the flask. 'There's no way Lucy will want him mixing with all the other guys she's sleeping with.'

'So, her and Damian,' he said, passing me the flask. 'Not serious?'

I took a long sip, flinching as the neat vodka hit the back of my throat, then handed it back. 'Why do you care?' I said, wiping my mouth.

'No reason. You told your parents about next year?'

'Not yet.' I turned to look out the window; we'd had this conversation several times already. Whilst everyone else had a clear vision of where they wanted to spend the next three years of their lives, I just couldn't bring myself to apply for a course that wouldn't be anything other than a complete waste of time. I wanted to write, I wanted to hear someone singing a song that I'd written, but a degree wasn't going to make that happen. Problem was, I had no real idea how to make the dream come true.

'I always thought you'd do music.'

'You and I both know I'm not Royal Academy material.' I yawned, then started tapping all over my skull because I'd once read somewhere it would keep you awake.

'I meant something less formulaic,' Isaac said.

'Like what?'

'I don't know,' he said with a non-committal shrug. 'You just always seem so much better when you play your own stuff.'

'Better than what?' I asked, rummaging in my bag for a lip gloss then squinting at my reflection and adding sticky pink to my lips.

'Better than trying to compete with your sister.'

I glared at him through the window, then added a bit more gloss. 'You're in a lovely mood.'

'I should be home finalising my UCAS application,' he said, picking at a rip in his jeans. 'Instead, I'm heading to some dodgy pub to listen to Tristan's dodgy band.'

'Can we not? You don't have to like him, but it would be nice if you could pretend. For me?' I needed Isaac to like him, because I needed this, the band, to work. Otherwise I was straight out of options and the last thing I wanted was to prove my mother right, that music, my music, could never be anything more than a hobby.

'Fine,' he said with a childish poke of his tongue, then crossed his arms and closed his eyes; the rest of the train journey was clearly going to be spent in silence.

The Half Moon pub was right next to the railway tracks on the very edge of London and opposite a park. The streetlights were just coming on as we crossed the road and Isaac grabbed my hand to pull me out of the way of a cyclist freewheeling around the corner.

'Remind me again why I'm here?' Isaac said as we joined the back of the queue, swiftly followed by a group of girls who were all wearing too much make-up and no doubt carried fake IDs.

'You're my wingman,' I said, noticing how a couple of the girls were looking from me to Isaac and back again.

'Does that make me Maverick or Goose?'

I laughed as I turned my head, ready with some quip about him not looking even remotely like Tom Cruise, but then I stopped short at the sight of his face. When did it change? When did that lopsided grin become sexy instead of goofy? And then there was the hair, the way his shoulders now filled his jacket instead of it hanging off him, and something else I couldn't find a name for, something that made me acutely aware of just how close he was standing to me.

'What?' he said with a frown, running both hands through his hair. 'Why are you looking at me like that?'

'No reason,' I said, shuffling forward in the queue and offering the bouncer my most dazzling smile. In return, he looked the full length of me, barely glanced at Isaac, then stepped aside to allow us through.

'Jesus, this place is a shithole,' Isaac said as I weaved through the crowd in the direction of the bar.

'It also never asks for ID,' I called over my shoulder as I squeezed in between two middle-aged men wearing faded band t-shirts that barely covered their girth. I smiled sweetly, then leant over the counter to catch the barman's eye.

Drinks in hand, we made our way to the back of the pub where barn-style doors were wide open to reveal a dark and decidedly dank space beyond. In the far corner was a makeshift stage, rammed full of speakers, wires, microphones and various instruments, including a keyboard that wouldn't have looked out of place in a kids' bedroom.

I peered through the gloom, searching the throng of people for the one I wanted most of all.

'Hey, babe,' Tristan said as he planted a kiss on my cheek. 'I see you brought your guard dog.'

'Tristan.' Isaac cleared his throat then took a long, slow drink.

'Actually' – Tristan smiled at us both – 'more like a lap dog.'

The two of them stared at each other and I imagined them as bucks squaring up for a fight. I was about to tell them as much when a whippet-thin girl with a heavy fringe and a bright red pout approached. She walked straight up to Tristan with barely a glance at me and rested her head on his shoulder.

'This is the songbird?' The girl lit a cigarette and waved it in my direction.

'Beth, Adrienne. Adrienne, Beth,' Tristan said, helping himself to my drink.

'Hi,' I said, deliberately not extending my hand, but I doubt she would have taken it if I had.

'Huh,' she said through an exhalation of smoke that I made a point of wafting away. 'I thought she would be pretty, like her sister.'

Her voice was heavily accented and her body was the kind of skinny that came from years of existing on little more than coffee and cigarettes. I hated her on sight.

'This one, however,' Adrienne went on, sidling up to Isaac, 'this one I would happily take home. But I may never let you leave.' She said the last bit against his ear and I felt my insides curl up with fury.

163

'Not now.' Tristan took hold of Adrienne's arm and steered her towards the stage. 'Got to go get ready.'

I watched them both disappear into the crowd, then stood on tip-toes and edged closer to the stage as I saw the band gather together, plugging in guitars and adjusting microphones. Adrienne hovered around Tristan like a mosquito in search of blood, sharing a cigarette and looking at him like he was something she wanted to eat.

She was the latest backing singer (the band had apparently gone through more than half a dozen that year alone) and I'd heard her sing on a couple of the tracks Tristan liked to play on repeat. I always thought her voice was a little shrill to balance the raw energy of Tristan's, but having met her, it was obvious she was there for more than just the music.

'I don't trust him.' Isaac was talking to me but looking at the stage. The lights dimmed as the first notes of the band's signature song, the one that Tristan claimed had record companies calling (although he'd never actually met any of the producers whose names he dropped into every conversation), blasted over our heads to fill the room.

'You sound jealous.'

'I mean it, Beth.' He bent down to shout against my ear. 'Don't let him suffocate you.'

'What's that supposed to mean?' I took a step back, searching his face for an answer.

Whatever Isaac was trying to tell me disappeared the moment Tristan started singing and I turned away from my best friend to watch him perform. He was hypnotic, with a kind of raw energy that more than made up for any wrong notes or missed beats from the band.

'The lead guitar is about half a second off every time!' Isaac shouted against my ear.

'Not everyone can be as talented as you!' I shouted back with a grin, then returned my attention to the stage, to Tristan and Adrienne, who was staring straight at me. 'I think she likes you.'

'Too thin. I like girls who like their food.'

I smiled, then held my breath as the song came to an end, because I knew what was coming next.

As soon as the opening bars of 'I Put a Spell on You' were struck, Isaac turned to me, then back to the stage as Tristan sang out the words to a song most people associated with Nina Simone.

But I had played him another version, one that was harder and with a rock edge that suited Tristan's voice far better than what he usually sang. It made him sound like Jim Morrison with a healthy dose of Jagger swagger thrown into the mix. It changed the whole dynamic of the band and meant that I was now included in all of their practice sessions, my opinion asked, instead of simply sitting on the sidelines.

'You played him the Creedence Clearwater version,' Isaac said, taking a long sip of his beer.

'Isn't it great?'

'I think I'm going to head home.' Isaac drained his pint whilst looking around for somewhere to dump the glass.

'What? Why?' I said, grabbing hold of his arm.

'It should be you up there,' Isaac said, pointing at the stage. 'You have more talent than the whole lot of them combined. And as for Tristan . . .'

'What about him?'

'I know you've heard the rumours.'

'It's different now.'

'Because you're falling for him?'

'No,' I scoffed. But of course he was right. He was always right and I hated being so transparent to him.

'Be careful, Beth,' he said. 'He has a habit of using people.'

I turned away so he wouldn't see the hurt on my face. I didn't see Isaac leave, but I felt it. The space where he had been only seconds before was cold and empty, and I told myself it didn't matter, because he'd always be there, no matter what.

165

19.

Isaac hasn't called or texted or anything, and I know I should be the one to reach out, but I just can't because I still don't understand what happened. It's been less than a week and he has a job, a very important job that keeps him incredibly busy, and that could be the reason he hasn't called. Or he's just avoiding me so we don't have to actually talk about why he kissed me, and why he thinks it was a mistake.

It's not just the kiss I want to talk about, but everything else that's happened and is still happening ever since Lucy sent me that puzzle box.

I've been going back through old pictures on my phone, including ones of Lucy, forcing myself to remember where each and every one of them was taken. It's acutely painful, seeing her face and not being able to talk to her, tell her about Isaac. The fact she's no longer alive is staggering in its absurdity, and I don't think I truly believe that I'll never see her again, nor hear her voice.

I don't want to live the rest of my life without her, but perhaps one day this won't be so excruciating. Perhaps one day I won't be so utterly bereft whenever I picture her face or her smile.

According to today's horoscope, I am about to receive a welcome surprise. Which could mean anything at all but of course only made me all the more nervous about this illustrious reunion

Isaac made me arrange. A quick glance at my watch tells me I'm early, which would be surprising if it wasn't for the fact I've been up since dawn.

It took me three days to work up the courage to call Tristan's parents and ask for his number – his mother at first thinking I was some crazed fan and then only realising who I was when I mentioned Lucy's name, which was embarrassing and also incredibly insulting given what I did for her son – and another full day and night to send him a text.

I was teaching when his reply came through, the soft ping making me startle and nearly fall off the piano stool. My student barely noticed, but I spent the rest of the lesson having heart palpitations as I tried to figure out what on earth I was supposed to do next.

Over the years, I have had countless conversations with Tristan in my head, possibly more than I've had with Isaac. They all end the same way, with him apologising profusely for what happened and saying that he'd made a terrible mistake, that he was nothing without me and my songs. I'm guessing the reality is likely to be somewhat different, which is why I have barely slept since he agreed to meet me here.

Kew Gardens on the outskirts of London was one of Lucy's favourite places in the world. We used to come here as kids, spent hours playing hide-and-seek in the Japanese Garden and following Dad through all the greenhouses as he tried to get us to show an interest in all things horticultural. It's also where she and Harry got married.

Perhaps she's the reason I chose to meet Tristan here, so that I might have her with me for luck.

Christ, I'm nervous to the point of feeling sick. What am I supposed to say to him? The fact he agreed to meet me without even asking why has to be a good thing, right? I wish Isaac was here, or I'd at least had the chance to practise my speech with him. But maybe he was right, maybe by coming here alone I might finally be able to put all my demons to rest.

Problem is, once that's happened, I then have to try and figure out what on earth I should say to Isaac, and the prospect of that conversation makes my entire body tremble.

Two girls brush past me, holding hands and giggling as they duck behind an enormous fern. A moment later a man follows, walking with arms in front of him and calling out that he's 'coming to get you'. I hear a laugh, turn to see a woman, not much older than me, with a toddler strapped to her chest. His chubby legs are pumping with delight, one fist curled around his mother's finger, the other shoved in his dribbly mouth. I'm halfway through a thought that starts off by imagining what it might be like to be so normal, so like everyone else, when I see him. He's standing at the end of the path next to a palm tree and looking straight at me.

Tristan.

It's like having a bomb go off inside me, pulling every single cell apart and then shoving me back together. It's incredibly strange seeing him in real life after so many years of seeing pixelated images of him on a TV screen or staring back from the cover of yet another magazine.

'Hi,' I say as he approaches. He looks the same, but different. Gone are the skin-tight jeans, biker boots and dishevelled hair, replaced with chinos, a fitted leather jacket and designer stubble. But it's not the clothes or even the beginnings of a receding hairline that strike me as odd, more the look behind his eyes, which seems so much less than before.

'Shit. This is awkward.' He's hovering a few feet away, clearly unsure as to whether it's safe to come closer.

'Just a bit.' I don't know where to look or what to do with my hands, or if I should be feeling all the feelings that are tumbling around inside of me. I hate him. I love him. No, I loved him, or at least I thought I did.

'I did think it was weird to hear from you after all this time.' He takes a step towards me, eyes moving from my lips to my cleavage and back again.

'It was Lucy's idea.'

'Lucy? But isn't she . . .'

'Dead. Yes.' His brother was at the funeral, no doubt passed on the news to the rest of the King family. I half expected Tristan to put in an appearance, or at the very least reach out to me, but that would involve him actually having a conscience, or a soul.

'Shit. Sorry. About Lucy, I mean.'

'Nothing else?'

It takes him a moment to understand what I'm referring to and I'm overwhelmed with the urge to hit him, hard and repeatedly, for being so stupid and selfish.

'Come on,' he says with a lopsided smile, one that always used to work but now just makes me want to retch. 'That was years ago.'

'They were my songs, Tristan.' I'm yelling now, fists balled by my sides as I let go of the fury I've been holding on to for what feels like a lifetime.

'We wrote them together.'

'Not all of them.'

'I didn't think you'd mind.' There it is. His arrogant, narcissistic streak that always meant he was never at fault.

'If you'd actually bothered to ask, I probably would have given them to you anyway.'

'Why?'

'Because of the way I felt about you.' I've finally said it and, even though he must have known it all along, must have deliberately used my feelings to his advantage, he has the decency to look shocked.

'But you must have realised . . .' He leaves the statement hanging, which is surprising because it's so very much out of character for him not to twist the knife a little further.

'I did it for you,' I say, backing away. 'I did everything for you.'

'I never asked you to.'

'And yet you were quite happy to take everything. Go off and have an amazing career and not once give credit to the person who made it all possible.'

'What, you think you could have done it better?' he says with a scoff, and I hate him for his arrogance, for his total lack of care for anyone other than himself. More than anything, I hate the fact he's right. 'You really think you were ever capable of standing on stage and making every single person in the audience want you? It's not just about the music, Beth. Surely you understand that.'

'Of course I do.'

'Face it, Beth. Anyone can write a decent song, but it takes so much more to become famous.'

'I never wanted to be famous.'

'Then what did you want?'

'To hear my songs on the radio.' As soon as I've said it, I realise I've lost.

'In that case, what are we even arguing about?'

'It's the principle of it, Tristan. You passed everything off as your own, without bothering to include me.'

'Oh, so you think you were the magic ingredient? That we never would have been successful without you?'

'Actually, yes, I do.'

'If that's the case, how come you never made it on your own?'

'I . . .' There are no words, only feelings. Feelings of regret and remorse and fury at my own stupidity for thinking that he ever cared about me. Most of all I'm angry at myself for letting him affect me even now.

'If you really cared,' he says, close enough for me to smell the stale coffee on his breath. 'You wouldn't have walked out on us.'

'You kicked me out of the band!'

'Because you screwed up, Beth,' he says, poking my shoulder, and I swat his hand away. 'You screwed up on the most important night of my life, so you can't blame me for being pissed off with you.'

'You know why I did what I did.' He didn't care back then, so what makes me think he'll give any kind of a shit now?

'And it shouldn't have mattered. You should have fought harder, proven yourself to us, because I thought you understood that music trumps it all.'

'Is this what helps you sleep at night?' I say, shaking my head in disbelief, because I wonder how many other people ever get to see the real Tristan King. The one so consumed with a need for adoration that he'll walk over everyone in order to get it and doesn't care what happens in the process. 'Do you tell yourself that I didn't care enough about my songs so therefore it was perfectly reasonable for you pretend you wrote them?'

I'm right. He knows I'm right; I can see it in the way he's looking at me, trying to decide what to say next.

'Why now?' His tone is soft, his features relaxed, but there's no kindness behind his words. 'Why are you only coming to me about this now and not before? Why didn't you contact me the minute the single launched, or the album, or the tour? Why wait eight years before trying to lay claim to something you were never going to do anything with?'

My jaw tightens as the words sink into my soul, because he's right. On some level I have always known that if it hadn't been for him and the band, my songs would have done nothing more than gather dust in a box under my bed. He may have gone about it in a completely cruel and inconsiderate way, but he is also the reason my songs have been played the world over.

'Lucy.' My tongue gets caught on her name and I turn my face away to try and hide the tears. 'Lucy made me come.'

'I figured she would have told you eventually.'

'Told me what?'

'About giving me "Hyacinth Girl".'

Everything stills. The entire world around me melts away as my mind tries to process what it is Tristan has just said.

'*Lucy.*' I whisper her name then clasp my hand across my mouth as if this will somehow stop his confession from being true. She wouldn't. She couldn't, because surely she would have told me?

I think I always knew it was her. Deep down I've always known, because how else would Tristan have got his hands on the cassettes that were in a box under my bed? What I still don't understand is why Lucy never told me. But maybe she didn't know, maybe she thought all along that I'd been the one to willingly give away my dream?

'I hate you,' I say, my hand coming out to strike him clean across the face before I've even thought about it.

'For fuck's sake, Beth,' he says, grabbing me by the wrists, and I kick out at him. 'Calm down.'

'Don't tell me to calm down!' I scream the words at him, see annoyance on his face, and it only fuels the fire within me.

'What does it matter, anyway? It's all over, for both of us.'

'It matters to me, Tristan,' I say, not bothering to wipe away the tears that are now streaming down my face. 'It matters because "Hyacinth Girl" is mine.' And Isaac's and Lucy's and even Dad's. They all had a part to play in creating that song because they all helped shape me into the girl who wrote it.

'Look, for what it's worth, I never meant to hurt you,' Tristan says, taking a step towards me, and I back away with both hands raised.

'But you did it anyway,' I say as I turn and walk away. I don't look back, I daren't look back, as I hurry between neat rows of rose bushes and over to the safety of an ancient oak tree. I go around to the other side, hidden from view, and sink down to the ground, resting the back of my head against the trunk and staring up to the canopy above.

My phone starts to ring and I turn it over to see Harry's name light up the screen. Is it coincidence or fate, or just pure bad luck that he's calling me the very second after I've walked away from the only person who I ever thought to blame?

'Hello?'

'Did you know?' I ask.

'Know what?'

'That Lucy gave Tristan "Hyacinth Girl".'

He hesitates before answering, which tells me everything. 'You've spoken to Tristan.'

'Why didn't she tell me herself?'

'I don't think you realise what it did to her. She thought she'd failed you.'

'That would have involved her actually giving a shit.'

'That's enough, Beth.' His voice is razor-sharp, reminding me of how Dad sounded whenever I pushed his patience a bit too far.

'She lied to me, Harry.'

'And you never gave her an opportunity to tell the truth, because if you'd known, would it have done anything other than drive you further apart? Shit happens, Beth, and you either learn from it, or you end up drowning.'

'So now I'm drowning in my own shit?'

I hear Harry sigh, can imagine him pacing up and down the hallway, asking himself why on earth he was still caught up in this ridiculous farce.

'Did Lucy ever tell you about her dissertation?'

The question throws me and I screw shut my eyes, searching for any kind of memory that might help answer him, because it feels like I should know this one. 'The one about fairy tales?'

'That's the one. Specifically about the need for them, even in modern society, because they teach us about fear and how we can overcome it.'

'I don't need a fairy tale to tell me Tristan was my demon.' There's a pause on the other end of the line and I check the screen to make sure we haven't been disconnected. 'Harry?'

'Actually,' he says, and I swear there's a smile in his voice, 'I think Lucy meant the demon is you.'

There is nothing, no words, no response. My mind is suddenly empty, and I think it's due to the fact that all the blood has rushed to my heart and is making it feel like I might explode.

'Look, I have to go,' Harry says, and I hear the faintest sound of keys being picked up and a door being opened. 'But please, Beth. Try to forgive her.'

And then he hangs up. No goodbye, nothing.

'Stupid, patronising piece of . . .' I stand up, turn around full circle with fists clenched and no doubt a certain madness on my face. I want to rip the tree from the earth, tear its branches off one by one and hurl them into the sky.

Instead, I look down at my phone, at a message that's just come through from my darling brother-in-law. It's a picture of a painting – Rosalind, a character from Shakespeare's play *As You Like It*. The play is about trying to trick someone out of love, one I had to study in my final year of A Levels but only finished reading the night before I had to sit the exam. But it's also about deception and the danger of falling in love with a liar.

Love is merely a madness, Harry has typed underneath. It's a line from the play, spoken by Rosalind to Orlando because she doubts that he truly loves her. At what point did I realise Tristan was using me, and why is it that Lucy seems so intent on making me remember?

There's no going back, no way to repair what the two of us broke without even realising it was happening. Is this why she sent me a box filled with the past? Is she asking for something more than forgiveness?

I want to ask her what happened. I want to ask her when she realised what she'd done and why she never said anything, never tried to apologise or explain. Except she did, only I thought her apology was for something else, something that I should have seen coming long before it happened.

20.

The weeks leading up to SuperKing's performance at the Dome in London were one of the most intensely exciting periods in my life. Ever since Tristan had taken my advice on board and changed up the band's sound, he'd been insatiable in his desire to come up with new material to send out to record companies, original songs that he wanted me to help write. For months we'd been writing and practising and deciding which songs worked best together, recording demos and videos in his makeshift studio and posting a couple of them online. Most had barely more than a few hits, but there was one video of Tristan singing an early version of 'Galaxy of Angels' a cappella that had over a thousand likes and dozens of comments about his natural, easy sex appeal.

It was that video which attracted the attention of Euphoric Records. I still remember Tristan showing me the email, how utterly overwhelming it was to think that because of something I'd written the band might actually sign a record deal. I lay on my bed that night, daring to imagine how it might feel to walk into a store and pick up an album that had my name written next to the lyrics of every song. It felt like we were on the cusp of something extraordinary, and I no longer cared about what people thought of my songs, because I knew that with Tristan singing them, they were more than enough.

My Easter holidays had been spent not revising in the library, as I claimed when I set off on my bike each morning, but holed up in Tristan's garage going over and over the set list. Flyers were printed and trips made into town to hand them out at tube stations, phone calls were made to all our friends asking them to tell their friends, and Tristan had convinced his dad to pay for the lot.

It was the day before the show and I was at home, tired and a little hung-over. I was supposed to have got up, gone to school, made meticulous notes about the recurring themes in Shakespeare's plays. Instead, I hid under the covers and feigned a migraine when Mum knocked on the door and asked if I was bothering to come down for breakfast. My obsession with Tristan had made me selfish and deceitful, believing that all the nights I snuck out to be with him and the band were of no consequence because I could see my future so clearly and it had absolutely nothing to do with academic achievement.

'Might be an idea to actually turn up every so often,' Isaac said as he came into my room. I was fresh out of the shower, sitting by the window and skim-reading As You Like It *in my half-arsed attempt at revising.*

'What for?' I said, stretching my arms up and twirling my wrists. 'Those revision classes are pointless.'

'You could at least pretend to give a shit.' Isaac dropped his bag on the floor and went over to my desk, flicking through the sheets of paper and empty crisp packets strewn all over its surface. 'Aren't you even trying?' he said, holding aloft a sheet containing lyrics to a song I'd been working on for Tristan.

I stood up and snatched it back, all too aware of where the conversation was heading. 'It's fine,' I said, folding the piece of paper in half and tucking it in between Shakespeare's own words.

'Is it?' He was leaning against my desk with arms folded, all self-righteous and superior, just like my darling sister.

'Don't be such a bore, Isaac.' I opened the drawer of my bedside table and took out a bottle of bright-red nail polish. Giving it a shake, I held it up to the light to see if there was enough left to paint my fingers as well as my toes.

'Well, forgive me for actually caring about your future.' He was peering at my calendar, at all the squares representing the coming days on which I'd scribbled the exams I'd barely done any revision for. I knew that his own version at home was neat and colour-coded, as were all the notebooks filled with pages and pages of everything he needed to know in order to become a doctor.

'Jesus, now you sound like my mother,' I said, unscrewing the lid and easing out the little brush covered with sticky liquid. 'I don't need a back-up, Isaac. The band's going to be huge.'

'Arrogant, much?' He walked over to the window and looked down at the garden, where we used to spend so much time. I think I missed him, or at least missed having him on my side, but he and Tristan so obviously despised one another and I hated being caught in the middle. Which of course meant I ended up choosing infatuation over friendship. Something all the stories and all the films and all the songs tell you is a very bad idea indeed.

'Look,' I said, dragging the brush down the centre of my biggest toenail, 'you know and I know that school doesn't actually teach me anything useful.'

'And hanging out with Tristan every night does?'

I filled in the nail on either side, chin rested on my knee so I didn't have to look at him, or all that judgement. 'Yes. You can't learn creativity from a textbook.'

He snorted. He actually snorted, and I bit back the urge to throw the bottle at him. I imagined it smashing against the windowpane, a vibrant splash of red, some of which would end up on his cheek, as if I'd cut him open to spill all that opinion on the floor.

'You have to live, Isaac.' (God, I sounded so pretentious). 'You have to discover and dare and risk it all in order to feel what it's really like to be alive.'

'But couldn't it wait? Just a few weeks?'

He had a valid point, but not one that I was willing to acknowledge, because if I did then he would see the crack, the slither of doubt, that I had been pushing down ever since my English teacher pulled me aside and gently reminded me that my entire future was resting on the coming months.

Mrs Gray was the only teacher who ever really encouraged me. She said I was good enough to study English at university. I wanted to believe her, told myself that studying poetry wasn't a million miles away from writing lyrics, but deep down I knew it was nothing more than a compromise.

'You do realise you need to actually pass the exams to be able to go to uni?' Isaac said, and I felt my jaw tighten because it was so typical of him to know exactly what I was thinking about. He was the one to help me fill out my UCAS application, telling me that any kind of degree would give me more options, at which point I flicked the side of his neck and told him off for being so boringly sensible. We even got on a train and headed out to Reading, because if I actually put the work in, my grades could be good enough to study there. Plus, it wasn't too far from London, meaning Isaac and I could visit one another as often as his medical degree would allow.

Problem was, as soon as I met Tristan, I figured neither my A Levels nor a degree was going to decide my future, so why worry about them?

'Tristan has a producer coming to the show.' A real, bona fide record producer, which meant that he'd barely left the garage, which his parents had so kindly converted into a rehearsal space, for weeks.

'Yeah, right.'

'No, he does. He showed me the email.'

'What's that got to do with you giving up on school?'

I slid the brush down another nail, wiping away the excess with my thumb. 'I've been helping him.'

'Helping him how?'

'I showed him a few songs,' I said with a shrug, as if this was the truth.

'Including "Hyacinth Girl"?'

'No, of course not.' Tristan had always been funny about that song, claiming that it should be hard and heavy with a bass guitar, not an acoustic. In turn, I'd always been fiercely protective of it and refused to show him the lyrics or play him the tape I'd recorded it on with Isaac.

I did so much of what he asked, even when I knew he was only playing with me, the way a cat might a mouse, and I willingly went back for more. But the more I feared losing him, the less control I had.

'He's using you. Surely you can see that?'

'Jealous, much?' I brought my head down between my knees and blew gently on each of my toes in turn.

'Did it ever occur to you that maybe, just maybe, I'm the only one looking out for you?'

'I don't need another parent, Isaac.'

'No, but you do need to grow up.'

His tone was condescending and patronising and I chose to completely ignore the fact that he might, in part, be right. 'Piss off.'

'You piss off,' he said, grabbing his bag and emptying the contents all over the floor. It was so uncharacteristic of him to make a mess, but before I could ask if he was ok, if he was annoyed about more than just Tristan, he chucked a book at me and I had to duck out of the way. 'I'm done covering for you. I'm done lying to your parents about where you spend your nights, or bringing books back from the library that I doubt you even read.'

'Isaac . . .' I began, picking up the book to see it was another copy of the play I needed to somehow memorise before nine a.m. on Monday.

'Do you not get how completely fucked up this is?' he said, shoving his stuff back in his bag and heading for the door. 'You're giving him everything, and he doesn't give a shit about you.'

'That's not true.'

'No?' he asked, hovering in the doorway and sending me a look. 'You sure about that?'

'Sure.' I had to be sure, because otherwise the past nine months would be nothing more than a complete waste of time.

Everyone I'd ever met seemed to be crammed into that room above a pub in North London. The space had morphed from being bland and empty to a thrumming mass of bodies crowding at the bar, all of them there to hear us play. Even Lucy had put in an appearance, travelling down from Oxford after I'd asked her about a thousand times if she would be able to come.

Standing backstage in the minutes before the band was due to play, I closed my eyes and just listened. I could hear laughter, snippets of conversations and the ting of the cash register as people ordered their drinks.

'That's a lot of people,' Graham, the band's drummer, said, peering over my shoulder at the crowd, which was growing more impatient by the second.

'It's fine,' I said, scanning the throng of bodies for Lucy. Over by the bar were a couple of middle-aged men wearing leather jackets and designer stubble, sipping their drinks and looking decidedly out of place. 'Is that the guy from Euphoric Records?' I asked Graham, pointing across to the bar.

'Christ, he actually came.' Graham blew out his cheeks and hopped from foot to foot. 'This is it, guys,' he said, looking around at the rest of the band. 'Hang on a sec, where's Ed?'

'Throwing up in the toilets,' Adrienne said as she applied another coat of lipstick to her already glossy lips. 'I told him shots were a bad idea, but he said they would help calm him down.'

'Calm him down?' Graham shouted. 'How the fuck is he supposed to play if he's wasted?'

'She could do it.' Adrienne nodded across at me, and I resisted the urge to slap her.

'No, I couldn't,' I replied, hands raised and backing away.

'Beth, you have to,' Graham said. 'You know the whole set better than any of us.'

'Come on, Beth,' Alex, the bass guitarist, chimed in. 'You can stand at the back. We'll even dim the lights so no one has to see you.'

'All you have to do is play,' Adrienne said, meeting my eye, and I swear she was laughing at me.

I could hear my heart beating erratically. It was true that I could play those chords in my sleep. The point was I never had any intention of standing up on stage and doing so. Glancing over at the bar, I couldn't help but think that there was no way in hell Tristan would introduce me to the guys from the record label, as he'd promised, if I let him down. If I didn't do this, then everything we'd spent all these months working towards, along with my dream of actually being able to do something worthwhile with my music, would be over.

'Where is Tristan?' I asked, suddenly aware that our lead singer was nowhere to be found. Losing a guitarist was one thing, losing Tristan would be nothing short of a catastrophe.

'I'd better go and look for him,' I said, smiling at Adrienne, who raised one eyebrow in response and then walked out on stage to a chorus of cheers and hollers, closely followed by the rest of the band.

I could hear them plugging in guitars, testing microphones and calling out to the crowd, asking if they were ready. But the band was nothing without their lead singer. I checked the dressing room, the toilets, even asked behind the bar, but no one had seen him. He needed to know about Ed. I needed him to tell me it was ok, that he trusted me not to screw up.

Shit, I thought to myself, seeing the guys from the record label checking their phones, we were running out of time. Just then, the door to the fire escape opened and Lucy stepped inside. I was about to go and ask her for help when I realised she wasn't alone.

As the door swung closed I ducked behind an amp and saw Tristan loop his arm around Lucy's waist. I shrunk further into the shadows, biting down on my fist to stop myself from screaming. They stopped right by me and I watched as Tristan kissed my sister in a way that suggested this wasn't a one-time thing.

'Thanks for coming, my little good luck charm,' I heard him say, and she smiled back in response. 'See you after the show?'

I held my breath as he walked out on stage, the roar of approval from the crowd vibrating up from the soles of my feet. He didn't even look around at his bandmates, didn't notice Ed wasn't where he was supposed to be. He simply waltzed up to the microphone and looked to the ceiling, signalling the start of 'Galaxy of Angels'.

In years to come, that movement alone would let the audience know which song was coming next. It was a song that I'd been working on instead of reading Shakespeare or spending time with my friends. A song that, along with all the others I gave him, I believed would be part of an album that would only be the beginning of an incredible partnership – me writing, him singing: the perfect combination.

But it never happened because I ran along the corridor, out on to the fire escape and down to the street below.

'Beth, wait!'

I turned around to see my sister chasing after me. I could have kept running, but we both knew she would always catch up.

'Where are you going?' she asked as she approached. 'The band's already started.'

'How long?' The words got caught in the back of my throat and I tucked my hands into my armpits for fear of what they might do.

'How long what?' She searched my face and I waited for her to understand. 'Didn't Tristan tell you?' she said, looking at me for only a second more before her eyes dipped to the ground.

'Yes. Of course. Silly me.' I started laughing, a shrill, jagged sound that didn't come out the way I'd intended. I scratched at my throat, then dug my fingernails into my palm. 'I completely forgot that he'd told me he was screwing my sister.'

'It's not what you think.'

'Oh really? So you haven't deliberately been hiding it from me?' All that time, Tristan hadn't said a word, and neither had Lucy. The betrayal hurt more than the lie, but only just.

'No. I mean, not really. It just sort of happened.'

'When?'

'Does it matter?' She took a packet of cigarettes from her pocket, no doubt a habit picked up from her latest conquest, and lit one.

'Of course it fucking matters, Lucy,' I said, watching as she blew smoke into the night sky and wondering how many other things there were in my sister's life I had absolutely no clue about. 'And what about Damian? How does he feel about you shacking up with his brother?'

'Damian and I were never serious,' she said with a dismissive wave of her hand.

It struck me then how utterly unfair it was that Lucy could cast someone aside without even stopping to think what it might do to them. Meanwhile, I was standing there, my heart in pieces, desperately hoping that someone might actually think I was worth loving.

'Did you come here tonight for me or for him?'

'That's not fair, Beth. I've always supported your music.'

'It's not about the music, Lucy. Ever since the tumour . . .' I stopped, all too aware that I was hovering on the edge of something and, if I took the leap, there might not be a way to climb back up.

'Go on,' she said, taking another drag of her cigarette and staring straight at me. 'Say what you were about to say.'

'Ever since the tumour, you've always got everything you wanted.'

'Oh Beth, come on. I never asked to get sick.'

'And yet you came out of it even more glorious than ever. Luck's always been on your side, Luce, and you make sure to use it to your advantage. You're the bright and shiny to my dull and ordinary, and you never, ever get in trouble for anything at all. Mum and Dad tiptoed around you for years, never commenting on all the parties you went to, or the boys you cheated on Thomas with.'

She flinched at this last comment, perhaps remembering how distraught he'd been when she finally got around to breaking up with him.

'The one thing . . .' I said, the words coming out between sobs. 'The one thing I had was my music.'

'You still have it.'

'No, I don't. Do you really think I can still be part of the band? Be anywhere near him, knowing that he'd rather be with you?'

'You like him.' Her eyes grew wide in realisation and I swear a small part of my heart fell away in that moment.

'I love him.' I balled my hands into fists and stared up at the sky.

'Beth,' she said, grabbing my arm, and I tried to pull myself free, but she refused to let go. 'Beth,' she said again, and I looked at her, saw all that pity behind her eyes, which only made me all the more enraged.

'You've ruined everything.' I wiped the back of my hand under my nose and wrenched my arm free from her grasp. 'This was my one chance, my one opportunity to become part of something incredible. But you couldn't even let me have that.'

'Beth, please.'

I turned and walked away, but this time she made no attempt to stop me and I told myself I didn't care.

The day after the gig, I steered my bike towards the far end of the village, down the hill and through the gates to Tristan's house.

I still wonder what would have happened if I'd stayed home as planned, eaten the quiche and salad Mum had left in the fridge and sat in the garden going over my revision notes. The problem with hindsight, though, is that it creates more questions than answers.

Wheeling my bike along the drive, I looked right, noticing that the garage door was shut, which meant Tristan was probably still in bed, having stayed up all night celebrating. Swallowing away the possibility that my sister had been keeping him warm, I rang the doorbell and waited.

'Beth? What are you doing here?' Mrs King asked as she opened the door.

'I was looking for Tristan,' I replied with a smile, but already I was starting to think that this was a bad idea. She was looking at me strangely, as if I were a wild animal ready to pounce.

'It's all right, Mum,' Tristan said as he came down the stairs, shrugging on a t-shirt over a pair of low-slung jeans. He stepped outside, closing the door behind him, leaving us alone and me with absolutely no idea what to say.

'Why are you here, Beth?'

'To apologise.'

'What for?' he said through a yawn and looking at anything but me.

'For walking out last night.'

'Oh, that.' He said it so dismissively, like it didn't matter I'd walked out on the most important night of the band's life. I told myself it was because he was angry, disappointed, and so I kept talking instead of turning around and going home.

'I know I shouldn't have.' I let go a nervous laugh. 'But I bet you were amazing. You're always amazing on stage.'

He looked at me, almost as if he couldn't believe I was still standing there.

'We were, actually.' He took a packet of cigarettes out of his back pocket and lit one. It was the same brand that Lucy had been smoking only the night before, and I glanced up at the house, wondered if she was in there somewhere, looking down on me. 'No thanks to you.'

My gaze snapped back to him. 'I said I was sorry.'

'It makes no difference, Elizabeth.' The way he said my name stung more than the way he was looking at me and I could feel the ground tilt underneath me as I forced myself to stay upright.

'What do you mean?'

'It means,' he said, blowing a couple of smoke circles into the sky and then picking a slither of tobacco from his tongue. 'It means we have a meeting next week with Euphoric Records.'

'That's amazing.' I reached out to put my hand on his arm. 'I've got exams, but I'm sure I can still make it.'

He removed my hand, slowly and with deliberate care. 'Don't you get it? You're not part of the band. Never have been.'

'But the songs.' My hand came up to my neck, fingernails scratching at skin that would bear the marks of my pain for days to come.

'What about them?'

'They're my songs, Tristan.'

'Oh, really?' He laughed at me, actually laughed in my face. 'You think the rest of us just sat around with our thumbs up our arses whilst you wrote an entire album?'

'Well, not quite, but . . .'

'You know what?' he said, flicking his cigarette into a nearby bush. 'Euphoric don't want half the songs you claim to have written. They don't even want the band. They just want me.'

'That's horrible.' Although Tristan looked as if it was the complete opposite.

'I convinced them to give the guys a chance.' He folded his arms over his chest and stared down at me. 'Said we'd been playing together for years. That, without them, there is no SuperKing.'

'But Adrienne . . .'

'Adrienne didn't walk out on us because she caught me kissing another girl.' He was furious. I'd never seen him so angry and it took me a moment to realise that he was more upset about my sister than he was about me walking out.

'Lucy told you.' Of course she bloody told him. Had to ease her conscience, didn't she, when it would have been far easier if she'd decided not to sleep with the guy I'd given everything to.

'She got the last train back to Oxford. Said it was all a mistake and that she couldn't come between you and your music.'

'She did?'

'But guess what, Beth,' he said, turning round to open the front door. 'You did that all by yourself.'

I launched myself at him, actually threw my arms around his waist in an attempt for him to stay. 'Tristan, please. I'm sorry. I'll talk to Lucy.' Even though it was the last thing I wanted to do. 'You can't do this, please, Tristan. The band is all I've got.'

'Go home, Beth,' he said, shoving me hard, and I stumbled backwards. 'There's nothing here for you any more.' And then he slammed the door, leaving me standing on the drive with my heart in my mouth and absolutely nowhere to go.

I barely remember cycling home, am astounded that I wasn't run over by a car for not checking when I took all those twists and turns. I do remember pausing at the junction where Isaac and I always said our goodbyes, trying to decide whether I should turn left or right, then kicked off from the kerb and headed for the river.

Bike tossed to the ground, clothes stripped from my skin, I stepped into the wet, gasped at the chill that lingered even in the hottest of summers, and waded out to the middle, to where the current began to pull. The water curled over my belly, my chest, then over my face, my eyes, my everything.

All became quiet. I held my breath and waited for the burn.

Pictures of memories filtered into my brain, of everything that had happened and everything I wanted to forget. I thought I understood pain, knew what it was to be scared of being hurt by someone you love. But what I felt in that moment was more than I thought I could endure.

It would have been so easy to stay under, to stay gone, to let my body and mind grow limp and be washed out to sea. There was a voice in my head saying I had nobody to blame but myself for choosing to love someone I knew all along was using me. There was another voice, one that belonged to a girl no more than ten, screaming at me to get up, to fight back.

The first breath pulled and ripped and hurt more than I was prepared for. As I dragged myself from the water, belched all that wet on to the bank, I wished more than anything I could somehow cut out my heart, just like the doctors had cut out Lucy's tumour, and throw it away.

21.

The streets are quiet as I head north towards the local pool; only a handful of joggers and dog-walkers are out, along with a couple of lads who look like they haven't yet made it back to bed.

I don't know why I chose today of all days to go for a swim. I honestly can't remember the last time I was in chlorinated water. I used to swim every morning during the summer, either in the river or at our local pool. And whenever we were on holiday I used to spend more time in the water than out of it.

Everything about the pool I have come to seems familiar – the smell, the damp changing rooms with a huge gap underneath the door, the slippery tiles and the old ladies wearing brightly coloured swim caps.

Poised at the edge, toes curling over the tiled lip of the pool, I take a long, slow breath before bending my knees and propelling myself up and into the water. It surrounds me, the initial shock of cold, passing along from the tips of my fingers over every inch of my body and down to my toes. It's like greeting an old friend, the sensation of moving through the wet, my muscles instinctively remembering what to do, and I find myself smiling as I turn my head to breathe.

Head down once more, arms reaching ever onward, my mind is filled with memories. Flashes of moments in time – in the bath making bubble beards with Lucy, jumping into the river from a rope strung from a nearby tree, getting my foot stuck in the drain of a hotel pool, and running through a freak rainstorm with Isaac.

One stroke from the end I tuck and roll, pushing hard against the wall with my feet and then turning sideways underwater. The burn comes slowly at first, a tickle in my lungs that fills and expands with every kick of my legs until I can feel it in my skull, pounding behind my eyes and forcing me back to the surface. I take in a huge gulp of air, making me cough and splutter, my nose and eyes burning from the chlorine.

'You all right?' a fellow swimmer asks as I move across to the side and rest my head on my arms.

'Yes, fine.' I attempt a smile in response and the woman looks at me with concern.

'I find it helps if you slow down,' she says, slipping on a nose clip and tightening her goggles. 'Listen to the water rather than trying to outswim whatever's bothering you.'

I don't reply, just watch her swim away, because it's so very much like something Dad used to say to me whenever I got stuck or frustrated with something I found I could not do. I once threw a tennis ball at my sister, giving her a black eye, and all because she refused to give me the answer to a riddle, and don't even get me started on Swedish flat-pack furniture. Dad was the one who told me to breathe, to close my eyes and just breathe, because trying to force your way out of a problem only creates more frustration.

But this isn't a problem like any I've had before. Finding out about what Lucy did is like opening an old wound, one that I don't know will ever heal.

Try to forgive her. Harry's words linger in my brain, but I don't know what to do with them. How are you supposed to forgive the dead? How do I move on from this, given Lucy had years to tell me the truth but chose not to?

Would it have made a difference if I'd known back then what she did? But I still don't know when she realised what had happened, because I barely spoke to her for years after I discovered she'd been sleeping with Tristan. It was easy enough to avoid one another, given she was living in a different city, madly in love and with no time to spare for her recalcitrant little sister.

What if I hadn't found out about them that night? If they'd stayed together, would it have mattered once SuperKing was a household name and I heard my songs being played in stadiums the world over?

The question that is shouting at me the loudest of all is *why* I found out about them. Once upon a time I would have blamed the universe or the stars, or simply put it down to bad luck. But Lucy got together with Tristan, just as she handed over my song, of her own free will. There was nothing I could have done to change it.

I lift myself out of the water and head for the showers. As I massage shampoo into my scalp, I think again of Lucy. Everything I do brings me back to her, to the years we spent together, and then apart. So many conversations had, and then missed because of what she did, what we both did.

Was any of this actually Tristan's fault, or would Lucy and I have drifted apart anyway because of how different we were?

I used to think he was perfect, but now I can't help but wonder what it was I was so in love with. Sure, he's good-looking, confident to the point of arrogance, but he was also never particularly nice to anyone. I saw it all the time, the way he'd flirt with everyone so openly, even in front of Adrienne. I told myself it was because they weren't suited. In reality I think he was simply addicted to having people adore him.

'What's the matter with you?' Sam asks as he comes in from out back, accompanied by the scent of stale tobacco.

'Nothing,' I lie. Picking up an old cloth, I start wiping down the bar, turning my back to him.

'I think that bit's clean,' Sam says, nodding at the spot I've been rubbing over and over whilst he watches me, waiting for a better response than 'nothing'. Because clearly it's not 'nothing' and Sam knows this even without me having to explain precisely how much of the opposite to 'nothing' it is.

'You ok?' he asks, cracking open a pistachio shell and popping the sweet nut into his mouth.

'I'm fine,' I reply, leaving the bar and heading for the piano, even though the hotel's main restaurant doesn't open for over an hour.

'You sure about that?' Sam calls across to me.

Running my fingers over the keys, I try to focus on which song I should play. Anything to get rid of the picture in my mind of how Isaac looked the precise moment before he kissed me.

I could confide in Sam, ask for his advice, but there are several problems I'm currently trying to negotiate, not least the invitation from Margot to Nathan's birthday drinks tomorrow night. I don't know if I can face it, or Isaac, as he's bound to ask if I've spoken to Tristan and I have no desire to tell him the truth. Not just about seeing Tristan, but how I would need to admit that my darling sister wasn't anywhere near as perfect as I once believed.

Tristan betrayed me because he didn't want to share even one bit of that limelight with anyone. Even though I would have given everything to him, already had, I see now that his narcissistic desire to always be the centre of attention is what made him turn against me.

But what Lucy did hurts even more. Not that I ever really believed Tristan would feel the same way about me as I did him, but that's not the point. She was my sister and she took him just like she took everything she wanted, and then barely offered up any kind of apology when I found out. And this is all before I even start to try and wrap my head around the fact she gave him the one song I never wanted him to have, without stopping to think just how much harm it would do.

'Look,' Sam says as he shrugs on his jacket and picks up his keys. 'I'm not one to interfere . . .'

'But?'

'Whatever it is you're going through, don't rush it.'

'Meaning?'

'Meaning you need to do it for you, and because you want to, not because someone else is telling you to.'

I stop playing, because this is remarkably astute given I've not even told him what the problem is. I also don't really know what the solution is, or if I'll ever be able to move on from the knowledge of what Lucy did.

'Maybe you need a fresh start.' He curls his arm around my shoulder, giving it a gentle squeeze, and I almost cry at his tenderness. 'A complete change of scene to give you the time and space to figure out what it is you want.'

'I have no idea what I want.'

'You sure about that?' he says, heading for the door. I turn to say something to him but am distracted by the sight of someone else, someone who walks straight up to the piano and sits down next to me on the stool.

'So this is where you've been hiding all these years,' he says with a grin.

'What are you doing here, Tristan?'

'I fancied a drink.' The smile stretches wider but doesn't make it up to those eyes.

I leave the piano and go back into the bar, start pouring him a pint to keep my hands busy, then turn around to find him watching me.

'And you knew I worked here how, exactly?'

He takes a sip of the pint I slide across to him, licking his top lip free of foam. 'I googled you.'

'You googled me?' I hate the idea of him looking me up on the internet, of the piecemeal information that would be there. It's humiliating to think of how little there is to show for the past eight years of my life, especially considering how much there is about his.

'Why are you really here, Tristan?'

'As I said, I fancied a drink,' he says, raising his glass at me with a wink, and I want to upend it all over his perfectly styled hair.

'And?' I turn away, aware that he's watching me the whole time.

'I felt bad about how we left things.'

This gets my attention.

'Now, or eight years ago?'

He takes another sip of his drink, and it feels deliberate, as if he's stretching out the moment for dramatic emphasis. He used to do the same thing on stage, just stand there, one hand on the microphone, looking out at the crowd. It was hypnotic back then; you couldn't take your eyes off him as he waited for the perfect moment before launching into the next song. Today, it's just annoying.

'Both?'

It's the closest he's ever come to an apology, but it's not enough. It will never be enough.

'You really hurt me.'

'I know. I'm sorry.'

Ok, so that was unexpected, and I'm not quite sure what to do with the words that are years too late. But I was the one to give up. I took the easy way out, told myself it didn't matter, because what was the point of writing songs nobody would ever get to hear?

'It wasn't Lucy's fault.' He tilts his head, trying to meet my eye.

'Which part?' I say, refusing to give him what he wants.

'I said you'd asked me to pop by and collect a tape.'

'How did you know about the tapes?'

He takes another sip of his pint, then pushes the glass aside. 'She told me how you used to record everything on a Dictaphone.'

Inside, my heart is racing, and I have to place one hand on the bar to stop myself sinking to the floor. The understanding that she talked to him about me is excruciating. To know that she shared details about our life, my life, with him makes me feel physically sick.

'She was really proud of you,' he says. 'Said you had this crazy ability to make a song feel like so much more than words and music.'

'When?' I ask, my mind racing through all the times when Lucy would have been at home and I wasn't. But there were so many times, so many moments when she could have given away the one thing I never wanted Tristan to have. 'When did she let you have the tape?'

'I don't know,' he says, moving his palms over the surface of the bar and turning his face to the door. 'Around Christmas sometime?'

'Christmas?' I say, thinking of the annual trip up to London we would make with Mum and Dad. We would always buy poinsettias from Covent Garden Market, drink hot chocolate whilst listening to the carollers and nearly fall asleep on the train home, surrounded by all the gifts we still had to wrap.

But one year, Lucy didn't come, claiming she had too much work to get through, and we sympathised at how demanding being an Oxford undergraduate was. Now it would seem she had an ulterior motive, and so did the person she was meeting in secret.

'But that means . . .' I say, staring over at Tristan as I finally put all the pieces of this particular puzzle together. 'That means you already had "Hyacinth Girl" before the gig at the Dome. Is that the real reason Euphoric came along? Because they'd already heard the very best you claimed to have on offer?'

He doesn't reply, just sits there looking back at me, and I know I should be mad, I should be positively seething, but right now all I feel is empty.

'Why did you do it?' He was enigmatic and brilliant and completely addictive when on stage, but without me, without my songs, he never would have had that time in the spotlight, and I hate him for it. But not nearly as much as I hate myself for still caring.

'Honestly?' He looks down at his hands, then back up at me. 'Because I could.'

'I was eighteen, Tristan. And you broke me.'

'Did you really think we would end up together?'

'No, but that's not the point.' The point is I loved being at the centre of what we created. I loved sitting in that space, watching and listening as together we came up with an album that we knew was special. Most of all, I loved how I felt when I heard him sing all the words I had put down on paper, believing I was one step closer to getting everything I'd ever dreamt of but been too scared to do on my own.

'Then what is the point?' he asks, reaching across the bar for my hand, and I let him. I let him run his thumb across my skin and stare at me long enough to make the rest of the world blur and fade. Someone calls out to me from the other end of the bar, a reminder that I work here. If ever there was a moment to show me just how badly I chose back then, this is it.

'How does it feel?' I ask, my eyes sweeping over a face I used to dream about every single night. 'How does it feel when your dreams come true?'

'Honestly?' he replies. 'They never really do. I mean, for a split second, it feels like you're the shit, the real deal, and all that bollocks. Then the dream changes; you want something else instead.'

It's what Dad tried to tell me only weeks ago, but I've been ignoring my dreams for years. Because how much of a dream is actually about hope and then the absence of hope? We all hoped Lucy would get better and she did, and then she didn't. I hoped Tristan was the answer to all the questions I had about my own life. Most of all, I hoped Isaac and I would always be friends.

'You need to go, Tristan,' I say, taking back my hand and going to the other end of the bar. Anything to put some distance between him and all those wretched memories.

'Do you still write?' he says, slipping from the bar stool.

'Not really.' I stopped because all it ever did was make me cry. There are so many songs I'm incapable of listening to because they all remind me of him. Even something as simple as sitting next to a father and playing a melody first learnt as a child felt impossible. Tristan ruined it all.

'I really am sorry for what happened, Beth,' he says, and for once he actually sounds genuine. 'I guess I always figured you didn't need me or the band, because "Hyacinth Girl" was so good.'

I watch him go, the half-hearted attempt at a compliment rattling around my brain. It leaves me feeling distorted, out of place, but most of all fuming.

Music used to be a part of me, was stitched through my soul and the only thing that made sense of the world. It showed me how to tell a story, to share all the feelings I didn't know how to convey. I opened myself up, showed Tristan my vulnerabilities, allowed myself to believe that together we could create something incredible. And we did, but then he took it from me, made me hate the music I carried inside me, that I could hear with every waking moment, no matter how hard I tried to drown it out.

Going into the main restaurant, I sit down at the piano, run my fingertips over the keys and force myself to take a long, slow breath. As soon as I start playing, I hear a couple of acknowledging murmurs from some nearby tables now that the restaurant is open, and then intuition takes over, spins me right back to the day Isaac and I recorded 'Hyacinth Girl', sitting at my dad's piano with him backing me up on guitar.

I don't look up, I don't allow myself to pay attention to anything other than the combination of piano and how my voice slips in between the notes, runs straight through the melody, and then the vibrations shoot through my fingers and hit me at the back of my throat.

It feels like forever, but I know it's only a few minutes and then it's over. My hands are shaking as I lift them from the keys, my whole body feels as if I've been shot with enough energy to make each and every part of me wake up. It's a feeling I haven't had for such a long time: the sweet release that playing one of my own songs gives me is like nothing else I have ever experienced, and I wish Lucy was here to see what she has done.

It takes me a second to realise where I am, that the sound of applause is directed at me, and then Natalie's beside me, tugging at my arm and pulling me up to take a bow.

'You'll never guess who's here,' she whispers in my ear, and my eye sweeps the room.

'That song sounds awfully familiar,' Tristan says as he approaches, and I can hear the whispers behind me about oh my goodness is that Tristan King and what's he doing here? I don't need to look to know that texts are being sent, photographs taken and posts being made to all manner of social media sites.

'Why are you still here?' I ask, even more aware now of all those phones pointed in our direction, snapping away for posterity.

'I was wondering,' he says with a raised brow, 'if you would play something with me? One of our songs, perhaps?'

It's such a simple invitation, one that should have been extended to me years ago, and I can't help but laugh at the irony of this whole stupid scenario.

'You are kidding?' I reply, whilst trying to come up with the perfect sentence to convey just how insulting his request is.

'Go on, Beth,' Natalie says as she comes up to the piano and stares across at Tristan. 'It would be, like, epic.'

'Exactly.' Tristan winks at Natalie as he stands up and shrugs off his jacket. Underneath he's wearing a plain white t-shirt, tight enough to let me know he's still in annoyingly good shape. He sees me looking, sends me a trademark smile. 'Come on, Beth. You know we were great together.'

Before I know what's happening, he's sitting next to me at the piano, accompanied by the sound of cheers and whistles as the crowd realises what it's about to witness.

'Hope you guys don't mind.' Tristan leans into the microphone. 'But I thought I'd sing a couple of songs.'

The audience respond in kind, the sound of all that adoration reverberating right through my centre.

What the hell should I do now? It would, perhaps, be the perfect opportunity to show Tristan up. To simply walk away. But then who would actually care or notice that I'd gone? And he'd just sing it a cappella and everyone would fall in love with him all over again.

Don't. The word appears in my head, in a tone that sounds remarkably like Mum's.

But maybe, the idea whispers in my mind. *Maybe I can get him to come clean. Admit what he did.*

And where would that leave you? My mother's voice persists, and I push it away, because she tried to help, tried to get me to speak to a lawyer, but I wouldn't let her.

Besides, it would make little difference – if I did manage to convince Tristan to fess up, then get him and his bandmates to hand over my share of all those royalties, what would it achieve? Sure, I'd have money, but I'd still be without my music.

'You ready?' Tristan says, and I have no idea what to say or do and so I give a small nod, my hands hovering over the keys as I try to calm the fear that's beating away inside me.

But it feels wrong, sitting here with him, and only moments after I'd finally found the courage to sing *my* song *my* way. I can't believe that he's doing it again, that I'm allowing him to do it again.

What would Lucy do? The idea appears out of nowhere, making me lift my head, almost as if I'm expecting to see her at one of the tables, watching. And she is there, or at least the memory of her is. It's not much, but it's enough to make me push back the piano stool and stand up.

'Beth?' Tristan says, grabbing me by the wrist.

'You said yourself you never needed me, Tristan,' I say, pulling myself free from his grasp. 'What makes you think I still need you?'

Walking out of the hotel lobby, I dial Isaac's number, only for it to go to voicemail.

'Hey,' I say, wondering if anyone ever leaves voicemails any more. 'I need to talk to you. About Lucy.' I need to tell him everything that's happened, that I know none of it was his fault and I'm more sorry than he can ever know.

After hanging up, I hold the phone in my hand, stare down at the screen as it fades back to black and try to give a name to what it is I'm feeling right now. I thought it would be bigger, somehow, that performing my song my way would leave me with a perfectly clear picture of what happens next. But there has been no epiphany, no light-bulb moment that suddenly appeared and said, 'Here you go, Beth, here is the magical solution to all your problems.'

I thought it would bring me peace, and perhaps a little joy. All it's done is make me realise that I was a fool to push Isaac away.

I wish I could go back to when my entire world caved in on itself, pulling me into a depression that took me years to escape from. But did I escape, or simply carry it around with me; the guilt and the shame weighing me down like a pocket full of pebbles? None of it was Isaac's fault, and yet I was so quick to blame him, to blame anyone other than myself for what happened.

Lucy gave Tristan my only copy of 'Hyacinth Girl', but I was the one who showed it to him in the first place. I was the one to offer myself up like some kind of willing sacrifice because I believed he and the band were the only way I would ever get my songs heard. And they were, just not in the way I'd dreamt of.

22.

Eight years ago ...

Exams are more than putting down words and symbols on a piece of paper. They're about the build-up, the focus, the whispers of good luck passed between friends as one by one you file into the sports hall at school. It's the rows of single desks and wobbly chairs, all the doors propped open in an attempt to quell the oppressive summer heat. It's the nervous jig of a leg, the soft sneezes of those struggling with hay fever or the tilt of heads as they search the ceiling for inspiration.

Most of all, exams are about the moment you walk out of the final one, the freedom that comes with the knowledge you have nothing to do in the coming weeks: no books to read, no facts to memorise, just a seemingly endless stretch of time until the day near the end of August ringed in red on the calendar of every student in the UK.

I think I knew even before I walked through the school entrance that morning what was going to happen. There was a prickling sensation at the base of my skull, in pretty much the exact same spot as Lucy's tumour. It felt like a premonition, or maybe a great big, glowing, fuck-off warning signal. All I know is that as soon as I entered the hall and locked eyes with Mrs Gray, my English teacher, all other sensations slipped away. Gone was the sound of shrieks and yells and overly excited voices as everyone around me hugged and cried and congratulated each other. I went up to Mrs Gray, deaf to any words she might have offered up, but not blind to the look on her face.

I took the envelope she was holding without saying thank you, pushed through the crowds, out to the parking lot, and mounted my bike. Pedalling hard, I refused to look back to where Isaac was standing calling my name.

I cycled all the way home without stopping, jumping several red lights and narrowly avoiding a cat that hissed its disapproval at me. I abandoned my bike in a clatter of still-spinning wheels and ran up to my room, pacing up and down as I looked at the envelope, scrunched it into a ball, then uncurled it, only to scrunch it up again.

'Come on, Beth,' I said to myself, standing by the window with my future in my hands. I can still hear the soft tear of paper as I finally slid my finger under the lip of the envelope. I still remember holding my breath as I took out the single sheet on which my subjects and cor-responding grades were typed. Most of all, I remember the emptiness I felt as I realised quite how badly I'd screwed up, again.

Isaac found me hiding in Dad's shed. I was underneath the work-bench, earphones in and listening to Joni Mitchell on repeat.

'Hi,' Isaac said, standing in the door to the shed and backlit by the sun, giving him the look of a guardian angel sent down to rescue one fallen from grace.

'I messed up,' I said between hiccups, banging my head as I crawled out from my hiding spot and disturbing an empty bottle of vodka. It clinked against a trowel, one I used as a child when helping Dad plant out all his seeds each spring. One year I had a favourite pair of bright-red wellies with daisies printed up the sides. The thought of those wellies, discarded somewhere, covered in dust and long forgotten, made me start crying all over again.

I'd started crying in the kitchen, tears splashing into the sink as I tried to fill the kettle. Then the phone calls began, an endless stream of messages on the answerphone, all wanting to know my good news.

After a while I gave up on making a cup of tea and raided the drinks cabinet instead. That's when Isaac started banging on the front door, asking what had happened, and so I grabbed my iPod and crept out to the garden, because I knew he'd sneak in through the garage and search the house for me.

What I didn't realise was that he would keep on searching until he found me.

'Come on,' Isaac said, hoisting me to my feet and gripping me firmly around the waist. 'Let's get you inside.'

'What now?' I asked, cradling the double espresso he'd made me and watching as he cut two thick slices of walnut cake.

'That's up to you,' he said, checking his phone then putting it on the counter, screen side down.

'I meant with my parents. What the hell am I supposed to tell them?'

'They love you,' Isaac said, passing me a slice of cake. 'It'll be fine.' He regarded me a moment, perhaps trying to figure out if I was still too drunk to process what he was about to say. 'Look, I know you think this is a disaster.'

'What else would you call it?'

'An opportunity. To start again.'

'I don't want to start again.' I wanted to go back, undo everything that had brought me to this point. Namely going to that stupid party and believing that someone like Tristan would be interested in someone like me. Except he was, just not in the way I wanted him to be.

'Then go through Clearing. Or resit your exams and apply for university next year.'

'I don't want to go to university.'

'I know. But staying here and listening to the most depressing songs in the world isn't going to change a thing.'

A second later, the song on the radio came to an end and the presenter started speaking about the soon-to-be-released second single from the year's hottest new band, SuperKing.

I heard the scrape of a chair leg, looked over in surprise to find Isaac still sitting at the table, then I closed my eyes as Tristan's voice spilt from the speakers, singing the words I had written, words that were never meant to be his.

You lit me up when I didn't have a clue
Just what it was that love could do
I saw myself reflected in your thoughts
A flower unsure how to bloom

The pain I felt in that moment was like nothing I had experienced either before or since. I thought Tristan had broken me, and even watching Lucy's recovery years before was excruciating in so many ways. But that's the thing about suffering, you think you're unhappy and then something worse happens to make you realise you were actually ok all along.

'What the——?' Isaac said, and I shot him a look before sprinting from the kitchen and upstairs to my room.

I pulled a box out from underneath my bed and emptied the contents on to the carpet.

'It's not here,' I said, going through all those tiny cassettes one by one, reading and rereading their labels.

'What's not where?' Isaac asked as he appeared in the doorway.

'"Hyacinth Girl".' I crawled under the bed and ran my hands all over the dusty carpet, but there was nothing there other than cobwebs and regret. 'Did you not just hear Tristan singing it on the radio?'

'Of course I did,' Isaac said as I came back out. 'What I want to know is what possessed you to give it to him?'

'You think I did this?' We were shouting at one another, and normally this would have been enough to make me cry, because Isaac never shouted.

'Why not? You gave him everything else.'

'What's that supposed to mean?' I got to my feet and looked around the room, but I don't know what for. I was so riled up it felt like I was about to burst.

'Did you write the others?' he asked, stepping into the room, and I noticed Mum hovering on the landing. Turned out she came home early from work to find out about my A Level results, only to discover something more. 'I'm willing to bet you wrote the entire bloody album.'

'How did you . . . ?'

'You mean apart from the fact you admitted you were writing for him? Or that the original version of "Hyacinth Girl" has more depth and emotion than he could ever possibly hope to put into a performance? Not to mention all the school you missed to sit in on their practice sessions.'

I glanced at Mum, who probably suspected I hadn't always been where I said I was, but this was the first time anyone had given voice to all the things I had done wrong.

'I told you not to give him anything, Beth. We wrote "Hyacinth Girl" together,' Isaac went on. 'I thought that meant something to you.'

'Is it true?' Mum asked, looking towards the stairs as if she couldn't quite believe that the song being played downstairs was mine.

I nodded in reply, because there were too many words and feelings for me to trust myself and actually answer her.

'Then we need to make this right. Speak to a lawyer.'

'There's no point,' I said, sinking to the floor and pressing the palms of my hands into my eye sockets. 'He has all the original recordings and now nobody will know those songs came from me.'

'I'm still going to call your father,' Mum said, turning around and heading back downstairs.

I wanted to run after her, tell her not to bother because I'd screwed up in more ways than one.

'So that's it?' Isaac said, leaning against the wall. 'You're giving up?'

When, when, did Tristan get hold of the tape? Was it some kind of revenge for me breaking up him and Lucy? But he wouldn't know where it was, or if it even existed, because I'd only ever played the song to him the night we met.

'What do you want me to do, Isaac? The songs are already out there.'

'With his name on them instead of yours. Instead of mine.' He said the last word with clenched jaw and balled fists and I could have sworn he was about to punch a hole in the wall. It frightened me, and then a split second later I realised how hypocritical he was actually being.

'Why do you care? It's not as if you ever wanted to pursue music.' He was so incredibly talented but chose not to do anything with that talent, that voice, and it annoyed me more then than ever before.

'But you did?' he asks, pushing himself away from the wall and coming towards me.

'You know I did. I still do.'

'You say you do,' he said with half a smile. 'But apart from selling your soul to Tristan King you haven't done a single thing to prove that you're serious enough to make a life, a career, out of songwriting.'

'That's not fair. I've always written. With Dad, with you . . .'

'And yet all those songs have simply sat in a box under your bed,' he said, pointing to the tapes strewn across the floor. 'What's the point if nobody gets to hear them, Beth?'

'You know I can't sing in public.' My voice was small, the same lump in my throat that always appeared whenever I thought about having to stand up in front of people and expose myself to them through music.

'There are other ways, Beth. Like going to music college, joining another band or, hell, I don't know, posting a video on YouTube.'

He'd suggested as much several times over the years; he even said he'd do one with me if that's what it took. I'd always shrugged him off, but perhaps there was more behind his suggestion than I'd originally thought.

'So it was you.'

'What was me?'

'You gave him "Hyacinth Girl".' It made perfect sense, or at least I thought it did.

'Give me one good reason why I would do that?'

'To get it out there, because you knew I couldn't. You just said it's your song as well, Isaac. Maybe this was your way of trying to claim it.'

'You're being delusional.'

'Am I?'

'You're seriously accusing me of giving "Hyacinth Girl" to Tristan behind your back?'

'Like I said, you were the only one who knew the tape even existed.' I knelt down on the carpet and put the tapes back in the box, one by one. Over half had been recorded with Isaac, me on piano and him picking out the melody with his guitar. There were so many memories captured on those strips of plastic, like a diary of my youth.

'Apart from Lucy.'

'Don't,' I said, even though a small part of me knew it was possible. I hadn't told him about Lucy and Tristan, was even less inclined to do so now.

'She's not as perfect as you make her out to be, Beth.'

'Says the boy who's had a crush on her for years.'

'Is that really what you think?' he said with a small, sharp laugh. 'God, you really can be stupid sometimes.'

'Stupid enough to think you actually cared about what happened to me.'

'I tried to warn you; I tried to make you see he was using you.'

'Perhaps you should have tried harder.' I thought Isaac understood how much I poured into every single one of my songs – each and every lyric was like a tiny piece of my soul.

'Tried harder? For fuck's sake, Beth, what else was I supposed to do? You were throwing your life away over some stupid crush on a guy who was never going to—'

'Never going to what?' I said, sitting back on my heels and brushing the hair from my face. 'Fancy me? Find me attractive? Oh, don't worry, Isaac, I'm painfully aware that there's only one person anyone pays attention to in my family.'

'Maybe if you actually did something with your life, instead of blaming everyone around you when it goes wrong, then you wouldn't feel the need to constantly compare yourself to Lucy.'

It was as if he'd slapped me, or stuck a knife in my heart, twisted it and then pushed it in deeper. My whole life I'd been compared to my sister; it happened the very second anyone realised we were related. Isaac had been the one person to never openly make comparisons, although it would seem he'd been doing it all along.

'I knew you'd take her side.'

'I'm not taking sides, Beth. Jesus, I'm trying to be your friend here, so would you please stop pushing me away?'

'I never asked you to be my friend.'

I watched the rise and fall of his Adam's apple, saw him turn his face away then look back at me in such a way as to make me draw breath.

'Well, now you'll never need to ask again.'

23.

When Margot texted me to say where she was having Nathan's birthday drinks, I told myself it was no big deal. Except it is, because it's the exact same pub where I spent too many evenings next to the stage and cradling a pint whilst I listened to Tristan sing.

From the outside, the Half Moon pub looks exactly the same, albeit with a fresh coat of paint and no bouncers by the door. Inside it is clean and bright, more refined art deco than *Peaky Blinders*, and the back room is gone. In its place is a restaurant serving artisan food, where before there used to be nothing other than a floor sticky with warm beer, which we drank from plastic glasses.

I hover by the end of the bar, scanning the crowd, which looks decidedly less intimidating than the weird mix of bikers, Goths and underage drinkers from when I last came here.

At the far end of the room there's a wall of glass doors that opens out on to a terrace. In the corner, sitting on a bench underneath a striped awning, is Isaac, along with Margot and Nathan and a group of people, only a few of whom I recognise. Margot waves a hand, beckoning me over.

'Happy birthday,' I say to Nathan, then look around the group, locking eyes with Isaac. He's wearing faded Levi's that he's probably had since we were teenagers, a dark blue shirt with the sleeves rolled up and his hair is still wet from the shower. My insides do a little flip. It's a mixture of nerves and excitement, a feeling I haven't had for years, and it takes me by surprise that I'm feeling it for him. Shit, now I'm in trouble.

Is he nervous? I can't tell. We haven't spoken since he kissed me, and then a stupid song put Tristan smack bang in the middle of everything, all over again.

'Nathan and I were having a discussion about whether Page or May is the better guitarist,' Isaac says, pulling out a chair for me to sit on, and I let go a small sigh of relief that he's including me in the conversation.

'You like Queen?' I ask, failing to hide the amusement in my voice.

'You say that like it's a bad thing,' Nathan says, draining his glass and then helping himself to a top-up.

'Not bad. More unexpected.'

'Because, let's face it, Led Zeppelin is infinitely cooler,' Isaac says with a grin, taking a sip of his beer.

I remember his dad regaling me with the story of how he met Isaac's mum at Knebworth in 1979 and they'd had their first kiss whilst Robert Plant was cavorting about on stage. Isaac grew up listening to seventies rock, just like I grew up listening to blues and jazz.

We swapped musical tastes, cycled out to the next town, whiling away the hours in a music store, flicking through vinyl records to spend our pocket money on, and he once spent an entire summer perfecting the guitar score of 'Stairway to Heaven'. I could play you every single one of Led Zeppelin's songs, having listened to them all hundreds of times. Their hypnotic melodies are like the backdrop to my early teenage years and had more than a passing influence on the songs I would go on to write.

'As brilliant as Page is,' I say, darting a look at Isaac, 'the originality, the essence of the band, doesn't come from him, or even Plant.'

'Not this again,' Isaac says with a groan.

'Not what?' Margot says, leaning forward on the table, her eyes darting between Isaac and me. For a second it feels like she's watching me for something, anticipating how she expects me to react.

'Beth is convinced that Zeppelin's songs are only successful, not because of Plant or Page, but their drummer, Bonham.'

'That's like saying The Stones would still have been successful without Jagger,' Margot says, eyeing me with amusement and making me feel like one of her patients.

I think of Tristan, of how he modelled himself on a mishmash of Jagger and Plant. He had so much presence and bravado on stage, but none of it was really him. Like he was hiding his true self, afraid it would never be enough, and I'm starting to see why.

They were my songs. He may have been the one to stand on stage in front of thousands and sing them, but music for him was only ever about the fame and fortune. For me, music was like breathing, or the beat of my heart.

'Remember watching Page playing with Foo Fighters at Wembley?' Isaac asks, and immediately I'm transported back to a night spent jostling in a crowd of thousands with hands in the sky and my throat raw from singing along to each and every word that tumbled from Dave Grohl's mouth and across the entire stadium.

'Now that was a concert.'

'You're the queen of my dreams,' he says, paraphrasing a Foo Fighters lyric and looking right at me. Then he bashes the table, announcing he is off to get more drinks, closely followed by Nathan.

'You two really love music,' Margot says, barely stifling a yawn.

'I guess,' I reply, turning to see Isaac stumble through the doorway, high-fiving Nathan as they laugh at his inebriation. He's always been a happy drunk, a happy stoner too. In fact, he's definitely a glass-half-full kind of person, whereas I tend to look for the bad before it has even begun.

'Can I ask you something?' Margot says, reaching out and touching me lightly on the arm. 'Why did you stop writing?'

'I ran out of things to write about.' Lucy once told me that Adele had made a fortune out of heartbreak, so there was no reason I couldn't do the same. I seem to remember telling her that Adele hadn't had her heart broken by her own flesh and blood and then slamming my bedroom door in her beautiful face.

'So you didn't love it?' Margot asks.

'Of course I did,' I say, meeting her eye and trying to see beyond the neutral, professional look on her face.

At this she smiles, sits back. 'A friend of mine is a sculptor. But art is hard to sell, so she does wedding photography to pay the bills. Which in turn gives her the ability to pursue her dream, even if it never comes to anything.'

There's more behind her words than she's willing to divulge, and I can't help but think it's deliberate, as if she's testing me for something.

'Answer me this,' she says, lighting a cigarette and brandishing it at me. 'Before your sister, before that guy screwed you over, why did you write?'

'There was never a why. I just did it because it was a part of me.'

'Then you have no reason to be so scared. Unless, of course, you don't know how to write without his help.'

She's talking about Isaac, which would be all kinds of insulting if she wasn't at least a teeny bit on point.

Right on cue, the sound of 'Galaxy of Angels' comes spilling out from all of the speakers dotted around the terrace. I never told anyone, not even Isaac – actually especially not Isaac – what it was really about. There's a line in there, right at the end, which nearly didn't make it into the song.

There will always be an invisible thread between
you and me,
Even if we end up peaking at seventeen.

Tristan believed me when I said it was about the feeling of first love, but really it was about Isaac, about how much I missed writing songs with him.

'You're lucky he forgave you,' Margot says, nodding back towards the pub, and I look over my shoulder to see Isaac, one hand clutching a bottle of beer, the other curled around the waist of a woman with hair as glossy as a thoroughbred and legs up to her ears. 'I'm not sure Kate will be so kind.'

I'm filled with an all-consuming jealousy I have no right to feel. The sight of her coiled around him and fiddling with his hair makes me want to puke.

I swallow away the lump that's appeared in my throat. 'Isaac didn't tell me she was coming.'

'Well, he wouldn't, would he?'

'He used to tell me everything.' He used to tell me in nauseating detail about all the girls he kissed. In turn, I would point out all of their failings, telling him that nobody would ever be good enough for him.

'Not everything,' Margot says with a little huff of derision, scrolling through her phone and deliberately avoiding my eye.

'Meaning?'

She turns her phone face down on the table and looks at me. 'Look, I've been friends with Isaac since Freshers' Week. The entire time I've known him he has been brilliant at absolutely everything he does, apart from one thing.'

'Which is?'

'Relationships.'

'Isaac's never been short of admirers.'

'But he's never been able to commit.'

'He and Kate were engaged.'

'Yes, and she called it off.'

I remember Dad telling me, via an email which I only read two days before the wedding I wasn't even invited to. What I don't remember is why the wedding never actually took place.

'What happened?'

'Nothing. Other than the fact he's clearly been in love with you his whole life.'

'That's not . . .' I don't finish my sentence, because I have no idea what to do with this little nugget of information. Pushing back my chair, I stand, catch sight of Isaac, who is watching me with a question on his face. I don't wait or give him any kind of answer, because I've known all along that he deserves so much better than me.

24.

My sister used to make scrapbooks that she would meticulously fill with remnants of her childhood. Everything from photos of friends, pressed flowers and the cinema ticket from her very first date. They were all carefully cut out, sorted into categories, covered with sticky-back plastic and surrounded by doodles and glitter. Her favourite, the one she would keep adding to long after her obsession with Barbies and boy bands had faded, was all about her dream wedding. Pages upon pages torn from magazines of dresses and tiaras and woodland settings strewn with so many fairy lights and scatter cushions it looked like Alice's tea party on steroids.

Apparently, she showed it to Harry the first time he went to meet my parents. He laughed and said she deserved a fairy tale every day, not just for her wedding. It made me nauseous, because if I had ever shown such an idealistic dream to a boyfriend less than six months into a relationship, they would have, quite literally, run a mile. Ok, so I haven't ever let anyone stick around for more than a few dates, but that's not the point.

The point is that Lucy got her happily ever after and I didn't.

On the day of her wedding, I stood up at the front of a chapel to read out some words about love and eternity and how the best people always get what they deserve, but inside all I kept thinking was how Lucy had got every tiny thing she ever wanted. Every hope, every wish she'd collected in those ridiculous scrapbooks had come true. I used to tell myself it was the universe's way of apologising for the tumour, but in reality it was simply a case of her knowing what she wanted and never hesitating to go after it.

'Your mum's really outdone herself,' Isaac said as he approached my hiding place by the bar. Temperate House at Kew Gardens was resplendent even without all the added details stipulated by the bride. There was a live band, a chequered dance floor, a tower of vintage glasses filled with chilled champagne and all three bridesmaids, myself included, were wearing drop-waisted gowns embellished with gold thread that wouldn't have looked out of place in The Great Gatsby.

He'd changed since I last saw him: the angles of his face had sharpened and he filled out his pale blue suit in all the right ways. But the hair was still messy and the creases of his eyes when he smiled were the same. If only nothing else had changed.

I'd been avoiding Isaac ever since he introduced me to Kate, his super-smiley girlfriend, outside the church. She had legs like a thoroughbred and a mane of hair to match. She delighted in informing me that they'd met at hot yoga and been inseparable ever since. I'd had the stupid notion that Isaac and I could get drunk together, break bread, forgive one another for what once was said, but clearly he was more interested in chakras and downward dogs than reconnecting with me.

'I think it's because she realises no one will ever want to marry me, so she's given the whole pot of money to Lucy.' I drained my glass of champagne and swallowed away some of the bitterness in my words.

'You ok?' Isaac asked, watching as I picked up another glass filled with crisp bubbles of escapism.

'Fine,' I lied, because being surrounded by so much happiness did nothing but highlight how little of it I had for myself.

'Hello, my dear.' I turned around to find the simpering face of my Aunt Helen. The tip of her nose was flushed pink and there was a strong scent of lavender emanating from the same pastel dress she'd worn to my cousin's wedding three years before.

'Hello, Aunt Helen,' I said, bending forward to kiss her on each cheek. 'You remember Isaac?'

She held out her hand to his, smiling up at his freshly shaven face. 'Indeed I do. I understand you're a doctor now?'

'In theory,' Isaac said, shifting beside me, because we both knew what was coming. 'Still have a few more years before they'll let me hold a scalpel.'

'Your parents must be so proud.' She said this whilst looking me up and down. 'You look rather dazzling, my dear. But isn't that dress a little too revealing for a wedding?'

'Lucy chose it,' I said, taking a long sip of my drink and fighting the urge to chuck the rest of it in her judgemental face.

'Well, it's not as if you could upstage her,' she said, looking over to where Lucy was laughing with her equally glorious husband. 'She's simply radiant. Don't you think she's radiant, Isaac?'

'Always,' he said with a lopsided smile at me.

'Your mother says you've started playing piano in a hotel bar.' She said 'bar' as if it was something shameful, like I was working in a brothel or some other such place of disrepute.

'I like the freedom it gives me.'

'Too much freedom can be dangerous for a girl like you. If you were my daughter . . .' She left the insult hanging, because it was always the same conversation, the same reminder of what a disappointment I was. And it didn't just come from her, but all the other friends and relations who commented on why on earth didn't I want to do something with my life.

'Not everyone wants to be like Lucy.'

'Not everyone can be like Lucy.'

I nearly slapped her. I was so very close to screaming at her, at everyone in the room, that I was a person too. A person with feelings who didn't need to be constantly reminded how much better her sister's life was. If it hadn't been for Isaac looping his arm around my waist and tugging me away, no doubt I would have caused the exact kind of scene that my aunt seemed to expect from me.

'God, she's insufferable,' I said as we made our way outside and sat down on a grassy verge next to a rosebush.

'She's also a bored, frustrated housewife who has nothing better to do than criticise other people.'

'True.' Isaac knew all about Aunt Helen and the sacrifices she claimed to have made to support her husband's career.

'You never called,' he said without looking at me. A simple enough statement, but with so much more in between the words.

'I didn't know what to say.' I couldn't tell him the real reason, but knowing Isaac, he already knew. He'd graduated from university, top of his class, and was now carving out a career which only the very best kind of people were capable of.

It felt like everyone I knew was marching ahead, charging towards a bright and successful future, whereas I was still stuck in the same place I'd been stuck in since I was eighteen.

'Don't you want something more than teaching piano?'

'Of course I do, Isaac. But that's hardly an option for me.'

'Why not? Your parents would help.'

I wasn't convinced that they would. They never said anything about me choosing not to go to university or doing anything at all meaningful with my life, but then I never gave them the chance to.

'I don't want to fight with you, Isaac.'

'No. You want to keep running away.'

'Whenever I see anyone from my past, I tell myself it will be different next time. That at some point I'll figure out a way to be happy.'

He didn't reply. Just sat and waited for me to keep talking. I had this fantasy that one day I'd disappear somewhere. Paris, perhaps. I would study at the Sorbonne, learn how to be as chic and elegant as the French and fall in love with someone handsome and rich. Then I'd come back transformed, the veritable swan, and nobody would ever look at me the way my aunt just had.

'But it's like even though I'm not the same person, even though I want to try and start again, everyone still sees me as Beth the screw-up.'

'Then prove them wrong.'

I so badly wanted to agree with him. To throw up my hands, say 'sod it' and start making plans for my shiny new life. But if I was being completely honest, I had no idea what that life might look like.

'Did you hear about SuperKing?' I asked, although the question was redundant because even if their demise hadn't been plastered across the front page of every newspaper, I'm sure Isaac would have found out.

'Serves the bastard right,' he said, finishing his drink and then lying down on the grass. I lay down next to him, turned my face towards his and willed him to do the same. 'Did he ever try to contact you?' he asked, staring straight up at the sky.

'No.'

'I thought he would.'

'Why?'

'Why do you think?' He looked straight at me, two brown eyes flicking between mine.

'He's never going to apologise for what he did.'

'Are you?'

'You know I didn't mean it, Isaac,' I said, sitting up and hugging my knees to my chest. It wasn't an apology, and I knew I should be saying sorry, clearing the air, paving the way towards us being friends again. But the sight of him with someone else, someone who clearly made him happy, made me think that perhaps he was better off without me in his life.

'We used to be friends,' he said, sitting up and leaning against me. 'Best friends.'

'I know.' I bit down on my bottom lip as I breathed in the scent of his skin. It's a scent I had smelt a thousand times before, but right then it seemed to be making me feel all kinds of feelings that I didn't know what to do with.

I'd thought about it more than I probably should have over the years, asking myself whether it would have been so much easier if Isaac and I actually fancied one another. I'd also thought about that night he went with me to one of Tristan's gigs, when I looked at him, properly, and saw a completely different person to the one who had been there before.

'But things change. People change, Isaac. And do we really have anything in common any more? I mean, when was the last time you played guitar or stayed up all night listening to "Kashmir" on repeat?' When was the last time I'd listened to any of the songs that were like the musical score to the film that was my life? When was the last time I'd sat down at a piano and played something that I had written?

I still woke in the middle of the night, music and words pulling me from my dreams. But instead of sneaking downstairs to hear them played out loud on Dad's piano, or cycling over to Isaac's to ask him to help me figure out the chorus, I would turn over and pray for sleep to claim me once more.

'It wasn't just about the music, Beth,' he said, his face only inches from mine.

We used to have so much: an understanding that meant he knew what I was thinking even before I'd said it. Sometimes I barely even got halfway through the first verse of a new song before he was harmonising with his voice, or picking out some different chords for us to try. It was instinctive and incredible and yet now it was gone because I'd taken it for granted.

'What if it was worth the risk?' I said, more to myself than him, because it was a question that had lingered in my mind for years. Everyone always assumed we were sleeping with each other, but I always told myself not to even try, because losing my best friend would be too painful if it went wrong.

'There you are.' We both jumped, literally jumped and sprang apart as if we'd been stuck with a red-hot poker and I looked up to see Kate smiling down at us. 'I've been looking everywhere for you.'

'Hi,' Isaac said as he got to his feet. 'Beth and I were just . . .'

'They're about to have their first dance,' she said as the sound of music filtered out to us.

'Oh. Right. Ok.' Isaac stood and offered me his hand, but I ignored it because Kate was watching me with intent.

'He's one of the good guys,' I said as I brushed past her without looking back. 'Take care of him for me.'

25.

'Beth, wait,' Isaac says, running after me as I leave the pub. 'Were you just going to leave without saying goodbye?'

'Sorry, I just suddenly felt completely out of place.' I need to talk to him, but I can't get the sight of him and Kate out of my mind.

'Did you solve the clue?' he asks before I can figure out where to begin.

'No.' In truth, I'd forgotten all about that stupid violin, ever since Tristan told me what Lucy did. 'No,' I say again, and then suddenly I'm crying, really crying. The sort of crying that bunches tight in your stomach and makes it hard to breathe.

'Beth?' Isaac says, stepping toward me. 'Beth, what's wrong?'

'Lucy did it.'

'Did what?' he says, searching my eyes for a clue.

'Gave Tristan the tape with "Hyacinth Girl" on it.'

'What?' He runs his hands through his hair, then starts pacing up and down. 'That makes no sense. Why would she . . . ?'

'She was screwing him. Or he was screwing her. It doesn't really matter.'

'Christ. When was this?'

'I don't know when it started. I only found out the night of SuperKing's gig at the Dome.'

'And you've never told me because . . . ?'

'Because I was embarrassed, ok? And angry. Because once again Lucy got exactly what she wanted and I didn't.'

He doesn't say anything, just stands there looking at me, and I want to peer inside his mind, listen in on all the thoughts he is having. Is he angry I didn't tell him about Lucy and Tristan, or wondering, just like I am, why Lucy never told me about the tape?

'Did she know what was on the tape?'

'I think so,' I say with a sniff. 'But Tristan told her I'd said it was ok for him to have it.'

'And she believed him?'

'It's not her fault, Isaac. It's mine.'

'How is it your fault?'

'Because, in all honesty, if it meant I could have been part of the band, I would have given him "Hyacinth Girl" anyway.'

'But it wasn't just yours to give.'

It's what has plagued me ever since I found out what Lucy did, the knowledge that at some point I probably would have given away the most perfect of songs, which Isaac and I created together, because I was so desperate to be a part of something that didn't belong to me in the first place.

'I know!' I shout the words, then close my eyes, take a breath, because I can't keep fighting with Isaac. I can't keep fighting about what happened all those years ago. 'I know all this now, just as I know I was an idiot to have ever thought someone like Tristan would be interested in someone like me.'

'Beth . . .'

'No, it's true,' I say, wiping away the tears that just won't stop, because this is what they call acceptance, isn't it? Taking responsibility for your actions because, ultimately, we all have a choice, no matter who we end up trying to blame. Nobody forced me to write those songs, to skip school and pour all of my focus on to Tristan. 'I was young and naive and so openly in love with him. But he didn't care about me. All he cared about was becoming rich and famous.'

I sit down on the edge of the pavement and Isaac sits beside me, just like he used to when we were young. It reminds me of all the conversations we had whilst playing music and dreaming of a future so full of possibilities. It also makes me sad to think how different that future turned out to be.

'I heard he had a meltdown,' he says, and I turn my head to look at him. 'Like, put in rehab sort of meltdown.'

'When?'

'When they were dropped from Euphoric. I mean, must have been tough to go from rock god to nobody overnight.'

I smile, only because this is the exact same thing Sam said to me, and it feels like a lifetime ago but is, in fact, mere weeks.

'I thought . . .' I drop my head to my knees because this is all a bit much to process. 'I thought it would be different, seeing him again.'

'Different how?' Isaac asks, knocking his leg against mine, but I don't lift my head. I can't, not yet.

'I don't really know,' I say, looking at all the dirt gathered in the gutter. It makes me think of Lucy, of how we would lie in the back garden with our cheeks to the ground, searching for ladybirds and fairies in amongst the blades of grass.

'Do you still have feelings for him?'

'No.' I sit back up and wipe the palms of my hands over my trousers. 'I mean sure, but not like that. If anything, I feel sorry for him.'

'You do?' Isaac bends his head down and around to meet my eye. 'Wow, if it was me he confessed to about stealing our song, a song that went on to sell millions worldwide, I might add, I would have punched him clean out.'

'And then one day he woke up and had nothing.' I never wanted to be famous, but I know only too well how much it hurts to have the thing you love most of all taken away from you, suddenly and without warning.

'Don't do that,' Isaac says, and I can't figure out if he's angry or disappointed. 'Don't give him your pity. He still had more than he ever should have because of you.'

'But was it though? Was it really because of my songs or just the way he sang them? I mean, Dad always said . . .'

'Your dad knows as well as anyone that even Beyoncé is nothing without the music.' He gets to his feet and offers me his hand.

We head north, through the quietening streets, neither of us saying anything, but our feet fall into step as we walk.

'Why do you think she did it, Isaac?' I ask as we stop at a crossroads.

'Gave him "Hyacinth Girl"?' he says, looking up and down the street and then taking me by the hand as we cross the road.

'No, why did she send me a box of memories instead of telling me herself?' He's still holding on to my hand and I can't help but hope he isn't going to let go. 'I mean, she must have known, or at least guessed, what she'd done when they released it as a single.'

'You never told me about her and Tristan.'

'True,' I say as we walk along the back streets of suburbia. Most of the windows are dark, but there's a light from an attic window that's open and I can hear the soft sound of a guitar being played. 'But what happened with the song is different.'

'Is it though?' We come to a stop by a row of black railings, beyond which is a park I last walked through months ago whilst on the phone to my mother, talking about Lucy. 'Maybe she never found a way to tell you the truth. But maybe . . .' he says, taking hold of both my hands and giving them a squeeze, and I just know he's going to tell me something I don't want to hear.

'Maybe it's also because she knew that "Hyacinth Girl" would have died without him.'

My first thought is, how dare he? How dare he forgive Tristan, and therefore Lucy, for what they did? Then I think back to the night when I went to a party, sat down at a piano and played the song I was too scared to sing in front of strangers, even with the help of my best friend.

'You always put Lucy on a pedestal,' he says, and I take my hands from his, reach behind me and curl them around the railings. 'Believed her to be perfect. But she was just as broken as the rest of us.'

I think about Lucy's drinking. About all the boys she gave herself to, the pills she took to keep her awake in order to study. She was determined not to let something as trivial as a tumour stop her from becoming everything she'd ever dreamt of, but somewhere along the line it made her obsessive, self-centred even.

'I'm so angry with her for dying, Isaac,' I say. 'Because I'll never be able to ask her what really happened.'

'Does it even matter any more?'

'I don't know if I can do this,' I whisper, and I see his jaw tighten.

'By "this", you mean us?'

'No, I've kind of realised that part's up to you.' I search his face for an answer I'm terrified to know. 'But I think Lucy wants me to take back control of my life. I think she wants me to stop ignoring all the songs that are still running around my mind.'

Harry told me to face my fears and then sent me a quote from a play Lucy wanted me to remember. Not just the play, but the time in my life when I was supposed to be concentrating on my future. And not just the exams, but all the music I was supposed to be writing – for me, instead of for Tristan.

'And how are you planning on doing that exactly?'

'I have no idea.'

'What is it you're afraid of?' Isaac asks, and of course he already knows what it is I'm thinking. He's always known.

'What happens if I screw up?'

'Then you try again.'

'And if that doesn't work?'

'There's no rule to say how many chances you get, Beth. But maybe this time you shouldn't be in such a hurry to get to the finish line. Be the tortoise, not the hare, just like it says in the book Lucy left for you.'

Lucy brought me to Isaac because she wanted me to remember what happened – all of it, not just the music. But remembering has done nothing other than remind me how easy it is for a heart to break.

I keep waiting for something to happen, for one thing to come along that changes my life.

'Isaac,' I say, and he steps closer, making my heart squeeze. 'You've been amazing.'

'But?' His face crumples and I hate myself for what I'm about to do.

'But you need to go back to Kate.'

'I thought you said it was up to me?'

'It is.' I stand on tiptoe to place a kiss on his cheek. 'But first I need to figure out a way to do this on my own.'

Back at the flat, I step into the shower, turn the water on full and rub soap into my hair and skin. Over and over I scrub, watching my body turn pink and blotchy. But just like Lady Macbeth, no amount of water can wash away the pain and so I slip to the floor, wrap my arms around my knees and close my eyes.

Countless images flood my brain: of my parents, Isaac and, of course, Lucy. All the moments she wanted me to remember feel like they belong not just to another person, but another lifetime. Like they're from a storybook or a film and not based in reality.

The water runs cold, mixing with my tears, but I don't know if I have the strength to stand, let alone try to figure out what I'm supposed to do now.

'I'm sorry, Lucy,' I whisper as I wrap myself in a towel and step across the hall into my bedroom. The sound of a siren flashes past the open window, like a bolt of lightning that appears and disappears before your eyes.

Sitting on the edge of the bed, I flip my hair over my head and use my hands to lift and squeeze all my curls. As I do so, my eye falls on the notebook Lucy asked me to write down all the memories in. It's tucked underneath the bed, just like the box in which I kept all the songs I once wrote.

You have to stop hiding, I think to myself as my hand reaches out. I have to stop hiding all my hopes and dreams in a dusty space where no one would care to look.

Flicking through the pages, my eyes fall on a couple of lines scribbled in the margin that I don't remember writing:

> Strawberry skies and mixed up lies,
> They make me think of you.

As I read the words, a familiar memory appears in my mind of a night when Isaac and I lay in a field full of poppies and thought we had nothing to worry about at all.

I turn the page, look at all the lyrics I've hidden in between the moments my sister asked me not to forget. The lyrics have been there all along, waiting for me to pay attention.

Going over to my nightstand, I open the drawer and look down at all the scraps of paper on which I would write a few words when they crept into my dreams and then shut them away again. Underneath is a fuchsia-pink notebook that contains the words to all the songs on the album that made Tristan a star. It's a notebook I could have given to a lawyer, if I'd had the courage to fight. A reminder, perhaps, of what could have been, of what I was too afraid to try and find again.

Taped to the inside front cover is a photo of Lucy and me as children, standing in the river with dresses tucked into our knickers. It's not unexpected, I knew it was there, but the sight of us so young and carefree makes me cry all over again.

Going across to the bookcase, I take down both of the puzzle boxes she left me, open them up and lay out all the clues on the floor. It doesn't look like much, just a few random objects that have no obvious connection. But each and every single one was about me. About a girl who carried music in her soul and dared to dream that one day she might be good enough to have her songs played on the radio.

And I was good enough. Lucy knew it, Isaac knew it. Seems like the only person who didn't was me. Sitting on the floor surrounded by all these forgotten moments, I open up my soul and finally, finally let go of all the grief. For my sister, for who I used to be, but mostly for the creativity I did everything I could to forget but which was yearning to break free. Just like the monster Dad always spoke about, a little creature who was there all along, begging me not to forget.

'I wish you were here,' I say, staring down at the photograph. 'I wish you were here so you could tell me what to do.'

I already did.

Her voice is in my head, as bright and clear as if she really were here with me, telling me to follow all the clues back to where it all began.

'Ok,' I say, looking around for my phone and noticing a new message from Isaac.

Tristan didn't steal everything from you.

As well as the message, there's a link to a video entitled 'Encore'.

You were always destined to write, Beth. It's a talent that shouldn't be kept in a box and hidden away, no matter how terrifying it may seem.

I already know what's on the video, the title alone gives it away. I also know what it is that he thinks I should do, what he's always thought but I was too scared to even try.

What's the worst that could happen? I mean, the worst has already happened, over and over again. And I owe it to the girl who would wake in the night and feel compelled to sit down and play the music in her soul. I owe her a second chance at making her dreams come true.

I remember the day Dad took Lucy and me down to the river, to where he'd tied a rope to the branch of a tree, long enough to swing us right out into the centre of the current. Lucy stood on the riverbank, toes curling into the damp grass and chewing on a thumbnail whilst I stripped off to just my pants. A second later, and before Dad could even tell us to be careful, I'd grabbed hold of the rope and gone running towards the water.

The air whizzed past my face as my feet left the ground and I cried out like a banshee, the sound startling a rabbit on the opposite bank. I felt the rope tighten, looked down to the river below and let go. For a split second it felt like I was suspended in mid-air, hovering like a hummingbird, and then I was falling, falling, before splashing into the water, the sudden hit of cold making me feel more alive than ever before.

When my head broke the surface, I turned to see Dad and Lucy, arms wrapped around one another and laughing. We spent all afternoon at the river, taking it in turns to launch ourselves into the current then stumbling home tired but exhilarated.

Later that evening, Lucy came into my room and sat on the end of my bed. She asked me if I'd even stopped to consider what might happen if the rope had broken, and I simply smiled and said no, because all I'd been able to think about in the moment was what it might feel like to be able to fly.

I never used to be afraid, which is what my sister has been trying to remind me of all along.

This one's for you, Lucy, I think as I copy and paste the link on to YouTube. She may never get to hear what's on that video, she may never know what it is that she's done, but it helps, just a little, to know that I'm only doing it because of her.

I should call Isaac. Tell him what I've done. Instead, I dial the first number I was ever told to remember. I hold my breath as the connection is made, close my eyes as the phone rings on the other end of the line. I picture him getting up from the sofa, or coming in from the garden to answer my call, and it's all I can do not to cry when he finally picks up and says hello.

'Dad?'

'Beth? Is everything ok?'

'No. Not really.' With one last glance around the space I've imprisoned myself in for far too long, I finally find the courage to do what I couldn't when I was eighteen. 'I need your help, Dad. I need to come home.'

26.

Four months ago . . .

I still remember where I was when Mum called me – standing in the freezer aisle of my local supermarket trying to decide if it was acceptable to have pizza for dinner three days in a row.

'Where are you?' she said when I picked up.

'Hello to you too, Mum.'

'It's Lucy.'

Two words, that's all it took for the world to tilt on its axis and flood my brain with all kinds of fear. I nearly dropped the basket I was holding, was only vaguely aware of someone asking me to move so they could get to the freezer behind me.

'Is she ok?'

'She collapsed whilst giving a lecture. Dehydrated. Spent the night in hospital.'

'But she's all right now?' Knowing Lucy, she'd been inhaling coffee and little else in the days before her lecture. She'd passed out a couple of times during her A Levels, making me swear not to tell Mum, and I convinced myself it was just Lucy putting too much pressure on herself, as per usual.

'Is that all you can say?'

'What do you want me to say?'

'Do you have any idea what it's like?' Her voice went up about an octave and I heard the sound of a door being slammed. 'Every time the phone rings, I flinch. Whenever Lucy tells me she's feeling run down or has a cold, my mind skips over all the rational parts and heads straight for the worst-case scenario.'

'Mum, it's fine,' I said, abandoning my basket and walking out of the supermarket. 'She'll be fine.'

'You don't know that, Elizabeth.' There was the scrape of chair and the distant hum of a mower, rewarding me with a picture of her sitting in the garden. It was small comfort, knowing where she was, and it made me wonder where Lucy was, right in that second. Because none of us had known if she would wake up after the operation and still be the same Lucy we knew and loved. The surgeon warned us of the risks – even without taking out the whole tumour, Lucy could have lost the power of speech or been mentally impacted in some way.

It was terrifying, the idea that even Lucy's luck could run out at any moment. Deep down I knew that touching wood or saluting magpies wouldn't change anything, that nobody really had that sort of power over the universe, but if I didn't do it and something bad happened, would that somehow make it my fault?

'I should have known,' Mum said, and I heard the sorrow in her voice.

'Known what?'

'I should have known it wasn't just hormones and headaches. If I'd done something sooner . . .'

'It wasn't your fault, Mum.'

'Perhaps not,' she said with a drawn-out sigh. 'But that doesn't make it any easier for me to forgive myself for what she had to go through.'

'We all went through it. You more than anyone.' Mum slept in the hospital practically every night until Lucy was discharged. Dad and

I were at home, propping one another up with music and junk food, which felt exciting but also wrong, because Lucy wasn't there with us.

Even when Lucy came home, it was Mum who shouldered the burden of looking after her. I might have read her stories and played her some songs, but Mum was the one who catalogued every tablet she took, every morsel of food she ate and how many steps she managed before collapsing.

'You two used to be so close. What happened?'

I stopped still in the middle of the pavement. I'd been walking without any concern as to where I was going, and I was only a little bit surprised to find myself by the boating lake in the park. Lucy and I used to take all kinds of things down to the river to see how far they could sail – home-made paper boats that sunk before they'd gone anywhere, plastic bowls that Mum used for baking and even Lucy's beloved dolls, one of which got swept down the river too quickly for us to catch.

We used to do everything together, but then the tumour, and later Tristan, pulled us apart.

'She moved on with her life,' I said. Lucy never looked back, never regretted a thing. Unlike me.

'Call her,' Mum said. 'I don't care what you two are still fighting about, you need to call her. Because none of us knows how much time we have left.'

As soon as I stepped inside the front door of Lucy's home I knew something was off. It wasn't any one thing that made me suspicious – there was a scented candle on the table in the hall, which couldn't disguise the scent of roasting meat emanating from the kitchen, along with something I recognised but was unable to name. It wasn't the too bright smile on Harry's face as he relieved me of my overnight bag and the bottle of wine I'd bought at Paddington Station. Nor was it the sound *of Miles Davis spilling from the stereo in the living room, where a fire was burning despite the unseasonably warm breeze I could still feel on the backs of my legs as Harry closed the front door.*

'Where's Lucy?' I asked, the words sounding strange, and the split second before Harry told me she was in the garden I realised what it was I could smell under roast chicken and melting wax. Antiseptic. More specifically, the kind Mum always used to scrub clean the bathroom whenever anyone was sick.

I didn't want to go and find my sister, had absolutely no desire to walk through the kitchen to see a table laid for three. Nor did I want to catch a glimpse of Lucy sitting on the back porch, her shoulders covered by a cashmere shawl and her platinum hair hidden underneath a peacock-blue scarf.

Because if I did go and sit next to her, if I did look at her sunken but still beautiful face, then I would know. And there's no going back once you know. It's not possible to unsee or unhear something just because it's too painful to bear.

'It's grown back?' I said, and it wasn't a question I wanted answering, but Lucy nodded at me anyway.

'Don't cry,' she said, cupping my face in her hands and resting her forehead against my own. I placed my hands on hers, registering the paper-thin skin under which I could feel her bones. It made me think of when she was recuperating after her operation, relearning all the things once taken for granted, when she would sit next to me at the piano and feel my fingers play.

'I don't know what else to do,' I said, because I'd never been any good at making things better or finding the right words to say.

'You carry on.'

'I can't. I don't know how without you.' I didn't want to. I didn't want to even contemplate for one second what my world would be like without her. I'd done it once before, lived through the highs and lows and watched my parents fall apart. And that was when she survived.

That was when she made it through the operation, spent weeks in the hospital and then several more at home. That's when the worst thing that happened was she abandoned me in favour of her friends. I would have taken that pain, that sorrow, all over again, because at least she was still alive.

'If anyone can do it, forge a new life out of one you fell into, it's you.'

'You should have let them cut it all out,' I said, sniffing loudly and staring out across the lawn. I needed someone to blame. I needed someone to fix her, even though I already knew it was impossible.

'I've had a wonderful life.'

'It's not enough.'

'It has to be.'

I stood up, then sat back down again, chewing at my thumbnail and kicking at the ground, wishing there was something I could break.

'It should be me instead of you.' I always thought this, from the very second I saw her by the river, doubled over in pain and speaking in tongues. I always believed that Lucy didn't deserve to get sick or fall over and scuff her knee because she was always so very, very good. 'You're the extraordinary one. You're the one who's done everything you're supposed to.'

'And yet I still wish I could be as brilliant, as talented, as you.' She put her hand on my arm and I glanced at her incredible face, sensing the pain, the fear behind her eyes. I wondered if she could see that fear reflected in my own.

'I'm not that person any more.'

'But you could be. You've always been incredible, Beth, but you never believed it.'

It felt like she was asking something of me that I couldn't give. As if she could keep living vicariously through her little sister, despite the fact I'd never amounted to anything at all.

'Seems little point, now.' I kicked again at the ground, upending a stone and watching a tiny beetle scurrying away. It made me think of Isaac, of a school trip we once went on to Brussels. We were on a tour of the Royal Palace when he stopped and looked up. Everyone else moved around him, but I stood by his side, craning my neck to gaze upon a ceiling that seemed to be covered in emeralds.

'They're beetle carcasses,' he said. 'Over a million of them.'

If it hadn't been Isaac telling me, I would have laughed, walked away and never given it any more thought. But he was always so good at making me look closer, at appreciating the little things the world had to offer. He was a firm believer in both the beauty and the resilience of nature, but in that moment, sitting next to my sister and searching for something to say, all I could think was how cruel and stupid nature could be.

'I need to know you'll be ok,' Lucy said.

'How? How can I be ok if you're . . .' I couldn't bring myself to say it, because then it would be true.

'Nobody stays the same their whole life, Beth. And you're stronger than you think. Every time life's thrown something at you, you've got back up and started again.'

'It feels like all I've done is run away.'

'So stop running.'

'And then what?'

'Then,' she said with a long, sad sigh, 'then perhaps you'll decide to write down all those songs I know you still carry around in your head.'

I didn't say anything, because she was right. I have always heard music in everything, from the roar of a motorbike engine to the turn of wing as swallows dipped through the sky. Or water flowing over a brook and the sound a girl makes as she lets go of a rope before crashing into the river below. Even the soft exhalation of breath a boy would take in the very moment before he started to play his guitar. It's there all the time, but I don't know how to do it any more, because every single time I try I'm reminded of what happened.

'Did you know,' Lucy said, shifting in her seat, and I adjusted her blanket, made sure she was all tucked in, just like I did when she spent all those days recuperating on our sofa, 'that the sound archive in the British Library only exists because of a lost song?'

I shook my head, no, and she smiled at me, which made a piece of my heart fall away, because how many more smiles did she have?

'In 1930, a man named Patrick Saul went into a music shop in London and asked for a gramophone recording of a violin sonata, only to be told that it was out of print. The song had effectively been deleted. He then went to the British Library, but there was nothing there either. The idea that music could disappear, he later said, was like experiencing death, and so he resolved to do something about it.'

'I'm guessing there's a point to this story?'

'Don't be such a philistine,' she said, laughing at me and punching me lightly on the arm. I could feel the soft imprint of her fist the moment she took it away, and I had to stop myself from grabbing on to her, just like I did in that hospital waiting room, and asking her not to die. 'Anyway, the point is that I would hate for all of your songs to disappear.'

'They didn't. That was the whole problem.'

'I'm not talking about Galaxy of Angels,' she said with a dismissive wave of her hand. 'I mean, sure, that album was incredible, but it wasn't the real you.'

'It was easier then.'

'Why?'

'Because . . . because I used to have something to write about.'

Lucy didn't say anything, and so we just sat, listening to the wind and unable to say all the things we should have been saying.

'Of all the sounds Patrick Saul catalogued,' she suddenly said with a laugh, 'his favourite was the mating call of a haddock.'

240

'A haddock?'

'Yes. Of all those thousands of recordings, he said he liked the fish the best.' And then she was laughing so hard that there were tears streaming down her face and I found myself joining in, even though I couldn't think of a single thing to be happy about.

My mind flooded with a lifetime of memories, pictures of the past that all included her. The idea of carrying on, of living in a world, making new memories, having the audacity to create music when she wasn't there to hear it was just too much.

'I'm sorry,' she said, resting her forehead against my own, and I breathed her in, felt the fear and the fury mixing inside me because I didn't know how many more times I'd ever get to be with her.

'I know,' I said, because Tristan and SuperKing and everything else I thought I'd suffered from simply wasn't important any more.

'I need to tell you something,' she said, sitting back and looking straight at me. 'It's about Tristan.' Whatever it was, I knew it couldn't be worse than the tumour, but there were tears in her eyes and in that moment I simply didn't want to hear whatever confession she thought she needed to make.

'I can't,' I said, rising from the chair I'd only just sat down in.

'I never meant to hurt you, Beth. I didn't know what I'd done until it was too late.' Lucy reached out her hand, but I didn't take it, because if she was trying to make things right between us, to tie up all those pesky loose ends, then it meant she was running out of time.

'I'm sorry,' I said as I turned and fled. The two most pathetic words I'd ever uttered, completely pointless and inadequate.

'Beth?' Harry said as I rushed past him in the kitchen, ignoring the fact he was carving a chicken and adding extra butter to the mashed potatoes. I laughed at the irony, a derisory laugh because Lucy and I had once discussed what we might choose to eat if we knew we were about to die. Hers was pepperoni pizza with extra chillies on the side, followed by apple pie. Mine was roast chicken and mashed potato with lashings of gravy and categorically no carrots.

Pausing in the hallway to collect my bag, I caught sight of myself in the mirror, then ducked my head in shame. Without looking back, I opened the front door and left.

I walked and cried, then walked and cried some more, stopping only when I reached the river. A mother and her young child were down by the water's edge, throwing bread to the ducks, which were fighting one another for crumbs. I watched as a couple of rowers skimmed past, their oars barely making a sound as they broke the surface. It was an ordinary day, filled with ordinary people doing ordinary things. Did none of them feel any pain, were none of them struggling under the weight of repressed grief, or were they just better at hiding it than me?

My head turned as a car sped along the road towards me, and for a split second I contemplated stepping out on to the tarmac. But it would be wrong; it would be selfishly destructive and not just for my family, but for whomever was driving that car. The car's stereo was turned up loud, the words of the only Oasis song Lucy knew lingering in the air long after the car had skidded around the corner.

'Don't look back in anger.' I said the words, but had no desire to listen. In that moment, I didn't think I could bear to listen to music ever again, because it would all remind me of her.

27.

Being back in my childhood home is strange and discomforting but also so very familiar. Everything looks and smells and sounds the same – from the scent of detergent on my bed linen to the gurgle of pipes and Dad padding downstairs to put the kettle on first thing every morning. I have slept more deeply, more soundly, than I have in years. Even though I still dream of Lucy, still picture her face every morning when I wake, it doesn't sting quite so sharply because she's here, stitched into the walls and the furniture and all the memories contained in this house.

I've been here a little over a week and the three of us have settled into the semblance of a routine. Domestic bliss, or at least I'm pretending it is – my days are filled with gardening, hanging out the washing, swimming every day in the local pool, cycling along familiar lanes and never once turning down the road that leads to the house where Isaac used to live.

A week in and my parents and I seem to have found a quiet sort of understanding, but I know I'm still hiding, still running from my life. But is being here any different from when I first moved up to London, thinking that somehow I could run away from what I'd done?

Yesterday Mum and I baked a lemon cake together. Such a simple thing, but I don't think we've ever done it before, just us two.

It made me think of Lucy, no doubt made Mum think of her too, and so I decided to show her and Dad the puzzle box. I think they need to know the truth of what has happened. I think I'm ready to tell them everything.

They're sitting in the back garden, drinking tea and eating the lemon cake Mum and I baked, when I come out, holding the box.

'When I came back here the last time,' I say, aware that my hands are shaking as I set the box down on the garden table, 'I was looking for something.'

'A book, yes,' Dad says as he turns the box around.

'But I never told you why.'

'You rarely tell us why you do the things you do,' Mum says, setting down her cup in its matching saucer.

'It's from Lucy.'

'What is?' Her hand comes up to her neck, fingers fiddling with the thin gold chain that always hangs there.

'The box.'

'But how?'

'She left it with Harry, who sent it to me.'

Mum looks away, staring out at nothing but no doubt picturing her elder girl.

'What was inside?' Dad asks.

'A card,' I say, swallowing away the lump in my throat. 'And a message.'

'A treasure hunt?' Dad says with a smile, and there's the smallest of glints in his eye, a pinch of excitement I haven't seen for a while. 'How does the box link to the book?'

I take the box from him, press down on the dragon's eye then hand it back, let him figure out the rest. Inside is the card, but also the photos, the postcard, all the clues and reminders Lucy wanted me to find.

'What does it all mean?'

'I think . . .' I say, then stop and take a breath, because I've been going over and over this for days. 'I think it's about a song I wrote.'

'"Hyacinth Girl",' Dad says.

'Yes. How did you . . . ?'

'Wait there,' he says, springing from his seat and disappearing back into the house.

'Why didn't you show us before?' Mum says, picking up each item in turn.

'I didn't want to hurt you more than I already have.'

'And what about you? If the contents of this box are anything to go by, I'd guess there's more than one reason you came home?'

'It's . . .' I begin, but then the words get caught around my heart because I've been trying not to think about it, about Isaac.

'Oh, Beth,' Mum says, reaching across the table for my hand, and it's enough to make me start crying. Really crying. Great, heaving sobs, tears that blur my vision and snorts that flow through my nose. She comes to sit beside me and pulls me close, just like she did when I was little; it's been so long since she touched me, let alone embraced me, but it all feels so wonderfully familiar, and safe.

'I'm sorry, Mum,' I stutter between my sobs, and when I look up at her I see she's been crying too. 'I'm so sorry for everything.'

'I know, my love. I'm sorry too.'

'I'm sorry for always shutting you out. But Lucy was so perfect, it felt like there was never any room left for me.'

'Is that . . .' Mum says, staring at me, then tilting back her head and blinking rapidly. The silence hangs between us and I busy myself with tidying up. 'You shouldn't think like that,' she says, resting her hand on my own. 'I know I probably focused too much on your sister, and I'm sorry for how that must have made you feel. And for not realising you needed my help just as much as Lucy, I truly am sorry.'

'I was so scared,' I say, the tears falling all over again. 'I was so scared of anything bad happening that I forgot how to try.'

'Everything all right?' Dad says as he comes back to the table. He's wearing a smile as he looks between us, hovering next to a chair as if he's reluctant to disturb this moment between Mum and me.

'I think so,' Mum says, wiping a tear from my cheek and tucking a strand of hair behind my ear.

'Good. Right then,' he says, putting another box, this one made from cardboard, on the table and taking off its lid.

I peer inside, discover dozens of tiny cassettes, each with a white sticky label attached to the front. I take one out, glance at the label then take out all the rest and line them up in date order. It's all the songs I wrote and recorded then stored away in a box. I can hear them, the melodies and words are so clear in my mind, along with the exact time and place I was in when I wrote them.

'It's still missing,' I say, going along the line, my hand pausing between the cassette called 'Silver Moon' and another with 'Messy Beginnings' crossed out and 'Hopeful Sunsets' written underneath.

Do I tell them what Lucy did, albeit inadvertently? But what good would it do?

'"Hyacinth Girl",' Dad says, taking out the last item from the box and passing it to me. It would seem he knows, perhaps not everything, but enough for him to realise that this is linked to what Tristan did.

It's a book. *The* book, the one that Lucy wanted me to find, and I realise it's no coincidence that it's been hiding alongside all the evidence of how once upon a time I actually knew what I wanted to do with my life.

'What is it?' Mum asks, leaning closer to read the book's title.

'Eliot,' I say, flicking through the pages in search of a particular poem. 'Lucy's favourite.'

'Yes,' Mum says, staying my hand and going back to the inside front cover, where a name and date are written. 'But she only ever came across him because of you.'

'Elizabeth Anastasia Franks,' I say, reading out my own name. This was my copy, the one I used to keep under my pillow and read every night before bed. Turning the page, I look at all the scribbles in the margin, all the phrases and stanzas underlined, done by my own hand. I keep turning, and as I do, I'm given a memory, one I haven't thought of in a while.

It was around the time Lucy got sick, when she'd ask me to read to her because staring at the TV for too long made her head hurt even more. I remember cycling to the library, eager to bring back something new and extraordinary, a story my sister had never heard before.

The librarian came across me as I was trying to decide whether Jodi Picoult or James Herbert was the better choice for a girl who'd had her brain sliced open. She asked me what I was looking for and I replied 'something completely different', to which her response was to lead me into the far corner of the library, reach on to one of the topmost shelves and hand me a book.

'What's it about?' I asked, and she smiled and said, 'You'll see.'

I began to read, eyes wide in disbelief as I took in words I understood but had never known could be put together in such a way.

'It's like music,' I gasped, and the librarian smiled again, wider this time.

'Look,' Dad says, pointing to a particular page. It's part of a poem about love and loss, the one Lucy based her PhD thesis on. Several sections are underlined, there's a mass of tiny stars drawn in the top-right-hand corner, but there's also a bright red circle drawn around two words – "hyacinth girl" – and then an arrow sneaking to the side where I'd written *go to back of book*. I do as I'm told and discover the original verse of the song that seems to be what Lucy keeps leading me back to, again and again.

'Do you know,' Mum says, 'Lucy and I used to sit on the stairs and listen to you and your father play. She was always so in awe of your talent.'

'She was?'

'I always knew you were extraordinary, so much so that I didn't know what to do with it. And yet you always put Lucy first, always took care of her instead of yourself.'

'Do you remember when you had appendicitis?' Dad asks.

'Not really,' I reply with a frown, searching my mind for a memory that is there, but fuzzy around the edges.

'Yes!' Mum says with an explosive laugh. 'You walked around all day, not once complaining because it was Lucy's birthday party and you refused to miss out on cake.'

'The doctors said you were lucky it didn't burst.'

'And when you came round after the operation you started singing that song you made up years before about a dirty bear.'

They're both laughing now, and smiling and happier than I can remember seeing them for far too long.

'You used to walk around singing to the birds, to your dolls,' Mum says, placing one hand on my father's arm and smiling up at him, before looking back to me. 'You used to sing instead of talking sometimes, and not always in tune. Drove me insane.'

'Sorry.'

'No,' she says, fixing me with a look, but for once it's filled with love, not regret. 'I'm sorry. I wish I could have helped you somehow.'

'I thought I didn't need help back then.'

'And now?'

'I need to try again. For Lucy.'

'I think she would have wanted you to do it for you,' Mum says, placing one hand on my arm and giving it the gentlest of squeezes.

I put my own hand on top, registering the warmth of her skin and remembering how I used to smell her when I was little, incredulous of the fact that she was my mother and yet her arm smelt completely different to my own. I would also smell Lucy, follow her around and sniff the air to see if any trace of her was left behind. She would swat at me as if I were a fly, then laugh and run away as fast as she could, daring me to try and catch her.

'I miss her,' I say. 'All the time.'

'Me too,' Mum says, the words catching in her throat. 'We all do. But I'm starting to realise that she'll never truly be gone, because we will always remember her.'

'It's not the same.'

'Of course not,' Dad says, shifting in his seat. 'But we can't stop living or dreaming or wasting time doing nothing at all.'

'What if it's too late?'

Mum points at the puzzle box, then across at me. 'She sent you that for a reason.'

'I wish I knew what it was.' I thought it was performing in front of people. I thought it was about finding the courage to sing one of my songs my way, but it still feels as if there's one more piece of the puzzle I need to figure out.

Mum stands, places a kiss on my head that's so tender it makes me bite down on the inside of my cheek to stop myself from crying. 'I think you already do,' she says, picking up the tea tray. 'You become a different person when you play. It's as if music is the only thing that truly makes you happy, or understands you in a way none of us ever could, except perhaps your father.'

And Isaac, I think to myself.

Somewhere inside a phone is ringing, but I don't bother to get up. I turned my mobile off days ago, given that I don't have anyone to call. Dad gets up, trots into the house, and a moment later his head appears out the door.

'Beth? It's for you.'

'Me?' I gasp, pushing back my chair, and half walk, half run into the garden room then through to the hall. I try not to think who could be calling, because there are only a handful of people who know where I am, who know which number to dial.

'Hello?'

'Beth? It's Harry.'

'Oh.' I can't help but be morbidly disappointed, even though I have no clue what I would have said or done if it was Isaac on the other end of the line.

'You're home.'

'I am.' I sit on the bottom stair and rest my head against the wall. 'And?'

'And it's ok,' I say, taking a deep breath then letting it go again. 'It hurts, but the three of us are making waves. Small ones, but it's a start.'

'That's good. Anything else?'

He knew what was here all along. It should annoy me, the fact he deliberately didn't tell me what it was Lucy wanted me to find, and I'm only half surprised to discover that, actually, I'm kind of glad I didn't know from the very beginning.

'The recordings.'

'Have you listened to them yet?'

'No.'

'You may want to.' There's an edge to his voice and it makes me nervous, but in a good way, like a child on Christmas Eve, too excited to sleep.

'Why?'

'Look in the box, Beth.'

'I already did.'

'Look again. At the tail.'

'Hang on.' I put down the phone, jog back out to the garden, retrieve the box then jog back to the phone. Turning the box upside down, I follow the length of the dragon's tail, trace over the carved, iridescent scales with my fingertips, searching for a clue. The tail curls all the way along the bottom of the box then up and around one edge, where it comes to an end next to a single lotus flower. I press down at its centre, but nothing happens, and then I notice the faintest of lines, a space even, between the flower and the tail.

Going back along the tail, I find another line, just before it curls over the base. With a fingernail in each tiny gap, I pull upwards, laughing when the whole section of tail comes loose to reveal a small, thin compartment inside of which is a rolled-up piece of paper tied with string. Pulling the string apart, I unfurl the paper to discover it is in fact a photograph of Lucy and me. We're sitting in her back garden, our faces in profile, and her hair is hidden underneath a peacock-blue silk scarf.

It was the last time I ever saw her, a snapshot of an afternoon last October that I have no memory of being taken.

Picking up the receiver, I'm about to ask Harry why Lucy sent it to me when I notice there's something written on the back. The name is familiar, too familiar, and there's a prickling sensation at the base of my skull when I realise who it belongs to.

'Harry,' I say as I pick up the phone slowly and with care, because it feels like something momentous is about to happen. But I don't know if I'm ready, if I'm prepared to hear what he's about to tell me.

'Beth?' I swear there's a smile in his voice and I take a deep breath, let all the air out long and slow before I ask him the question he knows I'm going to ask.

'Why is Peter Lugosi's telephone number written on the back of a photo?'

'His dad was a record producer.'

'I know.' Tristan practically stalked him, begged Peter for the chance to meet with his dad.

'Peter's taken over the label.'

'And?'

'And Lucy asked me to send him the original copy of "Hyacinth Girl".'

'How? When?' The words are no more than a whisper, because it seems ridiculous to say them, to even give thought to the idea that Harry has just given me.

'She called Tristan. Convinced him that he no longer had any need for the tape. But that's not the point, Beth. Peter's expecting your call.'

'Why?'

'Jesus, Beth,' Harry says with a long-drawn-out sigh. 'You can be insufferably stupid sometimes.'

'No,' I say, rolling my eyes even though Harry can't see. 'I mean, why didn't you tell me about this before?'

There's a pause, and the sound of something I can't quite picture. Perhaps a chair being moved or a cupboard being closed. I want to ask him where he is, even though it bears no relevance to the conversation. But still, if he's in their kitchen, making himself a cup of tea and going about his day in the most ordinary of ways, it feels comforting somehow.

'Lucy didn't want me to, not before you were ready,' he says, and I hear the sound of a tap being turned on and I smile, then look back down at the photograph and the box. A box that I have had for weeks now but dismissed as soon as I found the first clue.

'But what if I'd found it straightaway?'

'You can't go back, Beth. You can't undo what's already been done.'

'I know, but . . .'

'Would you want to? If you could, would you really go back and skip through everything that's happened over these last few weeks?'

Yes. But also no. So much has happened, and yet really nothing at all, other than me admitting to myself that my darling sister was right all along.

'She wanted me to remember.'

'She wanted you to feel.'

There's a rippling sensation going through me, starting at my toes and spreading all the way up to rattle around inside my skull as I think of everything that has happened. I think of the clues, the memories, but most of all of something Lucy said to me the last time we saw one another. Something that makes the scrap of paper with a drawing of a fish, a train, a violin and a boy with a scar on his head suddenly make perfect sense.

My songs aren't lost, but they may as well be, having spent over eight years hidden under my childhood bed. This has all been Lucy's way of telling me that starting again may be as simple as remembering what I've already done.

'Look, Lucy had no way of knowing whether you'd find Peter's number straightaway. But she told me that a part of her hoped the universe might be on your side, just this once.'

'Harry . . .' I say, but I can't find the right words to tell him what it is I'm feeling.

'It's ok, Beth.' I can hear the sorrow, the relief, in his voice. 'Just promise me you'll call him.'

'I promise.' I hang up, look over at the photo of my beautiful sister on her wedding day, me behind her, helping her with her dress, and thinking that there's more than one person she would want me to call. He was there for me on the worst possible of days, a day when it felt as if I was at the very bottom. He's been here all along.

28.

Fourteen weeks ago . . .

Lucy died on the fifteenth of February, just after what is supposed to be the most romantic day of the year. It was a Wednesday, which meant nothing and everything all at once. I'd spoken to her only the day before and she'd talked about how Harry had taken her punting on the river and they'd played Pooh sticks, just like we used to when we were girls. I remember asking her if everything was ok, because her voice sounded tilted and strange. She told me everything was going to be all right and that she'd speak to me again soon.

The next morning, I sat on a train surrounded by strangers, hating every single one of them because they weren't her. It was the same journey I'd made countless times before, but I didn't want this one to end, because waiting for me in the station car park was my father. And seeing him, seeing the raw pain etched all over his face, meant that Lucy really was gone.

The days that followed all blurred and slipped into one – we ate, we slept (neither of which we did particularly well), we moved around the topic of Lucy with pinched words and inadequate hugs. Most of all, I remember the silence that lingered in the corners of rooms. Dad had turned the radio off to answer Harry's call and hadn't turned it back on since.

I woke early on the day of her funeral, crept downstairs and put the kettle on to boil. I laid the kitchen table, put some croissants in the oven then went into the garage, grabbed my bike and cycled all the way down to the river.

Sitting at the river's edge, I took out my phone and scrolled through all the messages from her. They were just words on a screen, but I could hear her voice, see the way her face would crinkle when she laughed, feel the touch of her hand on mine. And it was gone. All of her was gone.

Pulling off my boots and socks, I dipped my toes into the current, gasping as the chill shot straight up my legs and through my centre. It made me think of the day I came here after Tristan tossed me aside and I thought my heart would never heal. It also made me remember the day I found Lucy in this very spot, talking in riddles because of the tumour inside her brain.

But there was good here, too. The river had borne witness to so much of our lives, moments we didn't think to hold on to because we assumed there were countless more to come.

'Hey,' Isaac said as he came to sit beside me, and I leant into his warmth. I didn't ask how he knew where I'd be, nor why he came to find me. We just sat, watching the river as the sun rose higher in the sky.

At some point he stood, offered me his hand, and we walked back along the familiar path, him wheeling my bike and me unable to focus on anything more than putting one foot in front of the other. He waited in the hall as I went upstairs to change, helped me on with my coat and escorted me to the car.

The church was full of muted conversations and the scent of too many lilies. I nodded and smiled at all the condolence on offer, all the while pressing my fingernails so hard into my palms there would be tiny semicircles of pink for days to come. But I couldn't stop the tears that fell as I heard the opening bars to Bob Marley's 'Three Little Birds', and he started singing about how every little thing was going to be all right.

The whole congregation turned to see my sister's coffin being carried up the aisle by four men, including her husband and our father. My mother let go a sound like nothing I'd ever heard before and I wrapped my arms around her centre, holding her tight as Dad turned to face us, his cheeks wet with grief.

He used to sing the same Bob Marley song to Lucy and me whenever we scraped a knee or bumped our heads or had a bad dream. It became our family mantra, a small piece of us that we would pass around like bread. It was also the very last thing my sister ever said to me.

She'd planned it all. Every single detail of the funeral and the wake had been written down in meticulous detail before Lucy died. It wasn't surprising, she was always careful to get everything just right, but it made me so incredibly sad to think she did it without including us. I get why she didn't include Mum and Dad, she was intelligent enough and selfless enough to understand how painful that would have been. But I could have helped her, and the fact she didn't think I was capable, that I was too fragile to cope with her death, was almost crippling in its accuracy.

The vicar began his sermon as Dad slipped in next to us and Mum melted into his side. He looked at me over the top of her head, eyes full of all the words that would never be enough to explain what it was we were feeling. And then all too soon it was Harry's turn to get up and speak.

'Lucy was one of the most extraordinary people I have ever met or will ever hope to meet,' he said, his voice carrying over and through every single person who was sitting looking up at him. 'Nothing I say will ever be enough to explain how deeply she loved and was loved.' He looked straight at me then and I felt a piece of my heart splinter in two.

'And so instead, I'm going to read you a poem, because Lucy adored poetry ever since she was a girl.'

I closed my eyes, held my breath whilst he read aloud the same words of Emily Dickinson that I once read to my sister as she was sitting on a dark green sofa with a six-inch scar in her skull.

> *If I should die,*
> *And you should live,*
> *And time should gurgle on,*

'I can't believe you're reading me a poem about death,' she'd said with a laugh. 'But I'll let you off, because it's rather beautiful, don't you think? The way she tells us that life carries on, no matter what.'

It's exactly what she did — carried on, kept moving and pursuing and living as much as she possibly could, and for as long as she possibly could.

'I miss you, Luce,' I whispered to the rafters. It wasn't enough, it would never be enough, and I wished more than anything we'd had more time.

29.

I am not the same person I was two months ago, nor do I want to be. I've been asking myself what would have happened if I'd found Peter's telephone number at the beginning? If I'd known what was going to happen, would I have chosen to do it anyway?

Harry said I can't go back, can't undo the mistakes I've made, but maybe in some way I can. Maybe this is my chance to tell my eighteen-year-old self that it is going to work out, just not the way I might expect.

The sun has disappeared behind a thin veil of cloud, but the air is hot and heavy, making my senses prickle with the anticipation of a storm. I glance up, thinking of another rainstorm, when Isaac nearly kissed me.

I'd intended to drive, went out to the garage with the keys to Lucy's old Mini in my hand. It had been sitting there for years as nobody had any use for it, and there was only a small complaint from the hinges as I opened the door. There was the same squeak of leather, along with a feeling of Lucy being with me as I gripped the steering wheel, my fingers touching the very spot hers once did.

Adjusting the rear-view mirror, I hitched the seat forward and started the engine, only for the stereo to burst into song. The sound of Fleetwood Mac filled the small car, making me laugh because I don't think Lucy ever bought a CD in her life, she just listened to whatever I gave her. I pressed the eject button, wondering if the CD has been stuck in there ever since she first drove up to Oxford, chasing her dreams.

Shifting the gear stick into reverse, I trundled out of the garage then promptly came to a stop halfway down the driveway. Another turn of the ignition proved fruitless and even when Dad appeared and told me to pop the bonnet we both knew I would have to find another means of transportation.

Cycling along the familiar lanes towards a house I must have passed a thousand times, I'm struck by the strangest sense of déjà vu. It would seem that I've been forever heading towards something, looking for something, and not just the clues Lucy left behind. Even before Tristan broke me, before Lucy got sick, I was always in a hurry to get to a certain point in my life without ever stopping to consider what it should be. Now I've come full circle, standing outside a house, still holding on to the handlebars of my old bike and trying to find the courage to ring the doorbell. Whatever is on the other side, whatever happens next, I owe it to Lucy to at least try.

'Christ, you haven't changed a bit,' Peter says as he opens the door with a smile. He looks pretty much the same as when we were teenagers, other than a little pot belly that protrudes from behind his crisp, white shirt.

'Hi, Peter,' I say, thinking how incredibly weird it is to be standing here with someone I haven't thought about in years.

'Are you coming in?' he says, stepping back, his eyes sweeping the full length of me, and I'm suddenly grateful for taking extra care with my outfit this morning, as well as remembering to wash my hair.

The house he invites me into has high ceilings, stripped mahogany floors and a wide, sweeping staircase. We bypass a kitchen, but not before I catch a glimpse of a marble-topped island and a cat asleep on a chair by the Aga. I want to ask if he lives here alone; it seems far too big for one person, and also decidedly middle-aged. Or maybe this is what most people decide to buy when they have enough money to make sensible, grown-up decisions?

Peter is chatting to me as we pass through a living room decorated in muted shades of green and then go out to the garden, where I spy what must once have been a garage but is now clad in weathered timber, complete with a glass window fully covering one side.

'I'm surprised you called,' he says, taking out a set of keys. 'Almost given up on you.'

'I've been a bit distracted,' I reply as I step through the door. Inside it couldn't be more different to the house, with walls the colour of midnight, deep-pile carpet and a U-shaped arrangement of keyboards, monitors and what looks like the cockpit of an aeroplane. At the far end is a glass pane, beyond which I can see a microphone hanging from the ceiling, along with two more on matt black stands around which a pair of oversized headphones are looped.

'I heard about your sister. I'm sorry.'

'Me too. But thank you.' I glance over at all the guitars lined up along one wall. 'Is that a Stratocaster?' I ask, moving closer and tilting my head for a better look. 'Do you play?'

'Sort of,' Peter replies. 'I'm more of a collector, really.'

'Wow. Isaac would be, like, insane with jealousy if he saw this. Did you know it's the exact same one Hendrix played on stage at Woodstock?' For a second, I think about calling him, telling him about the guitar, about all the guitars. But he still hasn't replied to the last text I sent him, after I'd figured out the answer to the riddle neither of us could solve. It's the exact sort of thing he would love, finding out the story behind a whole library of music, and it stings to know he's staying away, just like I asked him to.

'Why are you here, Beth?'

The question throws me, and I sit down on the chair Peter's offering and wait for him to do the same in order to try and come up with a response so exceptional he will sign me on the spot.

'Nothing else fits,' I say, looking around the space, taking in a drum kit, two keyboards and walls lined with photographs of album covers I used to listen to when I was younger. 'Music is the only thing that makes sense to me.'

'Then let's hear what you've got.' He gestures to the booth at the back of the room, waits for me to put down my bag and make my way inside.

As I shut the door behind me, the soft schlupp sealing me in, I'm aware that the only sound I can now hear is my own breathing. The space is completely soundproof and I think of how Isaac would claim it's the perfect place to get away with murder. Then I have to shake myself, because Peter's not a psychopath, he's a boy I used to know who now just so happens to be a record producer, giving me a chance I'm pretty sure I don't deserve.

'Whenever you're ready.' Peter's voice fills the small space and I look through the glass to where he's sitting, waiting for me to sing.

Here goes nothing. I slip on the headphones and allow myself to bathe in the silence, to feel the beat of my heart. Thinking of Lucy and all that she's done, I open my mouth and let out the song that's been both my undoing and my saviour. A song that belongs to me.

'Beth?'

Peter's voice startles me, not least because I've barely made it past the first verse before he's interrupted.

'Yes?'

'I need more.'

'More what? More feeling?'

'Something else.'

'I don't follow.'

He sits back in his chair, hands clasped in his lap. '"Hyacinth Girl" is what got you here. Now I want to hear what else you've got. Preferably something less fanciful, more real.'

'More real.' I repeat the words, as if by doing so I will be rewarded with a flash of inspiration, of anything at all. Problem is, every song I think of, all those recordings Dad found and we sat up listening to until late last night, none of them are real to me, not any more.

'I don't . . .'

'Look,' Peter says, and I close my eyes against what's coming next. 'I did this as a favour, because we know each other and your version of "Hyacinth Girl" is insanely good. But if that's all you have, then I can't help you.'

'Right. Sorry,' I say, taking off the headphones and leaving the booth to retrieve my bag. 'Sorry for wasting your time.'

'Can I ask you something?' he says, picking up one of the Fenders and running his thumb across the strings.

'I guess,' I reply, picturing Isaac's hands, the way they always seemed to dance over the strings of his guitar.

'*Galaxy of Angels*,' he says, and I must have gasped or jumped or something, because he laughs and apologises for startling me.

'What about it?'

'My dad told me how bad SuperKing's second album was. The whole industry was buzzing with the news they were dropped by Euphoric, climbing over one another to try and sign them instead. But when they heard the new material, it was obvious it wasn't written by the same person who created *Galaxy of Angels*.'

'Maybe they just had a bad case of writer's block?'

'Or maybe "Hyacinth Girl" wasn't the only one written by you.' He's looking at me with only half a question on his face. I should be flattered that he's even considered I might be SuperKing's secret weapon. I should be shouting at him, yes, it was me, it was all me, have him call his dad, tell the entire world just how much of a fraud Tristan King actually is. But it wouldn't change anything.

'It was years ago, Peter.'

'But still. That kind of talent doesn't just go away. And I have several new artists who I thought you might be interested in working with on some original material.'

'As I said, it was years ago,' I say, one hand reaching out for the door and wishing I'd come more prepared.

'Shame,' Peter says, leaning over and flicking on the stereo system in one corner of the room. 'I was hoping there was so much more still to come.'

It's like being hit over the head with a hammer or struck by lightning or being stabbed in the chest with a syringe full of adrenalin, because suddenly every single cell in my body is fully awake. In an instant, I'm catapulted back to Isaac's parents' garden, the night when the photograph of us sitting back to back was taken. We'd been playing around with some ideas I had for a song, something about hope, about never settling for less than you really want. But I couldn't find the words to express what it was I was trying to say, about how fearful I was that Lucy was going to Oxford, how scared I was about what would happen to us and, in a few years, Isaac and me, because life never stays the same.

Isaac caught me watching my sister, saw the uncertainty in my smile.

'Don't worry,' he said, giving me a nudge. 'There's so much more still to come.' At which point I grabbed his hand and we ran upstairs to fetch his guitar, recorded the song on his phone, me standing in the bath and him perched on the loo seat. It's the exact same song he sent me less than a week ago, one that Tristan never managed to steal.

The memory beats inside my head like a bird trying to escape from its cage. I laugh, a small inconsequential sound, but one that reverberates around my mind, my heart, every last part of me, as I realise that everything I ever needed, ever wanted, was already there. It's like remembering something that happened to someone else, a girl I used to know whose world was turned every which way because she chose to love the wrong boy.

'May I?' I ask with outstretched hand, nodding at the guitar Peter is still holding. He looks at me for a second before handing it over. Leaning against the wall, I pluck each string in turn, feeling the vibrations travel through my fingertips and into my soul. I dip my head, take two slow breaths and start to play.

An hour or so later, I'm cycling through the rain, hair stuck to my face and my clothes soaked right through. But I don't care.

'I don't care!' I yell at the sky, at the thunder rolling overhead and a fork of lightning that illuminates the world for a split second. I don't care that I will probably catch a chill and be snotty and disgusting for days, forced by my mother to eat a vat full of chicken soup. Today, now, this very second, it all ends and it all begins.

I may not have anything close to a record deal, but I have a chance. I have the promise of another opportunity, to go back to Peter when I have some new material. I never asked you to fix me, Lucy. I'd got used to carrying around all the pieces of me that are broken. You made every moment I got to spend with you memorable, but they were too difficult to hold on to and so I tried to drown them, just as I drowned myself.

I kept trying to forget all the pieces of you, bury them inside the darkness, but you are in everything I have ever loved, every memory, every song, and I carry that with me, safe in the knowledge that you will never truly be gone. I still hear your voice in the quiet moments. I still hear you saying that you won't give up on me, so now I have to promise I won't give up on myself.

At the crossroads, I pause, thinking of all the times I would cycle over to Isaac's house. I have to tell him, even if he doesn't pick up when I call, I have to tell him what's just happened because so much of it is because of him. Taking my phone from my pocket and turning it on for the first time in days, I notice a message from Harry.

She'd be so proud of you, it says, along with the link to the YouTube video I posted, which has already received thousands of likes and comments.

There are several more messages, some from friends I haven't thought of in years, all of them congratulating me on the song I wrote in my best friend's bedroom. The feeling it creates is a curious mixture of happiness and regret, but most of all relief. So much time was wasted because I was terrified of what people might think about my music. But thanks to my sister and Isaac, and even Tristan, I'm no longer afraid.

Wheeling my bike into the garage, I leave it propped up against the wall, next to Lucy's Mini. I squeeze out my hair, leaving small puddles of rainwater on the floor, and wonder whether Dad and I could somehow learn to fix that little green car? And perhaps Mum can teach me to bake, let me find some way to repay them both for all the lost years?

I look around the garage, at all the tins of odd nails, spare bulbs, garden furniture and Christmas decorations. Leaning against the wall, I breathe it all in, close my eyes and let my mind take me back through time and space to a morning when Lucy and I went down to the river in search of wildflowers. And not just then, but all the times before and all the times since. There's nothing special in this room, nothing of consequence, but put it all together and it adds up to an entire life, filled with memories and people and, most of all, music.

I have to speak to him. I have to speak to Isaac about what's on that YouTube video and the part he played in it all. I want him to know, even if it doesn't change anything, even if it's still too soon for us to be anything more than friends. I want him to know that I love him, that I've always loved him, that he is the very best thing that has ever happened to me. But first, I need to shower, or sink into a scalding-hot bath. And eat, and celebrate, and be with my family, just as Lucy wished.

Coming into the kitchen, I'm hit with the scent of baking and coffee and something else. One step more and I catch sight of my dad sitting at the kitchen table. Next to him is my mum and they've both got their heads turned towards someone, smiling at the person who is in the same seat he always sat in, because it's where he belongs. On the table in front of him, next to a half-eaten slice of cake, is a small cassette tape, the one Lucy gave away but has somehow managed to bring back home again.

'Hi,' Isaac says as I come into the room, and I swear I hear Lucy whisper, *Told you so*, in my ear.

30.

The first time I heard Isaac play it felt like the whole world had stopped to listen. He had a way of making the music sound new and different, no matter how many times it had been played before.

But whenever he played one of my songs, something I'd pulled from the corners of my mind, it was like nothing else on earth.

It was midsummer, late but light, the scent of roasting meat and spices lingering in the still-warm air. Isaac and I had been sitting on the lawn, back to back, as we tried to figure out a way to make the lyrics I'd been writing fit the melody he'd come up with.

I leant my head back against his, feeling the familiar curve of his skull that seemed to slot so neatly against my own. The sound of my sister's laughter carried over the garden towards us and I looked over to where she was sitting at the table, leaning forward so that her face was illuminated by candlelight.

'She's going to break my brother's heart,' Isaac said, following my gaze, and I looked away, ripped up a handful of grass and tossed it into the sky. 'It's ok,' Isaac went on, his fingertips hovering over the strings of his guitar. 'I think on some level he already knows.'

'Everything's changing.' I got to my feet, wiping stray bits of grass from my bare legs. 'It feels like it's all going by so fast, too quick for me to catch on to.'

'She'll always be your sister,' he said, swinging his guitar over one shoulder as we headed for the patio where a toast was being raised for the birthday boy. 'And don't worry. There's so much more still to come.'

'Say that again.' I grabbed his arm, felt the swell of muscle under his shirt.

'Say what again?' he said, looking at me in that way of his that made me think he already knew.

'There's so much more still to come.' I pulled him through the house and upstairs to his room.

It took us less than ten minutes to fix the chords around the lyric Isaac had just inspired. Perhaps five more were needed to go over the chorus, add in a harmony and sing it through once again, just to be sure.

'We should record it. Now, so we don't forget,' Isaac said, standing by the open window beyond which the sound of 'Happy Birthday' could be heard.

'I don't have my Dictaphone,' I said, flopping down on the bed and spreading out my arms.

'At some point you need to join the rest of us in the twenty-first century,' Isaac said, taking out his phone and waving it at me. 'The sound won't be great, but it's better than nothing.'

'Ok, but not here,' I said, pushing myself up and off the bed.

Standing in the bath (because even I could sound half decent with those acoustics), I waited as Isaac propped up his phone on the sink. Half of me wanted to tell him to stop, that I'd changed my mind, but I wouldn't have been able to explain why.

The other half of me was incapable of backing down, not once he picked out the opening notes to a song we called 'Encore'.

Looking back, those three minutes were the most intense I'd ever had. I don't really remember anything beyond the opening line, it's more *a feeling, an understanding that paradise exists. If not for ever, then at least for the length of a song.*

The very second after we finished, Isaac and I looked at one another as if we'd found the answer we all spend our entire lives looking for.

'We have to post it,' he said, looking at me with all kinds of expectation. 'Beth, I'm serious. This is really good. Better than anything else you've written.'

'You think?' The idea made me nervous, but inside I was grinning because I'd felt it too.

'Abso-fuckin-lutely,' he said, scrolling through his phone.

'Not yet.' I stepped out of the bath and covered his hand with my own.

'Why not?' he replied, and I could hear the frustration in his voice.

I wanted it to be good, I needed it to be good, but I was afraid that it was all in our heads. That if we posted it, people would laugh at us for believing we were anything more than average.

'I can't only post one song,' I said, looking in the mirror and pushing back my eyelashes with my fingertips. 'I need more.'

'I know you're stalling.' He was standing so close I could feel the warmth of his skin. 'But promise me one day you will.'

'Promise,' I said, turning around and holding out my pinkie finger for him to squeeze.

EPILOGUE

One year later . . .

Last night, just like every night, I dreamt of Lucy.

We were running, hair long and loose, bare feet kicking up dust and petals as a pair of skylarks flew overhead. I paused at the tree that will forever hold our initials carved with a penknife into its trunk, then I followed my sister's call as we headed for the river.

Lucy waded in, water licking at her skin and sticking the thin fabric of her summer dress to her legs. She turned around and smiled at me, her face changing from a girl to a woman and back again.

'Lucy, wait,' I said, looking down at the ever-flowing current, but hesitant, unsure as to whether I should step into the wet. My toes were painted a vivid red, my fingernails too, and I was holding a copy of *As You Like It* in my hands, but when I opened the cover, the pages inside were all blank.

'What's this?' I looked up to see Lucy wading further into the river, hands outstretched and surrounded by dozens of fireflies that cast tiny reflections on to both the water and her skin.

'It's the beginning,' she called over her shoulder, her voice sounding like a song. 'You have to write a new story.'

'Where are you going?' I cried out, because the water was up to her chest, catching on her hair and turning it a darker shade of pale.

'Nowhere,' she said. 'I'll always be right here, with you.'

'I miss you,' I said, reaching out my hand as she got further and further away.

'I miss you too. But now you need to wake up.'

It's late, or early; the half-light sneaking under the curtains makes it hard to tell. Rolling over to glance at the clock, my arm brushes up against Isaac's shoulder and he stirs in his sleep. I smile, trace my fingers over a scar on his arm, then slip from the bed and shrug on an old jumper.

Creeping down the stairs, I pause at the bottom to look at the photograph of Lucy and me that now hangs there, one taken when we were no more than girls and which used to be stuck to the inside cover of a notebook. We are standing side by side in the river, dresses tucked into knickers and holding nets aloft. There is such wild, expectant joy on our faces, a joy that used to be too difficult for me to remember but now always makes me smile.

There are dozens more photos decorating the walls, including several that Isaac and I have taken over this past year. So much has happened in such a short amount of time that sometimes I have to pause, take a breath and pinch myself into realising that yes, this is my life.

Kissing my fingertips, I press them to Lucy's face then pad along the hall and into the kitchen. I put the kettle on to boil, open the back door to let the morning in, then sit down at the piano that Isaac bought, just for me.

After I went home to discover Isaac sitting in my parents' kitchen, it was as if no time had passed at all. We stayed up half the night, listening to all my old recordings.

'Isaac,' I said, sitting next to him on the dark green sofa in my parents' house.

'Hmm?' he replied, half asleep and sugar-drunk on lemon cake.

'When did you first realise you liked me?'

'Liked you?' he said, turning his head to look at me with only one eye open. 'When have I ever not liked you?'

'I mean, *liked* me liked me.'

'Oh.' He sat up, rubbed his eyes and frowned at me. Then he ran both hands through his hair, looked over at the piano, then to the bookshelves filled with records, then back again to me.

'Probably the first time I ever saw you.'

'At school?' I asked, because, looking back on it, I probably knew too. His face was so interesting, plus there was the way I desperately hoped he wanted to be friends with me, delighted in our shared love of music. It all added up to something more, but I was simply too young to understand it.

'No,' he said with a shy smile, tucking a strand of hair behind my ear and looking at me in a way that made my insides curl up with delight. 'About a week before. I was walking the dog in the fields behind the river. I heard someone singing.'

'I was singing?'

'You came shooting down the lane on your bike, wearing dungarees and wellington boots,' he said with a low chuckle. 'Your hair was a halo of frizz and you were singing "Son of a Preacher Man" at the top of your lungs.'

'It is a pretty amazing song.' I wished I could see inside his mind, go back to that day and meet him all over again, but in a new and different way.

'I just stood there, completely dumbstruck as you whizzed straight past me,' he said, leaning across to kiss me gently. 'I think I fell for you right there and then, even before I knew your name or anything about you, or even what it meant to love someone.'

'You love me?'

'All I've ever wanted was for you to let me love you.' He kissed me again, then sat back with a yawn. 'But right now, I really need to go to bed. You coming?' he asked, getting to his feet and offering me his hand, and I nodded my head, yes.

I had no expectations as to what would happen next. If someone had told me that I would fall for Isaac, hard and fast and without fear, I would have shaken my head, no. If they'd then told me that I'd move in with him less than a month later, that he'd buy me a piano on which I would write song after song, the melodies and lyrics rushing out of me like an animal released into the wild, I would have laughed in their face.

What I categorically would not have believed is that he would love me right back, all of me, even the parts I'm still trying to figure out.

Sitting at the piano in Isaac's kitchen (or is it also mine now? I'm not sure), I lift my fingers from the keys because, somewhere, a phone is ringing. I turn my head, follow the sound into the hall and pick up the receiver of a landline that is barely ever used.

'Hello?'

'Turn on the radio!'

'Mum, is that you?'

'Elizabeth, just turn on the bloody radio!'

'Ok, ok, hang on.' I put the receiver down then trot back into the kitchen. My hand reaches out towards the radio on the counter, hovers there for just a second, because I need to remember this. I need to remember the good, not just the bad.

There's a fraction of time between my finger pressing down the 'on' button and sound escaping from the speaker, but when it does, it's like a puddle of warmth has appeared in my centre, slowly spreading out and wrapping me up in its joy.

This one's for you, Lucy, I think to myself as I listen to the song that I wrote because of her.

I sent over a dozen songs to Peter a week before Christmas, when the nights stretched long and heavy. He called me the very next morning, asked me to cycle through the frost and get on a train up to London, because there was someone he wanted me to meet.

That someone is a girl with music in her soul and an extra-special quality which means you can't help but notice her when she walks in a room. But that's nothing compared to when she sings – it's like she's a siren, pulling out everything from your very core and making you feel it in a completely different way.

I cried when I heard her sing one of my songs, which would have been more than embarrassing if I hadn't noticed Peter wiping at the corner of his own eye. I then cried some more when she told me it was as if I'd written it just for her.

That girl's voice now spills from the speaker of the radio on the countertop in the kitchen of the house where I live, with Isaac. It is so sublime and surreal and all other kinds of things I don't have the right words for.

'That was "The Other Half of Me",' the DJ on the radio says as the song comes to an end. 'The latest single by up-and-coming new artist Delilah Gray. And if you are as blown away by her voice as I am, then rumour has it she's set to appear at Glastonbury later in the year. Up next, it's the song you all made number one for the third consecutive week . . .'

I turn off the radio, feel the rise and fall of my chest as I try to process what it is that's just happened. 'The Other Half of Me' isn't just about Lucy, it's about Isaac, it's about music, but most of all it's about the side of myself I was always so scared to let out.

Half of me feels like I'm living in a dream, wading through the river with all the ghosts of my former self. The other half of me, the part I thought would forever be locked away, is daring to imagine what it might be like, to be standing in the crowd at Glastonbury and listening to Delilah play my song.

Outside in the garden, a bird begins its morning call, and I close my eyes, imagine a chorus of them hidden in the trees, a soft rustle of wind accompanying all that beautiful sound.

I think of a lyric, the first line of a song that I scribbled in the pages of a book my sister went to great lengths for me to find. I think of all the other songs I wrote, the ones that sat trapped in a box under my bed, the ones I wrote right here in this room, and all the ones I have yet to write.

I look back out to the hall, half expecting to see Lucy as a girl, sitting on the stairs, listening. She isn't there, and yet I know she'll never truly be gone. I picture Isaac asleep upstairs, smile at the knowledge that he'll be there every morning when I wake, and I don't think I've been this ok for a very long time.

Lucy may have sent me down this path of rediscovery, but it was Isaac who made me hear the music again, he was the one to make me realise all I had to do was listen.

From the songbook of Elizabeth Franks

THE OTHER HALF OF ME, by Elizabeth Franks

There is a part of me
That knows not how to be still
It whispers to me all those secrets I hide
It battles against my will

My loneliness, it shrouds me
Protects me from sorrow and pain
But the danger is I still may lose
The voice I can hear through the rain

When I am old, will I remember?
When I am old, will I know how to care?
What happens to the other half of me
If there's no more dreams left to share?

The moments spent in hiding
The music I kept in my soul

The girl who once lived for the promise of more
Is only one half of a whole

When I am old, will I remember?
When I am old, will I know how to care?
What happens to the other half of me
If my love then turns to despair?

I remember a field filled with fire
And reaching my hand to the sky
You walked with me
You are a part of me
Maybe one day I'll understand why

When I am old, will I remember?
When I am old, will I know how to care?
What happens to the other half of me
If my memories are no longer there?

ENCORE, by Elizabeth Franks & Isaac Hardy

I hope you still remember
That feeling of forever
When stars lit up the sky

You held my hand so tightly
As our future shone so brightly
Then we heard tomorrow sigh, sigh, sigh

Don't throw away the kisses
Keep searching evermore
There's so much more to come, my love
Don't run from our encore

There's an imprint on my heart
Like an invisible tattoo
A sign of me and you

Don't throw away the kisses
Keeping searching evermore
There's so much more to come, my love
Don't run from our encore

Notes and boats and longing and hopes
Of never feeling alone
To me you are my home

Don't throw away the kisses
Keeping searching evermore
There's so much more to come, my love
Don't run from our encore

There's so much more to come, my love
Don't run from our encore

HYACINTH GIRL, by Elizabeth Franks & Isaac Hardy

You lit me up, when I didn't have a clue
Just what it was that love could do
I saw myself reflected in your thoughts
A flower unsure how to bloom

Together, apart,
Don't run from the heart
Is it enough that you infect my soul?
You're here, after all

Joy and sadness dancing together
You called me your hyacinth girl
Said we'd be forever

Time shattered us, choice is a myth,
Hope is a fairy tale without an end
I need you to save me
I need you to be bad, so I can pretend

Who will be our witness, claim our love was real?
You called me your hyacinth girl
Taught me how to feel

The love affair, the high, the rollercoaster
Burnt souls, the embers of which glow long after

It only takes a second for love to tear
The things we weep for when there's no one left to hear
Fast-forward all the hours spent longing for you

My heart deserves something you don't know how to give
You called me your hyacinth girl
But she's dead and I want to live

GALAXY OF ANGELS, by Elizabeth Franks
We think we have forever to make all those mistakes
But no one intends to die
Even the angels who watch from above
One by one, they fall from the sky

I'll find you in between the stars
Where a galaxy of angels awaits
Come
Lead the way
To where possibilities play

Our dreams are just pieces scattered all over
With nowhere particular to go
Till our angels slip inside, whisper secret desires
The changeling of hope taking hold

I'll find you in between the stars
Where a galaxy of angels awaits
Come
Lead the way
To where possibilities play

The angels feed us pearls we've never tasted before
Like marbles in the playground
Small spheres of inspiration that pop in the night
Without which we might just drown

There will always be an invisible thread
Between you and me
Even if we end up peaking at seventeen
Come, walk swift into tomorrow
To where a galaxy of angels awaits

ACKNOWLEDGEMENTS

I wrote the first draft of this book during the lockdown of 2020, sitting at my garden table with only an old-fashioned fountain pen and notebook to hand, as my children had commandeered both computers for home-schooling. It feels very strange to think of what we have had to endure these past couple of years – it seems so close and yet intangible at the same time. Writing was the one thing that kept me sane throughout. The ability to escape to another world stopped me from worrying every minute of every day, and for that I am so incredibly grateful.

My thanks go out, as always, to my formidable agent, Hayley Steed, not least for knowing exactly what to say in order to calm my nerves and always being on my side.

This book wasn't easy or straightforward to write, not least because of all the interruptions from my kids about snacks and Wi-Fi, but it never would have come together at all were it not for the endless patience from my incredible editors, Victoria Oundjian and Sophie Wilson. Thank you for believing in me and the story throughout because I was ready to give up on more than one occasion!

Thank you to Gillian Holmes for your painstaking attention to detail during the editing process, and also to the entire team at

Lake Union Publishing for all your help and support both with this book and the last.

For the beautiful cover design, which perfectly captures the spirit of the story, my thanks go out to Emma Rogers.

Years ago, one of my dearest friends was diagnosed with a brain tumour and had to go through a similar recovery to Lucy's. She is, thank goodness, alive and just as enigmatic as always, but without her input, I was in danger of getting some of the details wrong. Thank you, Mandy, both for your help and for being one of the people who was such a huge part of my teenage years.

A special thank you goes to my extraordinary writing friend, Hannah Persaud, who not only read an early draft of this book but who always knows exactly what I need to hear whenever the doubt demons rear their ugly heads.

Finally, my heartfelt thanks goes out to my family, without whom I would have gone completely mad long ago.

If you loved *The Other Half of Me*, then please read on for an extract from Katherine Slee's novel *The Love We Left Behind.*

PROLOGUE

Oxford, 1996

The sky was slick with rain, the promise of more to come hanging in gunmetal clouds. Thousands of droplets fell, striking the alabaster stone of Queen's College clock tower under which a girl, just shy of twenty-one, stood waiting.

Her hair was tied at the nape of her neck, a handful of strands escaping from underneath the hood of her rain jacket. At her feet was a large backpack, military in style with the straps drawn tight, and she bent down to tuck something into the front pocket.

Every so often she drew back her sleeve and turned her wrist to check the time on her watch, absently running her finger around the silver face and fiddling with the dial, as if she didn't quite trust what the two thin hands were telling her.

On the other side of the road, a couple of students were hurrying against the rain, one with a book held over his head, laughing as they went. The girl followed them with her eyes and saw them duck inside the doorway of a café that was due to close when the clock struck six.

Tilting her head back, the girl stared up at the ancient bell that hung directly above and wondered what would happen if it were to fall. If there was no chime of the approaching hour would that somehow suspend time and give her a few more minutes to decide?

A soft boom on the horizon pulled her line of sight down and across, towards the river.

Brontide, she thought to herself. A sound like distant thunder. It was a word she first read whilst hidden away in the corner of her local library, a place she used in order to shelter from her real life. She never forgot its meaning, simply filed it away with all the others that were tucked neatly inside her brilliant mind.

But even a mind as brilliant as hers couldn't control another's will. It was a mistake to put all her trust, her faith, into one person. Because everyone gave up on her eventually, and she was stupid to think he might have been any different.

As she glanced once more at her watch, the bell began to call out how late the day had become. She shook her head, rubbing at the corner of her eye as she shouldered her rucksack and stepped towards the kerb, holding out her arm and waiting for the approaching coach to stop. She didn't look back as she climbed on board and paid her fare. Nor did she allow herself to cry as she sat down at a window seat and watched the familiar streets pass by in a blur.

If anyone had been able to search inside that mind, they might have heard it whispering a million words to her all at once: of sorrow, of regret, of the knowledge that she wasn't enough. But not a single one of those words was powerful enough to describe how it felt when her heart fractured into a thousand shards of pain; shards that she would carry within her soul every day and every night to come.

NIAMH

Mizpah (n.) – *a deep, emotional bond between people*

Oxford, 1995

It was an inconsequential type of day. At least, that's how it appeared to be at first sight. There was nothing unusual about the low-hung cloud that was suffocating the autumn sunshine, nor was it strange to see so many students whizzing along on their bikes.

Term had begun just shy of a week ago. Freshers' week had been and gone, a new collection of undergraduates arriving at their respective colleges with trunks and suitcases and pockets full of nerves. Introductions had been made, procedures and rules explained, ceremonies involving swearing in Latin about never bringing a naked flame into the Bodleian Library completed, and now it was Friday afternoon at the end of the first week.

In the middle of the city, on the south side of the High Street, stood the oldest college of them all. Founded in 1249, it was built with golden stone and thick oak doors, and currently home to several hundred students and professors. In a room up high, with slanted ceilings and leaded windows guarded from the outside by gargoyles, two girls sat cross-legged on the floor. One was smoking a hand-rolled cigarette, blowing out thin lines of smoke through the open window to the world below. The other was leaning forward to paint her friend's face with rouge and kohl, tilting her head to one side as she worked.

In the far corner sat an ancient wingback chair strewn with books, scarves and a burgundy fedora. Next to it was a bookcase filled with legends and tales of old, along with silver photo frames, stacks of CDs and all manner of knick-knacks collected over the years.

On every other conceivable surface, from the desk to the windowsill and even by the door, there were vases and jugs and a couple of empty bottles, each and every one filled with blood-red roses.

'Prosit,' the taller of the two girls said as her friend sneezed twice in a row. 'I didn't know you were allergic?'

'I'm not,' Niamh replied, rubbing the tip of her nose and looking around the room at the dozens and dozens of flowers. 'But there're so many of them.'

'There's more in Duncan's room,' Erika said as she rummaged through her make-up bag. 'Peter sent them this morning.'

'I thought you told him to stop.' Niamh took a last drag of her cigarette then stubbed it out on the window ledge.

'I want to make him think he might earn my forgiveness for just a little bit longer,' Erika said with a grin as she unscrewed a tube of lip gloss and held it out to Niamh.

'No thanks,' Niamh replied as she stood and went over to the mirror to appraise Erika's handiwork. 'It always sticks to my hair.'

'You could wear it up?' Erika came up behind Niamh and twisted all those curls into a knot at the back of her head, then let them go and wrapped her arms around her friend's waist. 'I am sorry about Peter.'

'Why? I'm not the one he cheated on.'

'But you are the one who I abandoned because I was stupid enough to fall in love with a total *kuk*.'

'He wasn't that bad.' Niamh looked around at the roses, a stream of non-verbal apologies that didn't really mean anything at all. Peter was the sort of person who was used to getting what he wanted, including Erika. What he hadn't bargained for was her strict moral compass; she was highly unlikely to ever forgive him, no matter how much money and sentiment was thrown her way.

'You tried to warn me and I refused to listen to all that wisdom inside your beautiful skull.' Erika rested her chin on Niamh's shoulder, her bottom lip sticking out in its own version of an apology.

'You can't help who you fall in love with,' Niamh said, looking at their reflection. If someone had told her a year ago that the two of them would end up being so close, she would have laughed or snorted, or done something to convey how completely ridiculous such an idea was. Not only was Erika gorgeous and popular and annoyingly confident, she was also disgustingly rich and privileged in a way Niamh couldn't begin to imagine. Girls like Erika simply didn't make friends with girls like her and, for what must have been the millionth time since they'd met, Niamh wondered if it was all too good to be true.

'I disagree.' Erika stepped away, going over to her wardrobe and proceeding to empty most of its contents on to the bed.

Niamh watched her in the mirror, noticing as she wiped at the corner of one eye, the pink of which she hadn't been able to disguise with concealer.

'Are you OK?' she asked, perching on the end of the chair and rolling another cigarette.

'I'm fine,' Erika replied with an exaggerated smile, which only made Niamh think she was the complete opposite.

Erika pulled off her sweatshirt and tossed it on to the floor, then picked up a leopard-print dress and turned to her.

'Too obvious?' she asked.

'Not for you,' Niamh said with a shake of her head. 'You could wear a bin liner and still look like a supermodel. Explain why you disagree about falling in love.'

'Do you remember that party?' Erika asked as she picked up another dress, bright pink and short enough to make anyone's mother blanch.

'You're going to have to be more specific.'

'The one in that converted church when Duncan spent most of the night arguing with the barman?'

'And then ended up snogging him in the loos. Yes, I remember.'

'Peter insisted on coming with me to meet you and Duncan. But I didn't want him to.'

'Why?'

'Because I knew I was falling for him, which meant I was afraid you would tell me he wasn't good enough.'

He wasn't. Niamh could still remember the very moment she first laid eyes on him. All tanned skin and sun-kissed hair with a smile that was more predatory than genuine. But when Erika had introduced them, she'd looked at her so expectantly that Niamh knew she had to be supportive of her friend's choice, no matter what.

Perhaps if she understood a little better what love actually felt like, she could have helped Erika see sooner that Peter was never going to be her knight in shining armour. Niamh's own love life had never amounted to more than a few stolen kisses or disappointing fumbles after too many drinks. Nobody had ever made her feel special or loved, despite how hard she'd wished for it.

Which was why it had hurt so very deeply when Erika had poured all of that vibrancy and attention on to someone Niamh knew wasn't deserving of it.

'Who are you dressing up for?' Niamh asked as Erika slipped her legs into a pair of micro leather shorts, then stood on tiptoe and turned around to peer at her backside in the mirror.

'You, my *älskling*,' she replied with a wink. 'Always you. Now, what are you planning to put on?'

'Who said I'm even going?'

'But you must.' Erika tugged on a pair of thigh-length boots and glared at Niamh in the mirror. 'Duncan is on one of his missions and I refuse to leave you behind with nothing but a pile of books for company.'

Spending an evening alone wasn't anything new for Niamh. She was more than accustomed to her own company, but ever since she had come to Oxford and become friends with an over-enthusiastic Swedish goddess, her social skills had slowly improved to being something close to normal. Besides, the inherent shyness she had battled with for years had absolutely no sway with someone who seemed to possess neither fear nor shame.

'I have no desire to watch you and Duncan stalk out some new prey.'

'Then join in,' Erika said as she began to apply gloss to her own lips. 'Let the three of us make a night that we will still talk about when we are too old to dance, let alone anything else.'

Niamh considered her options, knowing all too well that if she said no, Erika would only wait for Duncan to get back and then there would be no point at all in trying to resist.

'Fine. But I'm not staying all night.'

'Of course not. Wouldn't want you turning into a pumpkin. Here,' she said, reaching across to take something off a shelf and holding it out to Niamh. 'Take him with you.'

'What for?' Niamh asked as she looked down at the tiny plastic troll with mad spikey hair and a lopsided smile.

'For *lycka*.' Erika bent down to give Niamh a kiss on the cheek. 'I brought him back from Stockholm because he reminds me of . . .' She glanced at the photo frame on her bedside table, inside of which two girls were hanging upside down from the branch of a tree. Their smiles were wide, their knees scuffed with dirt and they were holding tight to one another's hands. Erika gave a small shake of her head, then turned back to Niamh with a smile. 'He reminds me of you, my beautiful, crazy little troll.'

Niamh looked across at the bookcase, at all the weird and wonderful things Erika kept as reminders of moments in her life she didn't want to forget. The sentimentality of it had surprised her at first, given how pragmatic Erika could be. When she had got to know her a little better, witnessed the tears shed whilst watching romantic comedies, and once having to stop her from punching someone who dared call Duncan a fag, the keepsakes didn't seem quite so strange. But it wasn't until last December that Niamh discovered why the collection existed at all.

She had gone into Erika's room and found her slumped in the corner clutching a photograph, a near-empty bottle of vodka at her feet. Through drunken tears Erika explained how it was supposed to be the birthday of her best friend, Astrid, but she had died two summers before from a brain aneurism. A here one minute, gone the next freak accident that leaves behind all kinds of damage. Not least because Erika and Astrid had argued the day before she'd died. A stupid, nonsensical argument about borrowing a dress for a party. But it was an argument that Erika could neither forgive herself for, nor forget.

It was the first time Niamh had met someone who understood the true meaning of loss. It was also the first time she ever told anyone the whole truth about her own childhood, not just the filtered-down version. Erika had hugged her tight, said they were bound together through grief, and Niamh finally began to experience the intoxicating pull of friendship.

'You think I look like a troll?' She took the strange plastic creature from Erika and twisted its hair into a peak. Glancing over at the photograph, Niamh noticed, as always, how similar she and

Astrid looked; they could even have passed for sisters. It should have been weird, given how quickly she and Erika became first close, then inseparable. But the joy of having a best friend was in such stark contrast to all the years before they'd met that Niamh refused to let herself worry about the ghost of someone she would never know.

'If you're going to be ungrateful,' Erika said, 'I shall simply pilchard him back.'

'Pilfer,' Niamh said with a smile as she tucked the little troll into her pocket and went out on to the landing, turning left in the direction of her room. 'Pilchard is a type of fish,' she called over her shoulder. 'Bit like herring, only smaller.'

'Pilfer,' Erika repeated to herself, following Niamh along the corridor and watching from the doorway as Niamh opened her own wardrobe and tried to figure out what to wear. 'Pilfer, pilfer, pilfer. It sounds silly when you say it over and over.'

'Then write it down.' Niamh tossed Erika a notebook bound in navy fabric and embroidered with tiny flowers. 'Write it all down so you never forget.'

'Tell me another one. One of your funny little words.' Erika went across and sat down on a small green sofa by the window and eased apart the pages, then brought the notebook to her face and inhaled deeply. It was a peculiar habit the two friends shared, one of several that had bound them ever tighter over the past year. A bond that occurred through happenstance – two souls in the same place at the same time for whatever reason, but who had stayed together out of love. Because they did love one another, though in a completely different way to how Erika had once told Niamh she felt whenever she kissed Peter.

'Mizpah,' Niamh said as she ran her fingers through her mane of hair, deciding that there wasn't much point in trying to tame it. 'It means a deep, emotional bond between two people.'

'Miz-pah,' Erika repeated, writing down the word and its meaning in looping script. 'I think I shall call you this from now on. Especially in public.'

'Please, don't,' Niamh said as she came out of the bedroom and gave a little twirl. 'What do you think?'

'I think' – Erika put down the notebook and came over to Niamh, unbuttoning the velvet waistcoat she had chosen and tossing it aside – 'that you should wear this instead.' Reaching into the wardrobe, she handed Niamh a thin black cape interwoven with stars, then walked over to a record player sitting on a table. 'And before you open that little mouth of yours to object, try it on. You will see that I am right. Now we should dance. And drink vodka. And find us each a handsome boy to kiss. But before that,' she said, whirling around as the first notes of a song closed the space between them, 'we should make a promise.'

'A promise?' Niamh asked as Erika took hold of her hands and they began to spin.

'Yes. That we will never again let anyone, especially a boy, come between us. Hoes before bros and all that.'

Niamh smiled at the mixed-up words, thinking of all the weird and wonderful things she loved about the girl with a gap-toothed smile and hugely optimistic view of the world. Being bound to her was just about the most amazingly sentimental thing that had ever happened in Niamh's life and the knowledge of it settled inside her like a golden nugget of hope.

'I promise,' Niamh said as she held out her little finger and waited for Erika to link it with her own. 'Hoes before bros, no matter what.'

ERIKA

ROSES

London, 2012

The scent of damp lingers in the early morning air. I can feel the soft splat of dew against my bare calves as I run across the lawns of Kensington Gardens. As always, I stop by the statue of Peter Pan and stretch my arms up high before bending forward, enjoying the gentle pull along my hamstrings.

My eye falls upon a fellow jogger, his breath heavy and laboured, his run more of a shuffle than a sprint. He gives me a small nod as he passes and I look away to the river, where a pair of coots is swimming side by side. Two lines of rippled water follow behind, muddling the reflection of the sky above into a swirl of blue and palest grey. It makes me turn around, seeking out whatever it is that seems to be missing.

There's something about the day that doesn't quite fit. The feeling was there when I woke, followed me as I shut the front door and tucked my key under the pot of begonias still in bloom. A sort of niggling sensation that stayed with me as I ran all the way along Portobello Road, swishing past me through rails of clothes that the stallholders were setting out for the day's market. It whispered to me as I turned the corner on to the High Street, which was already busy with traffic.

Perhaps it's due to the dog who trotted over as I entered the park, looking up at me in a way that suggested we'd met before. Or could it have been the song I heard playing on the radio of a car that was waiting at the lights as I crossed the road? It was a song that seemingly played on a loop throughout that long, hot summer when so much of my life suddenly changed.

I'm being ridiculous. It's nothing more than memories getting me a little spooked because so much is about to change all over again. No doubt it's just my subconscious, reminding me that in only a few short weeks I will be running through a different part of London, with a different person waiting for me back home. No more the pink mews house tucked away behind Portobello Road that has become a kind of sanctuary for Layla and me over the years. Every morning I run through the dawn, twice around the park and back again before standing in a claw-footed tub, praying there's hot water in the tank.

Soon enough my routine will have to change. I won't be coming back to the sound of a creaking floorboard as I cross the hallway into the bathroom, nor will there be the scent of coffee and spun sugar that seeps under the door from my favourite café only one street away. And no more shared bottles of chilled wine on a summer evening, the windows open to the night as Layla bustles around the kitchen throwing herbs into pots and trying not to burn everything in sight.

My life is about to become exposed brick and oversized windows in a converted warehouse all the way across town. There will be no silk scarves bought on a beach in India draped over the back of chairs, no Metallica played at full volume to welcome me home. Instead it will be the scent of beeswax and cologne, along with Miles Davis and the tapping of fingers on a keyboard.

The wedding is so close, so very real, but it sometimes feels as if it's happening to somebody else. Like I'm watching it from behind a curtain, peeping through the crack. Only yesterday I was standing in front of a mirror whilst a stick-thin sales assistant tightened the corset of my gown. (I'm convinced it was the same one who did Layla's fittings. A girl with a sharp, sour face who told Layla that all brides lose at least a couple of pounds before their big day.) I remember staring at my reflection and thinking that I didn't recognise the woman I'd become. A woman who was willing to stand up in church and declare my love, my fidelity, to a man who can swear like a trooper in four different languages, make the best scrambled eggs I've ever tasted, and who calls his mother every Sunday without fail.

Not that there's anything wrong with being close to your mother, it's just not something I can really relate to. Layla is my family, has been ever since we first worked together behind the bar of our local pub, and soon Hector will be too.

My feet have brought me back to the same spot where I always finish my run, even though my mind is clearly somewhere else. Going up on tiptoes, I look both ways across the street, almost as if I'm waiting for something to happen, something to appear that wasn't there a second ago.

Stepping off the pavement, I cross over and join the queue that's already snaking out of the door of my favourite artisan café.

Whilst I wait, I scroll through my phone, mentally mapping out the upcoming week and firing off a couple of replies to emails that came in overnight. There's a deal I've been working on ever since the start of the year, one that could prove to me that stepping away from the corporate world was actually a good idea. My salary may have been drastically slashed when I joined the non-profit sector, but my work-life balance, my mental health – all the crap you're told is actually the key to happiness – is literally bubbling over. I need this to work, but more importantly, I *want* this to work for all sorts of reasons that I never considered when my career consisted of doing nothing more than making rich people richer. I seem to have finally figured out where I want to be and who I want to share it all with.

Which is awfully clichéd, I know, this whole sense of self-worth, of finding your purpose and all that, and sometimes I have to laugh at how long it's taken me to realise that money really isn't the answer. So much of that is because of Hector and his everlasting patience with me. He's taking me out this evening to a new Catalan restaurant that's owned by someone he met on his last book tour. Before, I would worry about having nothing in common with his friends, the people he spends his time with – because, let's face it, finance is exceedingly dull to anyone who doesn't work in the industry. Now I feel included, part of the conversation, someone who actually has something worthwhile to say. It's liberating and I wish I'd had the guts to make the leap a long time ago.

Looking up, I scan the never-ending queue and the packed tables inside, my weight shifting from foot to foot like it does when I'm waiting at the lights, poised and ready to run.

'Drapetomania,' I mutter to myself. It's a word I collected during my undergraduate years from a fellow student who was writing a paper on racism during the American Civil War. But I have no need to flee, do I?

In the café I wait, listening to the sound of milk being frothed, spoons being stirred and music spilling from the radio that rests on a high shelf behind the polished wooden counter.

It's from this radio that a familiar song begins to play, the same song I heard as I crossed the street in front of a dark green sports car. Once again, it pulls my thoughts back to a summer years before when I was just a girl with a heart full of hope.

I move forward to collect my order, and that's when I see him.

Leo.

Shit. What am I supposed to do?

Of all the people in all the places, why him, why now?

Another second goes by, during which my heart squeezes so tight it makes me gasp, then I spin on my heels and push my way back out of the café.

But it can't be Leo, not after all this time. There is simply no way he could be there, in *my* café, just sitting by the window, sipping his coffee as if it were the most natural thing in the world.

My laughter soon turns to tears and I rub them away, my shaking hand blocking my line of sight so that I trip over a bucket full of roses and land with a cry and a thud of knee against concrete.

I hate roses.

'You all right, love?' the florist asks as he pokes his head out from behind an enormous bunch of lilies, watching as I scramble to my feet, righting the bucket and muttering an apology before sprinting away.

'Layla?' I call out as I slam the front door behind me and run straight upstairs.

A creak of floorboard makes me turn my head towards the door at the other end of the landing, underneath which a shadow passes, along with the sound of someone opening and closing a drawer, turning on a tap and brushing their teeth with an electric toothbrush. I picture the room beyond, with black-tiled floor, roll-top bath and a hanging pot of ivy that trails almost to the ground.

'Everything will be OK,' I say to myself with a slow inhale as I wait for my world to fall back into place. Then the bathroom door opens and Layla steps out wrapped in a bright-pink towel.

'Jesus,' she shrieks, leaning against the doorframe. 'You scared the crap out of me.'

'Sorry,' I reply, staring at her face, at the full lips, tanned skin and eyes as blue as the Caribbean Sea.

'Everything all right?' Layla says, running her fingers through damp curls.

'Yes. I mean, I think so.' Because there are so many memories rushing around inside my head. All those neat little boxes I carefully and meticulously filed away that are now open and fighting for my attention.

'What happened to your leg?' Layla steps towards me and I back away.

I look down to see a trail of dried blood running down my shin. I turn and go to my room, sitting down on the edge of the bed to peel off my running shorts.

Layla is hovering on the landing, tiny droplets of water falling from her hair to the carpet.

'Did someone hurt you?'

'No,' I say, but my heart would seem to disagree because its rhythm is off. Two slow beats followed by one that skips and falters, making my whole body feel on edge.

'Let me get dressed. Then you can tell me what happened.'

'I'm fine.' I peer at my knee. The cut isn't deep, not much more than a graze, but there's a pulling sensation when I press against the skin.

I stand up and walk across to the wall of wardrobes and slide one open to reveal row upon row of designer clothes, each item carefully organised into colours, styles and seasons. I rub the hem of a black silk blouse between finger and thumb, then pull down a skirt from the very last hanger and shut the door, only to open it again and tilt my head to look up.

At the top is a shelf, bare of anything other than dust if you only look the once. With one hand on the shelf and a foot on an open drawer, I pull myself up to the top of the wardrobe and stretch my arm back into the dark space. My fingers creep over cobwebs, and no doubt a couple of dead spiders, before they find what I'm searching for.

I sink down on to the bed. In my lap is a tapestry bag with a drawstring neck, embroidered with brightly coloured bumblebees and butterflies.

One by one I take out all the contents and line them up on the windowsill, neat and ordered like soldiers, winking back at me in the morning sunshine. The feeling they arouse in me is a bit like finding a long-lost earring stuffed down the side of the sofa. Something you haven't thought of in ages, but recognise nonetheless.

Picking up a miniature porcelain boot, I slip it on to my thumb then put it back down. Next to it is a thimble made out of emerald glass with a golden rim that always makes me think of a wishing well, toasted chestnuts and a bitter caramel sweet I once broke my tooth on. A tooth I seek out with my tongue, feeling the chip worn smooth, and I try not to go back to the day it happened, because she was with me.

Going back to the wardrobes, I open them each in turn, tossing aside t-shirts and pyjamas, pulling open drawers and peering inside boxes. Then I move across to the dressing table, glancing at a tube of hand cream as I open the top drawer where a notebook and a small velvet box are waiting.

There is no need for me to open the notebook to know all the words hidden inside. Instead I reach for the box to find a pear-drop diamond ring as large as my thumbnail, which I slip on to my finger, turning my hand towards the light. It's comforting and makes it easier to shut the notebook away.

'Is that new?' Layla asks as she comes back, holding two steaming mugs of coffee and nodding her head at my skirt.

'What's wrong with it?' I say, smoothing my hands over the layers of lace, just as the memory of another day and a visit to a second-hand clothes shop appears in my mind.

'Nothing.' Layla passes me one of the mugs. 'I like it. It's just not very you.'

Maybe it is, I think to myself. Maybe what I saw, *who* I saw, in the café was precisely what I needed to make me finally own up to what is missing from my so-called perfect life.

Layla's at my side, watching me in that inquisitive (some would say downright nosey) way of hers and I can smell eucalyptus, a branch of which always hangs from the shower head and permeates her skin with its scent.

'Whatever it is, you can tell me.'

Opening my palm, I let go of the small emerald thimble that I picked out of the line on the mantelpiece. It falls to the floor, rolling across to bump against the wall.

'Is that a thimble?' Layla asks, crouching down to retrieve it, then holding it to the light, turning it round so that thin lines of green glance over her hand.

'It reminds me of someone I used to know.' I clear my throat and pick up my mug. The bitter scent fills my nose and I'm transported back to a small café in Oxford that sold sugary pastries and coffee so thick you could stand a teaspoon in it.

'Do you ever get the feeling,' I say, 'that you've woken up in someone else's life? That you're not quite where you're supposed to be?'

'What's going on?' Layla puts the thimble down and perches on the end of my bed.

I let out a sigh, trying not to think of the reason I started collecting all these random things in the first place.

'I can't do it,' I say as I take a long sip of coffee and stare at my reflection. Suddenly I'm struck with the strangest sense of time slowing down, then spinning around and flinging me back in time – back to an attic room in Oxford where two girls were getting ready to go out, completely unaware of what was about to happen.

'Do what?'

'Marry Hector.'

'Not this again,' she says. 'Yes, you could get hurt, but you could also end up living happily ever after.'

'There're no such things as fairy tales.'

'Nor is there such a thing as perfect, but for some strange reason, nobody is ever good enough for you.' There is a distinct undertone of disapproval in her voice, one that I know has more to do with her past relationships than me and Hector.

'Surely it's better to walk away now?' I ask, taking another sip of my coffee and wincing as the heat hits the back of my throat.

'If you do, it will destroy him.'

Walking away is so much easier than admitting life hasn't quite worked out the way I thought it would. On the surface all the boxes are ticked – rewarding job, financially secure, gorgeous fiancé with an adoring, stable family. But it's still not enough.

'Layla,' I say as I put my mug down and turn to face her, 'there's something I need to tell you.' Something I should have told her years ago, perhaps back when we first met. But secrets are so easy to keep when you think they're protecting you from harm. And for a while they did, but now I need to be honest about the real reason I left Oxford, and everyone in it, behind.

'I think you need to talk to Hector, not me.'

Except I don't want to talk to Hector. Because if I do then I would have to tell him everything, not just the bits about my life I've filtered and polished to look their very best.

I go across to the window, looking at my collection one by one before putting the thimble back in place.

Layla comes to stand next to me, no doubt trying to figure out how the line of unfamiliar objects is relevant to me announcing that I no longer want to get married.

'All of these things are linked to a specific moment in my life that made me stop and think.'

'What's this really about, Erika?' Layla asks as she picks up a tiny silver key, then puts it down next to a hand-painted turtle.

'There were three of us back then.' I reach into the tapestry bag, take out a crumpled Polaroid and hand it to her.

Layla peers at the faces, bright with youth and possibility, only one of which she knows. She looks at me, then back at the photograph, reading aloud the names written on the strip of white at the bottom.

'Erika, Duncan and Niamh,' she says, her eyes travelling back and forth between us. 'Oxford, 1996.'

'They were like my family,' I say, looking at the people I find so impossible to forget. 'We used to be so close.'

'What happened?' Layla asks as she gives the photo back, and I can imagine her noticing both the similarities and subtle differences between the woman standing before her and the one smiling back from the past. 'Why haven't you ever told me about them?'

'Because of Leo.'

'Who's Leo?'

'For fifteen years I've wondered if I should have chosen differently,' I say with a glance at the watch wrapped around my wrist. It feels like time is running away from me, too quick to catch on to. As if stumbling across Leo was only the beginning of something more.

'If it weren't for him, everything would have stayed exactly the way it was supposed to.'

ABOUT THE AUTHOR

Katherine has a master's in Modern History from Oxford University, is a member of Mensa and used to work as an investment banker. She lives in Kent with her husband, two children and a disobedient dog.